"What's the plan?"

"Plan?" He tried to sound nonchalant. "What—"

"You had a list of options already mapped out before you called me," Wren accused. "One for if I bailed on you and told you to handle your own mess. One if I didn't answer the phone. And one if I agreed to help. Let's get option C out into the open. Where are we going and what's our plan when we get there?"

"Ah." Now came the tricky part. "We'll be going to Splendor, Alaska. A small town on the west coast, population a whopping four hundred and forty-three."

"Wow. Okay. Well, I guess that'll limit our suspect pool. What?" She narrowed her gaze, pointed her finger in between his eyes. "What's that look?"

He swallowed harder than he meant to and almost choked. "I, ah, may have already laid the groundwork for our cover story." He reached into his pocket and pulled out two gold rings. He watched the shock register first, then dismayed amusement, followed immediately by her *you have got to be kidding me* look. "What do you say, partner? Will you marry me?"

Dear Reader,

When I wrote the final Honor Bound book, I had no idea a character would appear who would launch The McKenna Code series. Love when that happens. But— that hero (Aiden McKenna) is going to have to wait a bit. His law-enforcement siblings are going to get their stories first, beginning with his sister, FBI special agent Wren McKenna.

For years I've wanted to set a suspense in a locale inspired by Whittier, Alaska. So much about this town fascinated me, so of course I had to create my own version. Hence, Splendor, Alaska, population 443, was born. Sending longtime FBI partners Wren McKenna and Ty Savakis on an off-the-books case to protect Ty's former witness was the perfect fit, and personally, I love writing friends to lovers. Or in this case, best friends to lovers.

Wren and Ty are fearless in their jobs, but when it comes to love and taking a chance on each other, that's a different story. These two are definitely made for one another. Even her family thinks so, and as Wren knows, family is always right. I hope you enjoy their roller-coaster journey to happily-ever-after.

Happy reading,

Anna J.

ARCTIC PURSUIT

ANNA J. STEWART

Harlequin

ROMANTIC SUSPENSE

Harlequin®
ROMANTIC
SUSPENSE™

Recycling programs
for this product may
not exist in your area.

ISBN-13: 978-1-335-50268-1

Arctic Pursuit

Copyright © 2025 by Anna J. Stewart

For questions and comments about the quality of this book, please contact us at CustomerService@Harlequin.com.

TM and ® are trademarks of Harlequin Enterprises ULC.

 Harlequin Enterprises ULC
22 Adelaide St. West, 41st Floor
Toronto, Ontario M5H 4E3, Canada
www.Harlequin.com

Printed in U.S.A.

Bestselling author **Anna J. Stewart** honestly believes she was born with a book in her hand. After growing up devouring every story she could get her hands on, now she gets to make her living making up stories and fulfilling happily-ever-afters of her own. Her dreams have most definitely come true. Anna lives in Northern California (only a ninety-minute flight from Disneyland, her favorite place on earth) with two monstrous, devious, adorable cats named Sherlock and Rosie.

Books by Anna J. Stewart

Harlequin Romantic Suspense

The McKenna Code

Arctic Pursuit

The Coltons of Owl Creek

Hunting Colton's Witness

The Coltons of Roaring Springs

Colton on the Run

Colton 911: Chicago

Undercover Heat

Visit the Author Profile page
at Harlequin.com for more titles.

For Mom

I miss you every day.

Chapter 1

"No! Wait, Wren, don't go chasing him without..."

The rest of her brother's command fizzled in Wren's ear as she slammed out the back door of The Murky Mermaid and ran face-first into a winter storm. She pivoted, sweeping the rain out of her eyes as she scanned the back alley. There! The shadow shifted just out of sight around the corner.

FBI special agent Wren McKenna's sneakered feet barely hit the pavement as she raced after their drug-trafficking suspect; a suspect she'd been keeping under surveillance for the past four days. Normally she didn't mind surveillance duty, but in this instance it required her to take a bartending job in one of the seediest establishments in all of Seattle. She'd be washing off the grime, stink and misogyny for weeks.

Her earpiece crackled and popped before the static settled in, no doubt taking exception to the rain that had drenched her from head to toe. She ran full bore, lungs burning for an instant before her breathing found a familiar rhythm. Arms pumping, her skin puckered against the chill, Wren rounded the corner just as her suspect stopped and turned, unfortunately for him directly under one of the few working streetlamps in the area. Even from here Wren could see the panic in his darting eyes, see his hands shaking in a telltale sign he'd been doing far too much sampling of his own product.

He spun, lost his footing, did a bit of a flail before he caught himself and beat it around the corner and out of sight. At two in the morning, the nonexistent traffic allowed Wren to make easy work of the remaining distance. She ran across the street in a diagonal path, cutting through a pair of parked dilapidated sedans, stopped at the corner, panting a bit as she peeked around the side of the building.

He ducked inside an abandoned warehouse in the center of the block. She looked up. Eight stories. She shook her head, reached into her back pocket for her cell and quickly texted Aiden an update of her location. She was on the move again when his response came in.

We're two minutes out. Wait for backup.

Can't. She texted back even as she heard her big brother's voice echoing in her head.

Might be a back exit. Catch up.

Her confidence wasn't arrogance or even rebellion. It was seven years' experience as an FBI agent specializing in drug trafficking and distribution cases that had her dismissing the order. She'd worked everything from deep undercover to van surveillance. She knew how these guys thought, she knew their tendency to panic, and she knew what they were capable of when they were cornered.

She turned her phone to Silent, slipped it back into her pocket and pulled out the 9 mm Glock she'd been issued upon graduating from the FBI Academy. Before she ducked inside the building, she could hear the rumble of the surveillance van Aiden and his team had been living out of for the past few days. The engine had an odd clinking to it and the sound told her the team would be right on her heels.

She sucked in her stomach, squeezed carefully between the wall and the askew plywood covering the doorway. A button scraped against the wood, echoing up and into the emptiness of the dank, musty building. She froze, waiting. Listening.

Something plinked in the distance, scurried. Weapon raised, finger posed against the side of the barrel, Wren shook her wet hair back and stepped carefully forward. Another step, then another, until she was deep in the building's belly, turning, scanning.

A gentle thud had her spinning, weapon aimed at the door beneath a dead exit sign. She advanced, heard the rustle of footsteps back at the entrance. She pushed down on the metal bar, shoved gently to open the door to the emergency staircase.

"Wren." Her brother's hushed, irritated voice echoed behind her. She held a finger up to her lips as he approached and pointed up.

"I've got three men circling around back," Aiden said. "Blueprints we pulled up don't show a back way out."

"Meaning he could only go up or down." Two choices were better than three.

"Trapped either way," Aiden confirmed. Two Minotaur Security agents from Aiden's private security firm joined them. "You want up or down?" His smile reminded her of when they were kids and dedicated to challenging one another. He knew exactly which she'd prefer. She'd take rats and a sewer over a fire escape and a roof.

"I'll take up."

His brow arched and she rolled her eyes. "The best way to deal with a phobia is to confront it, right?" Anything over three stories and she got the lurches. Even now, the thought of eight stories up had her stomach pitching and her toes tingling. "Besides, I've been stuck behind a bar for four days. I need the workout."

"Your choice." Aiden shrugged. "Talbert, on her six."

"Sir." Rico Talbert, a former navy SEAL with a sometimes unpredictable temper, nodded once, then looked to Wren. "On your go."

Wren shoved the door all the way open and moved through. "Go!"

She and Rico made quick work of the first three floors, circling up and around, aiming their weapons in preparation for a sneak attack. Her suspect wasn't known for being armed, but he hadn't been tagged by a special investigative unit before. Word was a major meth shipment was hitting the West Coast in the next twenty-four hours and this guy was their best shot at gleaning any details.

She hadn't heard any other doors open, but every once in a while she thought she could pick up the distinct shuffling of feet above them. As they rounded the fourth floor, she stopped, inclined her head, looked back at Rico.

The man was the very definition of intense with his

dark lock-jawed features. Given that buff physique and curly black hair, not to mention an all-assessing gaze, she might have found herself tempted were it not for the fact that he had an equally buff navy JAG husband waiting for him at home.

More scampering overhead, slower now, and Wren sighed. "He's going all the way up."

Rico nodded. "Sounds like."

"Let's hit it." She picked up her pace, taking the stairs double time now, and had to admit that when they reached the roof level, she was feeling the burn. "You take right." She stood on the left side of the closed metal door. "I'll go left."

Rico nodded, placed his hand on the bar and shoved the door open.

The rain was still pounding when she spun out. Weapon raised, she moved forward, squinting against the weather. The temperature had dropped in the last few minutes, but she was too charged up to shiver. She stopped at the outcropping of a brick wall, back pressed up against it as she crouched, leaned out and peered around.

The suspect was standing on the top rung of an old fire escape, looking down but not moving. She could hear the pounding of footsteps on the metal rungs far below.

She swore, leaned her head back and drew in a steadying breath. "You're locked in, Jackson!" Wren called as she slowly rose to her feet, held her weapon out to her side as he spun around. Moonlight caught him in its grip, cast him in light as he stood far too close to the edge for her liking. "Just come in with me." She held out her free hand. "Let's talk. You help us, we'll help you."

Jackson swooped strands of damp hair out of his eyes. "How can you help me?" he called into the wind. "You're just a bartender. And a crappy one at that."

He wasn't wrong.

"My name is Wren McKenna, Jackson. FBI special agent Wren McKenna. I work with Ty Savakis. You know Ty, don't you?"

"Yeah." Jackson trembled, looked back down as the arc of flashlights from street level cut through the midnight darkness. "I know Ty."

"I can take you to him," Wren lied. "He's down in the van overseeing the entire operation. You want to talk to Ty? All you have to do is come with me."

"No, man." Jackson shoved his hands in his pockets, took a step backward and nearly toppled off the edge. Wren lurched forward, ready to reach for him, but he grabbed hold of the rounded railing and caught himself. Only then did he cast a longing gaze to the roof across the alley.

Wren holstered her weapon, felt Rico come up behind her. He laid a hand on her shoulder, letting her know he had her back.

"You won't make it," Wren called as the rain finally began to ease. "You can't make that jump, Jackson." She inched forward, mentally willing Jackson to come down off the edge of the roof. She really, *really* didn't want to have to look down. "It's wet, it's slippery, and no matter how much you want to, you can't fly." Another step. She was just inches from him now. She could smell the booze and street wafting off him.

Rico circled around her, looked down the fire escape. "We've got him!"

Wren winced. She wasn't so sure. Her gaze locked on Jackson's. She saw the desperation on his face, the panic in his eyes. He was weighing his increasingly limited options.

"Come with me, Jackson. Please." She was almost close enough to touch him, almost close enough to—"Jackson, don't! There's a way out of this. I promise. Let us help—"

"Ain't no way out," Jackson laughed, and in that moment, she saw the manic acceptance. "Vex doesn't let anyone talk."

"You can be the first," Wren said quietly, desperately. She needed this guy alive. Ty had been trying to get him to turn for months, but Jackson had disappeared three weeks ago, right before Ty's mandatory vacation had started. She'd promised Ty she'd keep an eye out for Jackson, do what she could to finish the job he'd started. One thing she would never do was let her partner down. "Give us a chance to help you, Jackson." One more step.

She locked her hand around his wrist, felt rather than heard his gasp of surprise. "I've got you, Jackson." *Don't look down. Don't look down.* She resisted the impulse to squeeze her eyes shut.

The tension in Jackson's body lessened and he let out something that sounded like a sob. "You can really help me? You can keep me safe from Vex?"

"I really can." It always disturbed her how easily the lies came. "Give me a chance, Jackson. I won't let you down."

"You got him?" Rico asked as Jackson grabbed hold of her with his other hand.

"Yeah," Wren said quietly. "I've got—"

A shot rang out, loud even against the rain. She jolted, tightened her hold on Jackson, but as she met his gaze again, she saw the dazed, dead look coming across his face.

He looked down as a large red pool seeped across his shirt.

Jackson fell back, his grip still tight on Wren. She cried out as he pulled her forward, nearly off her feet. She slammed hard into the edge of the roof, the cement cutting into her stomach as Rico reached around and pried Jackson's hand free. He dragged Wren back and down behind the cover of the roofline just in case the shooter took another shot.

"No!" Wren pounded frustrated fists against her knees as she sat beside Rico, purposely blocking out the abject fear of nearly pitching off an eight-story roof. "Almost had him."

"Yeah, I don't think we did." Rico poked his head over as three armed Minotaur security specialists reached the top of the fire escape. Their guns were poised and pivoting back and forth, looking for any sign of the gunman. "You see anything?" he yelled at them.

"Nothing," a female specialist shouted back.

Rico clicked on his shoulder radio. "Sweep a three-block radius, rooftops included." But Wren heard it in his voice. Whoever had taken Jackson out had been a professional. He was gone seconds after he fired the shot. Rico swore, let out a slow whistle. "Long way down."

Wren gulped. Very long way. She shoved herself up,

promised herself one very big glass of Jack Daniel's when she got home. "Well, that's three months of Ty's life he won't get back." Her partner had made the conviction of Dante Vex his life's mission for more than three years. The case had eaten away at his soul, not to mention eviscerated Ty's marriage, and had their superiors at the agency wondering if, once again, Ty had gotten too personally involved. All she'd had to do was get this one witness to turn—

"You okay?" Aiden approached, flanked by two of his men. He touched her arm, flexed his fingers once, an action the McKenna siblings had developed decades before to silently check in.

"I'm fine." Her temper snapped through the words. "How'd they know he was up here?"

"Not sure. Something more to look into where Vex is concerned." The drug supplier had been making steady progress up the criminal racketeering ladder ever since Ty had locked up his boss, Ambrose Treyhern, almost ten years ago.

Wren shook her head. "Jackson was the only potential source Ty could come close to locking in. No one else would talk to him." She knew what was going to happen when Ty found out what had happened. "He's going to blame himself."

"Then he'd be wrong," her brother said, moving closer and resting a hand on her shoulder. "If what you told me about Ty's investigation is true, chances are they'd have taken him out, too. Might just be lucky they missed you."

"Or they figured I wasn't worth the effort," Wren said. "Treyhern got charged with almost killing Ty. Vex would have learned from his boss's mistake."

"Doesn't mean he won't next time," Aiden commented. "You get in his way enough, you won't leave him a choice."

"Right." Wren sighed. "Next time." She shivered, the cold of the night finally seeping into her bones. "I'd better call this in. Thanks for lending a hand. Sorry it was a waste of time."

"Hey, when my baby sister calls—"

"Regan is the baby." Wren cut her brother off with a gentle slug to the shoulder. "Although don't let her hear you say that."

"All the same, we McKennas stick together. You ask for help, you've got it. No questions asked."

"There might be some questions," Wren said. "I didn't exactly clear your involvement with my bosses."

"Typical Wren." He slung an arm around her shoulders and led her back to the stairs. "Rather ask forgiveness than permission. You want my help explaining?"

"No." She'd gotten herself into this mess. She'd get herself out of it. Besides, dealing with her superiors at the agency was going to be far less painful than telling Ty she'd lost his best lead. "When are you headed back to Boston?"

"Tomorrow afternoon. You want to hitch a ride on my plane?"

"Well, duh." She rolled her eyes. "You really think I'm going to risk missing another family dinner?"

"I think Mom would understand," Aiden said.

"That's because you never miss," Wren countered. "But then I guess that goes with being your own boss." One of the perks to being one of the premier private security experts in the country meant her big brother could come and go at his leisure. An added bonus? Setting his own hours pretty much ensured he'd never miss the mandatory monthly McKenna dinners that kept the tight-knit family on an even keel.

They ducked inside, made quick work of the eight flights down, but once they got to the bottom, the adrenaline coursing through Wren's system was evaporating. She was ready to crash.

"You going to call Ty tonight?" Aiden asked as they walked outside and into the carnival of flashing police lights surrounding the building.

"I—" She was cut off by her cell phone buzzing against her butt. She pulled it free, stared at the screen for a good long moment and muttered, "I swear my partner is psychic." Ty always knew when something was seriously messed up.

"Or," Aiden said in too innocent a tone, "he's just that into you that he can read your mind."

"Stop it." The warning wasn't the first one she'd given. For years, Aiden—okay, all three of her siblings—had teased her about her relationship with Tyrone Savakis. Thankfully they knew to keep their comments under control this past holiday season when Ty had come for Christmas dinner at the McKenna house. It had been difficult enough to convince him to spend the day with her family without him knowing what all of them somewhat believed about their relationship.

It wasn't as if there had ever been anything romantic between them. She'd been married when they first became partners and he'd gotten married a year after. Didn't matter neither marriage survived; they were each other's best friend.

And, okay, she'd be lying if she didn't admit to hav-

ing had a major crush on him at one point. And she'd
have to be foolish not to genuinely appreciate a tall, in-
credibly fit blue-eyed man who gave his godlike Greek
ancestors something to be proud of.

Getting involved with one another was only going to
make their professional lives messy and complicated.
Neither of them wanted that. Still…there were times
when she let herself think maybe—

"You going to answer or just speak to him telepathi-
cally?" Aiden asked.

"Shut up." She glared at her brother as she answered
her phone. "Ty, hey. We were, um…" She shoved her
sopping hair out of her face once more. "Aiden and I
were just talking about you." She frowned when he
didn't immediately respond. "Ty?"

"Yeah, I'm here."

Wren straightened. Ty sounded distracted. He rarely
sounded distracted. He was arrow straight on concentration 24/7. Heck, he could probably set a world record
for not blinking. It was one of the qualities that made
him such a good agent. "What's wrong?"

The teasing light in Aiden's eyes faded.

"What isn't wrong?" Ty said in a frustrated tone. "There's
way too much…" He trailed off. "Sorry. I haven't slept in a
couple of days. You still in Seattle?"

"Yeah." She stepped back as the rest of Aiden's men
filed out of the abandoned building. "Um, I've got some
cleaning up to do here before I head home to Boston."

"Okay, when you're done, and before you head back,
I need you to meet me." He rattled off the name of some
private airport outside of Seattle she'd never heard of.

"Sunrise. A friend is going to fly me back in time. I'll grab some sleep when we land."

"Fly you back from where?" As far as she knew, Ty had been holed up in his Boston apartment serving out his forced vacation time as if it were a prison sentence. "Where are you?"

"Right now? Anchorage. I'll explain when I see you, okay?"

"Ty? What's going on?"

"I don't want to get into it on the phone. Just meet me, yeah? I really need your help, Wren. As always, you're the only person I can trust."

"Okay." He had a tendency to get a bit overdramatic when a case wasn't going his way. Was it possible he'd already heard about Jackson? Not likely since it was still in local law enforcement jurisdiction. "Just tell me one thing. Are you all right?"

"Yeah, I'm okay. For now. I'll see you in a few hours. Thanks, Wren. Oh, one more thing?"

"What?" She didn't like the uneasy, queasy sensation in her belly.

"Don't tell anyone official we spoke, okay? No one. Especially anyone at the FBI." He hung up.

Wren stared at her cell, then looked up at Aiden.

"Trouble?" Aiden asked.

"Looks like. For you, too," she added as she headed toward the alley to speak with the officers on scene. "You'll have to tell Mom I'm missing this month's dinner."

Chapter 2

The knots in Ty Savakis's stomach didn't loosen until he saw headlights turn in his direction. His breath erupted in thick puffs of white, disappearing into the cold February air that had frozen his face to the point of numbness. Hands shoved deep into the pockets of his fleece-lined jacket, he remained stone-still, standing in front of the private airplane hangar that housed a friend's impressive aircraft collection.

He had no doubt Wren was behind the wheel of the approaching car. He'd always been able to tell when she was near and, given the way he was finally starting to relax, the car couldn't be carrying anyone else. As she pulled the dark sedan to a stop, his gaze shifted to the passenger seat. He'd set the odds at fifty-fifty she'd bring her brother Aiden along for the ride.

But she'd come alone. He hadn't asked her to, but the request had been implicit. There truly was no one else in the world he could trust more than his partner.

His hands clenched as she shoved open the door and climbed out. Her fit five-foot-five frame, primarily constructed of muscle and sass, was bundled up cozily in snug jeans, black tactical work boots and a puffy dark jacket. The knit cap tugged onto her head covered some but not all of her sandy blond hair she normally wore in a messy ponytail to keep it out of her face. She slammed the door and headed in his direction. "You okay?"

Wren wasn't a worrier, so the fact that she asked told him he'd sounded more frazzled on the phone than he'd hoped. "Not remotely. Coffee?"

"Bathroom," she corrected as she followed him into the dimly lit hangar. Half a dozen aircrafts ranging from restored historic models to a modern-day two-seater sat on display. "I drank a tankard of coffee on the drive up."

"Over there." He pointed to the restroom in the back corner of the metal industrial-style building. He didn't ask a second time if she wanted more coffee; Wren McKenna had it running through her veins. Her drug of choice, if one didn't count the occasional Jack Daniel's she downed after nastier resolutions to cases.

He rotated his neck, then his shoulders, trying to work out the exhaustion that had been creeping over him the past few days. That sleep he'd hoped to catch hadn't materialized as his mind wouldn't shut down long enough to reboot. Rubbing his palm across his whisker-covered face, he shoved at the guilt trying its best to grab hold of his throat and choke him.

These days he seemed to spiral from one disaster to another, with bad luck nipping at his heels every step of the way. Given how the last couple of days had gone, that wasn't going to change anytime soon. But now, with Wren by his side, the odds were more in his favor.

"Okay, whew." Wren reappeared, her cuddly jacket unzipped to reveal the thin rock band–inspired T-shirt she wore. "That feels better. That for me?" She pointed to the steaming paper cup near his hand.

"Yeah." He stood back, offered her the cup. He should have realized.

She eyed him over the rising steam. "You heard about Jackson?" She sipped and, true to form, let out a sigh that rivaled that of a woman in ecstasy. An electric jolt shot through his body; an increasingly familiar sensation he found himself experiencing when the two of them were together.

"I heard."

"I'm so sorry. The last thing I expected was for someone to take him out. Not like that."

"Not your fault. I mean it," he added at her scoff. "If anyone's to blame, it's me. I let my focus get foggy. The agency was right to bench me. I should have done a better job. Brought Jackson in on my own, through procedure instead of getting creative and letting him convince me he was fine on his own."

"You only got creative because you couldn't get Jackson the guarantees he wanted," Wren reminded him. "You were looking out for your informant."

"Guess I'm off the hook now." The bitterness in his voice was only countered by the warming air around them.

"Jackson didn't have to run," Wren told him. "He made his choice, and it cost him his life. Still trying to figure out how someone knew to take that shot, though. We had the surveillance locked down tight," she muttered. "Only a handful of people at the FBI knew what I was doing."

"What're Aiden's thoughts?"

"Many and varied." She winced. "You ticked I brought him in?"

"Not remotely." He only wished he'd thought of bringing Wren's brother in sooner. Maybe then Ty would have managed things better. Wren's older brother had the habit of getting through Ty's stubbornness more effectively than most. "Glad he was there. Sorry you got saddled with it."

Wren glared at him. "That sounds disturbingly like self-pity, which you don't do. What's going on? What's with the cloak-and-dagger conclave?"

Every emotion Ty had been struggling to keep under control began to cyclone inside him. "You remember me telling you about Alice Hawkins?" Stupid question. Wren never forgot anything.

"Sure." Wren's blue eyes sharpened as she accessed her memory banks. "She was the main witness who testified against Ambrose Treyhern, one of the biggest drug traffickers on the East Coast. She helped put him behind bars for the murder of one of his dealers." She inclined her head. "Which allowed for Dante Vex and his ilk to slither up Treyhern's organization to take it over, and thus here we are."

Right on the nose. Now came the tricky part. "Treyhern was granted a new trial three weeks ago. His new lawyers are claiming prosecutorial misconduct." Not entirely surprising given the federal prosecutor in charge of the case had recently been indicted on bribery charges.

"Three—" Wren set her coffee down, eyes wide with surprise and more than a little anger. "Three weeks ago and you're just telling me this now? That was the biggest case of your career. You got your promotion because of it. You got partnered with me because of it. What the what, Ty?"

Ty nodded. All true. "I can't—"

Wren swore, held up a hand, began pacing in a circle the way she always did when she was trying to work something out in her head. "Three weeks ago. That's when you started going loopy-loo on me. Why didn't you tell me?"

"Because I was under the misguided perception that I was handling the information okay." It never occurred to him to lie. He and Wren had a long-standing agreement. No lies. No matter what. Omissions, on the other hand... "I messed up."

"Ya think?" She stopped, looked him dead in the eye and arched one brow.

Ty sighed. He didn't think. He knew. That mistake in judgment had resulted in a forced two-week "vacation" that, if he weren't careful, would be changed in his record to a forced leave of absence. A notation like that could turn any promise of advancement into a long shot. "I fully deserve whatever lambasting you're about to give me, Wren, but it's five in the morning. I haven't slept in three days and right now I'm standing upright out of sheer will."

The irritation faded from her eyes, but her suspicion remained. "What is going on with you?"

"Someone ran Alice Hawkins down in the street last week." Considering he wasn't entirely sure what day this was, he couldn't be more precise than that. "Shortly after she agreed to testify against Treyhern in the second trial."

Wren's posture shifted. Her spine went steel straight

and her eyes sharpened to the point of slicing through metal. "Is she dead?"

"No. But it's close. She's in a coma. So far the local sheriff's been able to keep her condition quiet, but it won't be long before whoever went after her realizes he didn't finish the job."

"And you think Ambrose Treyhern's behind the accident? Hasn't he been in solitary for the past two years?"

"So we've been told." But as anyone in law enforcement knew, solitary didn't mean powerful prisoners didn't have their way of communicating with the outside world.

"How did you find out? About Alice?"

Ty could all but hear the wheels turning in her brain.

That now-familiar slick, sick sensation slid through him. "I was on the phone with her when it happened." Even now, the haunting screech of tires, Alice's scream, that decidedly heavy thump replayed in his mind. Those horrifying seconds had been on a nonstop loop in his head. "She called me, needing some reassurance about her testifying again. She was concerned for her family."

"Considering what happened, she was right to be."

Ty swallowed hard. "We were talking when it happened. When she was hit. I heard her...land." The sickening sound was going to haunt him if not forever, certainly for the near future.

Wren shook her head, eyes filled with disbelief, irritation and pity. "Ty."

"I know." He ducked his head in shame. There wasn't anything she could say that he hadn't already said to himself. "I spent the entire time getting up to Splendor, trying to come up with a story about how Alice and I met. Shouldn't have worried over it. She'd already come up with one. Her husband knew who I was immediately."

Wren's brows shot up.

"She'd told him I was a friend from her old neighborhood. The only one she kept in touch with. She also told him if anything ever happened to her that I should be his first call."

"He didn't question how you knew she'd been hurt? Or the, what? Six-year age difference between you?"

"They've got three kids," Ty said. "He wasn't thinking about anything other than them and Alice."

"Lucky for you."

She wasn't wrong. They needed to get their stories straight and do it fast.

Wren eyed him in the same way she did a suspect. "I seem to recall you telling me Alice had a bit of a sketchy past. Is it possible something or someone else caught up with her?"

"No. No doubt in my mind Treyhern's behind this. I get that my opinion might not carry much weight at the moment." He hated having to rehash this again, but he didn't have any choice. "Alice was a messed-up eighteen-year-old when I was working the Treyhern case. And, okay, I was new to the job and desperate to prove myself." He'd spent his entire life trying to do just that one way or another. The only person he'd never had to do that with was the woman standing in front of him. "Sure, she had a record, but for petty stuff. Vandalism, pickpocketing. Petty theft. Doing whatever she needed to survive. She'd been living on the street for over a year when Treyhern found her, gave her a job at his nightclub. He paid her enough that she didn't have to live in alleys and share a cardboard box with the rats. But she had, or she has, a code, Wren. Watering down drinks was one thing. Seeing Treyhern kill someone in cold blood crossed a line for her. She wanted to do the right thing and I was more than happy to take her help."

"I seem to recall you telling me she refused witness protection."

"She did." It had been an argument he'd been devastated to lose. What was happening now had been his nightmare scenario come to life, but Alice had been adamant. "She'd finally gotten her life together and knew what she wanted. She didn't want Treyhern messing with her future. She'd just started dating the man who would become her husband. She was happy, and testifying felt like closing the book on a big chapter of her life. Said she knew how to disappear and still keep her identity intact."

"Brave woman. Wrong, but brave."

"I told her she'd be safe," Ty said. "I promised her Treyhern would never get out, that he couldn't hurt her anymore and I'd make sure she could have that life she wanted so desperately." The layers of guilt that continued to build threatened to pull him under. "I went so far as to visit Treyhern in prison and told him that whatever beef he had, it was with me. That I was the one who made her testify. I made him believe she didn't have a choice."

"Something tells me you didn't quite succeed."

"Alice is still alive, Wren." Right now that fact was the only thing holding him together. "She's clinging to it with her fingertips, but she's alive. She has a good life, a wonderful family. I can't walk away from this. From her. Not again. Whoever's gunning for her works for Treyhern and he probably doesn't take failure well. They're going to finish the job, maybe even hurt her family to get to her again. I need to be there when they try."

"You?" Wren picked her coffee back up. "You mean we, don't you?" She sipped, sipped again. "That's why you called me, right?"

"I'd appreciate the assist." A new layer of uncertainty unfolded inside him. "But I also don't want to put you in the position of having to lie. I called Frisco, asked for permission to head up to Alaska to look into this, to make sure Alice and her family stay safe."

"Let me guess," Wren said slowly. "Our commanding officer denied your request."

Not only denied it, but Frisco told Ty if he did pursue the investigation, he could pretty much kiss his career in the agency goodbye. After his insubordination regarding Dante Vex, it made sense the agency would want him far away from the Treyhern retrial. "I promised her she'd be safe. And you know I never break—"

"Your promises." Wren nodded. "Yes, I am aware."

"I just need you watching my back up there. And maybe covering for me with Frisco when he asks where I am. Just say you don't know."

"Well, that'll be a bald-faced lie since I'm coming with you." The ease with which she said it both erased the tension in his bones and awakened new concerns.

Deep down he'd known Wren wouldn't let him do this alone. She'd never let him down. Not in seven years. "You don't have to."

"Please." She rolled her eyes. "Of course I do. If for no other reason than to make sure you don't mess this up. Plus, I really don't want to have to break in a new partner. So." She finished her coffee. "What's the plan?"

"Plan?" He tried to sound nonchalant. "What—"

"You had a list of options mapped out before you even called me," Wren accused. "One option if I bailed on you and told you to handle your own mess. One if I didn't answer the phone, and another for when I agreed to help. Let's get option C out in the open. Where are we going and what's our plan when we get there?"

"Ah." Now came the tricky part. "We'll be going to Splendor, Alaska. A small town on the West Coast, population a whopping four hundred and forty-three."

"Wow. Okay. Well, I guess that'll limit our suspect pool. What?" She narrowed her gaze, pointed her finger in between his eyes. "What's that look?"

He swallowed harder than he meant to and almost choked. "I, ah, may have already laid the groundwork for our cover story." He reached into his pocket and pulled out two gold rings. He watched the shock register first, then dismayed amusement, followed immediately by her you-have-got-to-be-kidding-me look. "What do you say, partner? Will you marry me?"

Wren had flown in military cargo planes with only a thin metal bench as a seat during category two winds. She'd found herself dangling off the side of a helicopter with only Ty's hand locked around her wrist as security. And she'd flown coast to coast in a massive jetliner that lost one engine during a particularly nasty summer storm.

Right now she'd take any of those scenarios over the single-engine 1946 Piper Super Cruiser—suspiciously similar to a tin can—she currently found herself in.

The only reason she could even identify the plane

was because its pilot, one forty-something Gabriel Haw-thorne, had given her an extensive rundown on the plane's capabilities. No doubt the abject look of horror she'd been unable to conceal when she first spotted the red-and-white-painted aircraft was the reason for the history lesson.

Hawthorne seemed to believe that the fact his grand-father had flown the plane for more than forty years was an endorsement of safety. She might have felt better if the plane had just rolled off the assembly line.

Her pilot slipped right into the stereotype explana-tion she'd imagined hearing about how she'd be trans-ported north. Big, a bit on the burly side, fully bearded and flannel-wearing cold-weather enthusiast, Hawthorne projected confidence in both his plane and his abilities, which took a bit of the edge off her fear.

A very little bit.

Hugging her stuffed duffel bag in front of her like an already exploded airbag, Wren bounced around on the thinly padded bench behind the pilot's seat. The narrow belt across her thighs dug into her denim-clad legs. Even now, she could feel the pressure bruises forming, but at least they were a reminder she hadn't traveled into the great beyond. The ride had been bumpy since they first coasted into the air, and more than once her head had just missed connecting with the roof. The engine rum-bled loudly all around her and she could feel the vibra-tions through her work boots.

"You doing okay back there?" Hawthorne yelled over his shoulder as they hit yet another air pocket that set the plane to trembling and Wren to grabbing the top of her head with her hand.

"Fine." She really didn't want to talk. It was taking most of her concentration to hold on to the breakfast she'd forced herself to eat before returning to the airstrip. It had been close to thirty hours since she'd left Ty, promising to try to get some sleep at the hangar. At least twenty since he'd returned ahead of her to Splendor, Alaska, no doubt to avoid having to climb into a plane with her.

She couldn't blame him. She was a nightmare to fly with. She imagined every bump and whine was going to lead to certain death. Fliers like her were partly why the pharmaceutical industry did a gangbuster business. Somehow, miraculously, her brothers would say, she'd managed to hide her anxiety well enough where her job was concerned.

"Ty didn't mention you were a nervous flier." Even though Hawthorne shouted, she could barely hear him through the headset she wore.

"I'm not nervous." Petrified maybe, but she'd left nervous back on the tarmac. "How do you know Ty?" Distraction, she told herself, could work far better than drugs.

"Met him on a wildlife excursion about ten years back. Flew him and four other CSOs up north during the salmon run."

"CSOs?"

"City slicker outdoorsmen." Hawthorne's laughter crackled in her ears. "They like to think of themselves as urban adventurers. Gotta admit, for a townie, Ty has a pretty good grasp of the natural way of living. He and I got along from the jump. Man respects the wilderness. He enjoys it when he comes up here and never loses sight of the fact it can be dangerous."

"Does he?" Wren frowned. She knew Ty took off on his own a few times a year, mostly to decompress and get away. She had no idea he made his way north into the wilderness Alaska had to offer. The engine seemed to strain, causing the entire cabin to rattle. "Well, I appreciate you getting me to Splendor." *Hopefully in one piece.*

She'd done some destination research in the spare hours she'd had after packing. She knew it was a very, *very* small town, but boasted a surprising amount of art and culture pulling from both those of native Indigenous ancestry and other residents. Fishing was a primary source of income for a lot of people, as was the tourist trade, thanks to cruise ships making Splendor a stop along their routes in the warmer months. From what she'd gleaned off the city's official website, the art studios and galleries outnumbered the restaurants about two to one. Skyway Tower, where Alice Hawkins and her family lived, was a bit of a unicorn when it came to apartment buildings.

Considered a self-contained community, the main and first floor of the six-story complex that housed more than a hundred residents included everything from a school to a post office, from a grocery store to even a movie theater in the basement. The library offered not only books but also cooking equipment, board games, puzzles, and hosted numerous classes in countless subjects. In theory, one never had to step outside to get everything they might need.

That didn't mean the surrounding area didn't have its aesthetic offerings as well. But in the dead winter months, when the snow didn't stop and the sun didn't shine, it provided a safe if not locked-down environment for its residents both in and around Skyway Tower.

"You live in Splendor?"

"About thirty miles north," Hawthorne shouted. "This here's my car." He slapped a hand down on the console. "Gets me anywhere I need to go. I like Splendor, though. It's different. Everyone knows everyone. It's both hard and easy to get lost there."

"That's what I'm counting on." Wren's murmur earned her another over-the-shoulder glance. "I'm looking forward to experiencing it," she called. "Where's the best coffee?"

Hawthorne veered the plane east. "Now, that there's a bone of contention. You ask me, Mountain Morning's got the best brews. But Morning Sun Coffee Company's giving them a run for their money these days. Can't go wrong with either."

"That's all I need to know." Although at the moment she couldn't anticipate a time when her stomach would feel settled enough to imbibe anything.

"You like fresh fish cooked well, put The Hungry Halibut on your list, and the Salmon Run Café has an excellent salmon, bacon and tomato on fresh-baked whole grain."

"So we won't go hungry, huh?"

"Definitely not. Not much to do in Splendor if you ain't on a boat or throwing clay on a potter's wheel. Food's a way of life and they take it serious."

"Noted." Always helpful to know she wouldn't starve. "How much longer?"

"We should be landing in about forty-five minutes. Long as those clouds stay at a distance." He gestured out the windshield to the bank of gray. "We should beat it, though."

Beat it they did, but not by much. By the time Hawthorne brought the plane in for a relatively smooth landing, Wren closed her eyes in silent thanks. Her arms had gone numb with how tightly she'd been holding on to her bag. Even as he steered the plane to the dock at the end of the marina, she was unsnapping her belt and scooting to the edge of the seat to make a break for it.

Whatever unease she still felt evaporated as she caught her first glimpse of Splendor. The marina itself was both typical and a bit ethereal. With the way the midmorning sun hit the boats, it set the gleaming paint and the blue of the surrounding sea to glistening. She could smell diesel mingling with the briny air, an intoxicating combination that made her lungs eagerly expand. As the engine on the plane died back, the silence set in and offered a kind of peace she hadn't been expecting or prepared for.

She spotted Ty heading down a marina gangplank and immediately her stomach jumped. The flight had distracted her from the other point of contention on this particular job. Pretending to be married to Ty Savakis. What a can of worms that could open up. They'd had their share of undercover assignments, but nothing quite so…intimate before.

Wren glanced down at the gold band on her finger. It felt oddly heavy. She'd never worn one when she and Antony were married, which had been one of the many points of contention between them. Her then-husband had always accused her of not wanting the reminder of him when she was working. He hadn't been wrong, but by the time she realized her marriage was on life support, she'd lost any desire to resuscitate it. Which made it even stranger she should look upon this ring so fondly. And her heart really needed to stop skipping every time she glanced at Ty.

"Thanks for the lift," Wren said as Hawthorne pulled the plane to a stop right in front of where Ty stood. "Sorry if I was a bit freaked out."

"I've had worse passengers," Hawthorne assured her as he flipped a switch and killed the engine. "All you want is the landings to equal the takeoffs. Anything that happens in between those two things means nothing."

Wren actually laughed. The door popped open, splitting into two, one panel going up, the other providing a solitary narrow step out.

"You made it in one piece, I see." Ty's grin had Wren chucking her duffel straight into his chest. He caught it with a grunt of surprise as she hauled herself out. "Want to kiss the ground?"

"We aren't on ground yet." She could feel the walkway swaying a bit in the barely-there waves. "But when I get there, you bet. You get any sleep?" It sure didn't look it. She hadn't thought he could look more exhausted than he had in Seattle.

"Some. Worried I'd be late to pick you up."

Fat chance. Her partner was predictably punctual. "How's Alice?" She'd half been hoping by the time she landed Alice would be well on her way to recovery.

"Thought we'd head over now and check," Ty said. "This all you brought?" The disbelief in his voice barely reached her ears as she ducked back inside for the wheeled suitcase she'd also packed. "Ah, that's more like it."

"Half of this is courtesy of Aiden," she told him. Her brother hadn't been overly thrilled at the idea of her heading to Splendor off book, but he knew her well enough not to fight her on it. Instead he'd made sure she had plenty of artillery to supplement her Glock and backup piece.

"Love your brother," Ty said. "Always thinking ahead."

"Yeah, well, keep in mind he's not overly thrilled with you at the moment." She thanked Hawthorne again, and after he and Ty settled up in cash, Wren was following the latter through the marina. "He said to call him if we needed help. He's putting Howell on alert."

"And here I thought Aiden had more faith in me. We don't need a marshal running backup."

"Howell might be a US marshal, but he's got more connections than even Aiden has. We might need help if this thing goes feet up." The FBI had a long-standing thing going with the Marshals Service. Personally Wren had never had a problem with them, but that was because she understood them better than most FBI agents. Her brother Howell was one of the best people she'd ever known and that wasn't just familial affection talking. There was a reason Howell McKenna had the respect of every law enforcement officer he'd ever worked with— in and out of the Marshals Service. But then the same could easily be said for any of the McKennas.

Her family covered the law enforcement agencies like a well-worn blanket, and while they had the reputation for being tenacious and tough, they also erred on the side of cautious consistency. McKennas in law enforcement went all the way back to the very first police department in Boston. Their mother, Elizabeth McKenna, had become the first female police commissioner in the city nearly a decade ago and still served in the office with distinction. To say they took their jobs seriously, and with the utmost responsibility, was a massive understatement. Genetics, if nothing else, demanded it.

"Hopefully we won't need the reinforcements. Speaking of which." Ty suddenly seemed very interested in a fishing boat unloading its morning haul. "You talk to Frisco?"

"Nope." She flashed him a smile. "Sent our boss an email, though, said I'd be out of touch for a while. Family emergency." It hadn't been a lie. Exactly. Ty was family and this was an emergency. "Timed the send to correspond with when I climbed on that monstrosity." She pointed back to the plane. "And funny enough, the Wi-Fi and cell service around here sucks." That said, if Supervisory Special Agent Jack Frisco wanted to track her down, he could. Easily.

Ty slung her duffel over his shoulder as a light rain began to fall. When he slipped his free hand into hers and squeezed, she nearly lost her breath. "Keeping up appearances," he said when she tensed. "Been mentioning how my wife is on her way to meet me so I can convince her we need to move here."

"We still going with you having sold off your IT company for a small fortune and therefore have time to play?"

"It's worked before." Ty's smile was tight. "It's a legend I know forward and backward. It's just using my real name that'll be weird."

"Still doesn't sit well with me." Wren kept turning her head, memorizing where things were and how they were set up. The marina displayed an array of various watercraft from large fishing boats to dinghy-sized vessels. There were sailboats with aquatic and ironic names and an actual thirty-foot yacht named the *Titanic Ego*. *Ugh.* She rolled her eyes. *Seriously?*

She watched as additional craft, likely with their morning catch, made their way to dock. She'd bet she'd find a stellar fish-and-chips somewhere in the area. "I'd feel better with an alias."

"Yeah, well, Alice locked us into the real thing. Should have come up with a fake name for her to use at the beginning."

"At least that's one lie we won't have to remember." She didn't particularly care; she just wanted to be prepared. Her hand tightened around his and the rumble of the wheels on her suitcase offered a bit of a distraction. "Have you seen her husband since we met down in Seattle?"

"Couple of times. Once at the hospital, then once at Skyway Tower. He's bopping back and forth because of the kids. I told him I'd stay close in case they needed anything." He checked his watch. "If we get to the hospital soon, you can probably meet him. Kids'll be in school, though."

"Right. The kids. There's three of them?" Cases with kids always put her on edge.

Ty nodded. "Esme's seven. Bodhi's five, and River is three." He winced into the cloud-covered sun. "Esme's the only one who seems to have a grasp of what's going on. She's a little withdrawn but is playing mama to the little ones."

"Poor kid."

"Their neighbors are helping, keeping them entertained. And they have their classroom in the same building."

"Noted." Keeping them all in the same place where they felt safe was going to be important. "So what's my story?"

"Lawyer. White-collar. Figure I'd keep it to something you have a shot at." He grinned at her. "Serves you right for always talking about maybe going to law school."

"I only say that when I'm frustrated with my job." It never failed to impress her how he actually listened. The very idea she'd become a lawyer, however, would never sit well with her family. A McKenna lawyer? Perish the thought. "I can lawyer-speak well enough to pull that off. I think."

"There is one thing you should probably know."

"Only one?"

"I met the local sheriff." He paused. "I didn't tell him I'm FBI."

"Okay." She noodled that for a moment. "Considering you're usually pretty big on not stepping on the locals' toes, I'm guessing you have a good reason."

"Honestly?" For a flash of a second, he looked utterly defeated. "I went with my gut, but we both know that hasn't been acting in my best interests lately."

Understatement of the year.

"Alice's accident has got people spooked," Ty went on. "And you and I have been in enough small towns to know that nothing stays secret forever."

"Hearing the FBI is in town, even unofficially, will only cause more problems."

"And could drive whoever hurt Alice underground."

There it was. The rationale he probably needed.

"You did what you thought was right at the time," she assured him, even as she doubted his decision. Ticking off the local sheriff could, in the long run, turn around and bite them. "You get a feel for the sheriff otherwise?"

"I've kept an eye on him. He's good. He's not wearing the badge because it looks pretty. Near as I can tell, he cares. He knows everyone by name, checks in on people, does morning rounds with the shops and stores. He'd notice an unfamiliar face and he definitely noticed mine."

"Ah." Wren ducked her head to hide her grin. "He made you." No wonder Ty's gut was telling him to stay quiet.

"Pretty much," Ty admitted.

They stopped at a park bench that, according to the brass plaque bolted to the back, was dedicated to a Cyrus Ebscomb, who worked the Splendor waterway for more than fifty years. Seemed fitting his bench overlooked the entirety of the marina not far from the central hub of town.

"Things like what happened to Alice don't happen here," Ty said.

"Until they do." Wren stretched her stiff arms over her head, twisted back and forth as she took in her surroundings. "And they always do."

The cool breeze wafting off the sea behind her shifted her focus to the town in front of her. Three streets that she could see, each branching off from the center of Splendor. Not a lot of cars parked in the area, but she suspected that was because there was only one road into the town and that road came through a nearly three-mile-long tunnel that was shared by the railroad.

The buildings were mostly stone gray in color, and didn't climb much above two stories. She saw homey curtains in some second-story windows, indicating people living there. First levels appeared to be relegated to shops, stores and local businesses, including a real-estate office that boasted photos of rentals in their front window.

"That's Skyway, I assume." She jutted her chin toward the massive building that looked closer than it probably was. She knew it had been built originally as military housing, but after a massive shift in defense funding and priorities, the town had bought it for a fraction of its value and turned it into housing.

Since it was past the usual season of darkness— Alaska had had its annual sixty-day-plus period of no sun—it felt a bit brighter than she'd expected. The gray cloud cover that continued to advance, along with the increasing snow-threatening sprinkles from beyond, eked away some of that sunshine, though.

"I found an apartment in Skyway Tower to sublet through that real-estate office," Ty said. "We're on the fourth floor, same floor as the Hawkins family. Place is furnished. Nothing fancy, but we've dealt with a lot worse. Kitchen seems great."

She should have known he'd find a way for Wren to cook. It was a matter of survival for him since he could barely zap a microwave meal without scorching it. "How long are we in for, do you think?"

"Had to pay for the month." Ty shrugged. "It'll be worth it to keep us close to the family. It's a one bedroom."

"Keeping up appearances." She repeated his earlier

comment. "That's fine." No need to stand out with multiple bedrooms for a short stay. "The sheriff probably doesn't have any problems, but do you have an idea as to how we figure out who belongs here and who doesn't?"

"Given the attention Sheriff Egbert showered on me, right now, I'm it."

"Man. Egbert. Now, that's a name." Wren laughed and swiped at her tired eyes. "Since I've got my land legs back, let's say we head over to the hospital and check on Alice."

"You don't want to drop off your bags first?" Ty asked.

"Sooner we figure out what's going on with her, the sooner we can both get back home." Wren tugged her jacket tighter together beneath her chin and shivered. There was cold, and then there was Alaska cold, but she didn't have much time to think on it. Barely three blocks later Ty was headed inside a single-story building. "I thought—"

"Hospital and medical clinic are all one facility," Ty told her as he pulled open the glass door. "Full service, open twenty-four hours. They've got enough beds for twenty-three people. More if they double up in the rooms. Only three ICU beds. Any more who need it are sent to Anchorage."

He'd definitely done his homework. "Personnel?" She could only imagine a facility like this had to be short-staffed.

"Decent. Three on-call doctors, all GPs, specialists get brought in occasionally, otherwise…"

"Anchorage." Wren was sensing a theme.

"Eleven nurses on staff, rotating shifts and departments. Then you have the usual custodial, office, management. All told, twenty-six employees."

He'd definitely done his due diligence. If he'd been hanging around the hospital enough to gather this kind of information, no wonder the sheriff tagged him.

Despite its outside appearance, once inside the Splendor Medical Facility it looked like a welcoming, highly organized and efficient space. Perhaps more so than most big-city hospitals and clinics she'd been in. One thing that wasn't different was that familiar stale, almost too clean medicinal air and overly bright polished floors. The directional signs gave the option of visiting the outpatient clinic to the left or the inpatient services, including the ICU, to the right.

The demarcation between the two was a small desk labeled Security but with a current be-back-in-a-half-hour sign taped on the wall above.

"Alice's room is just there." Ty pointed to a closed door near the nurses' station. "Room eleven."

"Good morning, ladies." Ty set Wren's bag down and greeted the pair of female nurses sitting behind a scarred half-round desk. One wore scrubs in a rainbow pattern while the other was clad in a simple maroon-colored set.

"Hey there, Ty." The older of the two flashed overly interested dark eyes in his direction until she caught sight of Wren. The way she deflated was almost comical.

"Good morning, Aiyana." He leaned an arm on the counter. "How're things going with Alice?"

"Bradley just got finished speaking with Dr. Johansen. No change in her condition, I'm afraid."

Wren resisted the urge to arch a brow. Did HIPAA regulations not make it this far north? Then she realized

Ty had no doubt turned his charm on full blast on his previous visits and managed to wiggle his way around medical privacy issues.

Letting the two of them chat, Wren set her wheelie suitcase against the wall and did a quick assessment of her surroundings. Despite its limited size, the facility appeared to be up-to-date and, for the most part, impressive. The noise level wasn't bad, which made sense considering the patient capacity. What noise there was seemed to come from far down in the other direction where the clinic was located.

The halls were quite narrow and didn't echo the way so many hospitals did. Each hospital room appeared to have a window that allowed the patient to see out into the hallway and, more importantly perhaps, for the patients to be observed.

She spotted a male orderly mopping the floor farther down the hallway, past where a nurse's portable computer station was parked just under the exit sign. An elderly woman made her way out of her room aided by a nurse. Another nurse was at the woman's side, wheeling the patient's squeaky portable oxygen tank behind them. Toward the clinic, a tall, thin man in a white medical coat chatted with a mother and her two children.

Wren pushed her hands into her pockets, feigned slight boredom as she paced a bit, nearly running into a doctor coming out of what she saw was a supply closet. Out of habit, she looked down to the ID badge that wasn't where it should have been. He knocked into her, murmured a distracted "Sorry" before moving on.

Tall, a bit on the bulky side, he wore a long white lab jacket over navy blue scrubs. His black work boots squeaked as he strode down the hall before pausing at Alice's window, where he knocked quietly before pushing open the door.

Something niggled in Wren's mind. Chills erupted on the back of her neck. Wren's gaze dropped again to the doctor's shoes. She leaned over, looked at the nurses' feet. They both wore soft-soled shoes, comfortable. Colorful. Quiet.

The plastic blinds covering Alice's window closed.

Adrenaline kicking in, Wren bolted for Alice's door. She slammed it open, catching the two men inside off guard.

The younger and slighter of the two jumped out of his chair, still clinging to Alice's limp hand. The machines attached to Alice's vitals beeped at regular intervals.

"Who are you?" Bradley Hawkins was instantly recognizable from the photos Ty had messaged her. The man was a little on the thin side, more than a bit geeky and had the appearance of someone who had been kicked by life a good couple of times in the past few days.

"Hi, Bradley. Wren Savakis." She gave him a quick smile. "Ty's wife."

"Oh, sure, yeah." Bradley offered a weak apologetic smile. "Sorry. Ty mentioned you were headed up. Thanks for coming." He glanced at his wife. "I'm sure she'll thank you herself when she's awake." The hope clinging to his words made her heart ache even as it continued to pound in dread.

Alice Hawkins lay stone-still in the bed, the ventilator next to her keeping her breathing. Her left leg was elevated with metal pins held in place by circular metal frames in three different positions. Her right arm was in a cast and lying across her chest. A thick bandage was wrapped around her head, obscuring most of her light brown hair. She was so pale it was almost impossible to see where the stark white sheets began.

She could only imagine Ty's initial reaction to seeing Alice like this. Wren already understood his commitment to the case, but looking at his witness in this condition, she realized just how hard her job would be to keep Ty focused on not taking matters into his own hands. Any more than he already had, anyway.

"Everything all right, Doctor?" Wren asked the physician currently examining Alice's IV bags.

"Fine. Just adding her new medication." He didn't look once in her direction as he reached into his pocket.

Bradley shifted. "Dr. Johansen didn't mention any new medication. What are you doing?"

"My job." The man turned, choosing now to look at Wren directly.

Her eyes narrowed. She flicked a gaze to the hypodermic needle in his left hand. Her eyebrow twitched up.

The man pivoted and instantly locked an arm around Bradley's throat.

Bradley gasped, kicking out as the man dragged him toward the open bathroom door. The move sent Bradley's chair crashing to the floor. Alice's husband's eyes went wide and bulging, clawing at the arm around his neck as he struggled to breathe.

"Stop!" Wren took a step around the bed, heading for them, both hands up as if in surrender. "Think about this. There's nowhere for you to go."

The man's eyes darted to the door, but he remained silent.

"What's happening?" Bradley gasped as his face lost color.

"Let him go," Wren ordered as she continued to advance. She felt Ty move in behind her. She inclined her head to the right, hoping Ty, even off his game, would get the message. Behind Ty, she heard the kerfuffle of voices rising and footsteps echoing. "Let. Him. Go." She didn't flinch as she met the man's gaze over the top of Bradley's curly head.

The closer she got, moving around the foot of the bed, the more clear she could see the man's plan.

Out of the corner of her eye, Ty shifted away. Wren debated about using the gun she had stuffed into the back of her jeans. She didn't want to out herself completely. Not yet, anyway. And a gun in close quarters with a lot of innocents was rarely the wise play. She reached out, caught one of Bradley's flailing hands and tugged.

The man released him with a giant shove. Bradley catapulted into her. They fell back and Wren managed to control the landing so that her head didn't crack into the tiled floor.

Wren rolled Bradley off her, pushed to her feet and dived forward into the bathroom just as the man exited through the connecting door.

She heard a crash and a lot of yelling. Ty had tripped the man and sent him falling face-first into a cleaning cart. The pushback had Ty on the floor as well. The racket brought patients to their doors, bed alarms clanging and nurses scrambling to keep their charges safe and calm.

Ty reached out, attempted to grab the man's ankles as he stumbled to his feet, but he darted out of Ty's grip and raced off. His feet barely touched the ground as he ran for the emergency exit at the far end of the hall.

Ty practically bounced up, giving chase, as Wren fell in behind him.

The emergency alarm exploded overhead as they bolted outside, mere feet behind their suspect.

Their suspect picked up speed as he ran along the meandering footpath through the courtyard leading to an anemic parking lot. A white SUV sat parked on the other side of the waist-high exit gate.

From behind Ty, Wren saw the driver lean down. At first she assumed they were ducking out of the way, but then they popped back up, flung the door open, gun in hand, and aimed directly at them.

Chapter 3

"Down!" Wren tackled Ty from behind, sent them both tumbling over one another as a bullet whizzed past their heads.

Another shot, then another kept them pinned down as the suspect leaped over the short exit gate and threw himself into the car. They sped away with the passenger door still flailing. Ty untangled himself from Wren, shoved to his feet and ran out to try to get a look at the car. "No plates. White SUV. In Alaska, that's probably like finding a snowflake on an iceberg."

Adrenaline still coursing through her system, Wren got up onto her knees. "We should get back. Check on Bradley. And Alice." She didn't think the man had injected anything into Alice's IV line, but they couldn't be too careful.

Ty grabbed her arms and hauled her up. "I missed something, didn't I?"

She loathed the guilt and self-pity she heard in his voice. "You were charming the nurses to get information we needed." She shrugged. "One of them mentioned the doctor had just left after seeing Alice. Didn't make sense there'd be another one coming in to see her again so soon."

"Damn." His hands tightened around her upper arms and he hauled her onto her toes, pulled her close and pressed his lips against hers.

Her entire body locked down. There wasn't a muscle she could move or a thought she could process. The only thing that seemed to be getting through was the idea that Ty Savakis had finally, after more than seven years...kissed her.

"Um." It was all she could say once he set her back on her feet. She blinked, uncertain where that kiss had come from or what it even meant. It had to be cover... didn't it? But one quick glance told her there wasn't anyone to witness the moment. That meant... She struggled not to frown. What, exactly?

"You are amazing," he said before he moved around her and headed back inside through the now-open emergency exit door.

"Right. Amazing." She couldn't stop blinking, as if her body was trying to reboot her brain. What on earth was she supposed to do with *that*?

Embrace it, silly girl. Embrace it?! When had her subconscious jumped on board whatever crazy train she'd landed on? She stopped short before reaching the emergency door, lifted a finger to examine one of the wooden pillars and the bullets lodged in it.

She wedged the door open and ducked into an empty patient room. She snapped a pair of purple latex gloves out of the dispenser hanging on the wall. She grabbed a few extra, along with a pen resting on top of an admissions form.

Letting Ty deal with the initial fallout—they knew him better, after all—she returned to the pillar and, as flashbacks from her forensics training assaulted her, carefully pried the first bullet free. She wrapped it in one of the extra gloves, trying not to handle it very much. The heat of the bullet seeped into her fingers, helping to warm them against the chill.

It took longer to get the other two, but they soon joined the first one. She peeled off the gloves and stuffed everything into her jacket pocket. One of the orderlies turned up to pull the door closed and reset the alarm.

"Hang on!" Wren hurried inside. "Thanks."

The incident had brought everyone out of their offices and cubicles. Nurses focused on keeping the patients calm and getting them back into their rooms. The clinic patients had emptied into the hall. Voices remained raised and a bit panicked.

"I heard gunshots!" someone cried. "Did anyone else hear them? Is someone hurt?"

Wren avoided the pointed looks she received as she returned to Alice's room. The first thing she noticed, other than Ty's visible concern over Bradley, was that Alice herself remained completely and blissfully unaware of what had transpired. Good news, Wren supposed. Best she not know someone had tried to finish the job they'd started last week.

Alice's husband, on the other hand...

Ty crouched beside Bradley, who was still on the floor, only now he held an oxygen mask over his face and was breathing deeply.

"Prone to panic attacks," Ty told Wren as she stepped farther into the room. The nurse Ty had been chatting with previously was on the other side, resting a comforting hand on Bradley's shoulder.

"Did you check Alice's IV?" Wren asked the nurse, who nodded.

"First thing." She gestured to the disconnected line. "I pulled it to be safe. Our supervisor is getting a new setup."

Wren nodded.

Bradley tugged the mask off long enough to gasp at Ty. "Why would someone try to kill Alice?" he demanded. "Especially after..." He turned to his wife, his eyes wide with fear. "What on earth is going on?"

"An excellent question."

Wren spun at the deep, gravelly male voice that belonged to an older man standing in the doorway of Alice's hospital room. His hair was thick, more salt than pepper, and he wore a khaki uniform from his pressed trousers to the top of his wide-rimmed Smokey Bear hat. The sharp eagle-eyed expression on his narrow face assessed Wren in the blink of an eye, shifted to Ty before he settled on Bradley.

"Bradley? You and Alice all right?"

Bradley looked a bit confused at the question at first, then nodded. "Uh-huh." He rubbed a hand across his forehead. "Wren broke my fall. Thanks for that."

"No problem." Wren walked around the bed, stepping carefully past the trio of people huddled on the floor, and approached Alice's IV bag. The nurse was right. She didn't find any holes in the IV line or any indication the infusion tube had been tampered with.

Something caught her attention on the floor and she bent down. Peering under the bed, she found the hypodermic needle and the safety cap lying nearby. "Sheriff Egbert?" Wren asked and straightened to face the town's number one law enforcement officer.

"And you'd be Wren...Savakis." The pause in his voice and even narrower gaze suggested he was reevaluating Ty's previous story.

"That's me." She pulled a fresh pair of gloves out of her pocket and shoved her fingers into them.

"You got something?" he asked when she ducked out of sight again, picked up the needle and cap and topped the sharp end. The plunger was high, yet the tube itself was empty.

"Where did that come from?" the nurse asked as Bradley sat up and pushed the mask off his face again.

"Our assailant. It's evidence. Hopefully." She looked to the sheriff. "You'll be wanting this for prints, I presume?"

Sheriff Egbert eyed her for a moment. "Best we discuss that on my turf."

Wren removed the gloves, covering the needle with them to protect it.

"Shall we?" the sheriff asked as Bradley and Ty both pushed to their feet.

"Hang on." Bradley grabbed hold of the foot of Alice's bed as if to steady himself. "I don't know what is going on, but before I forget. Thank you." He looked to Wren. "It didn't occur to me he was anything other than a doctor. This is all so confusing. It's...incredible!"

"I'm just glad you're okay." Wren didn't want to generate more questions than the man already had.

"Yeah." He ran a hand across the back of his neck. "Might need a chiropractor after that, but yeah, I think I am." He looked at his wife. Tears filled his eyes. "Why would anyone want to hurt her?"

Wren's chest tightened with sympathy and more than

a little guilt. It was obvious Bradley had no clue about big chunks of his wife's past, which added a layer to the deception that she and Ty were spinning.

"I'm hoping we can figure that out," Ty said. "Remember what I told you, Bradley. Alice is my friend. I'm not going to leave until I know she and the rest of your family are safe."

"The kids." Bradley balked and lost what color was left in his face. "I didn't even… I need to check on the kids. They're supposed to go on a field trip today."

"Deputy Adjuk's gone over to Skyway Tower to check on them," Sheriff Egbert said. "But we can give Mrs. Caldwell a call if it would make you feel better. Ask her to keep them at the tower."

"Okay." Bradley raised a trembling hand to his throat. "It would, thanks."

"I'll do that right now," the nurse offered. "You just stay here with Alice. I'm going to have one of the doctors give you a once-over. Just to be safe."

"Good idea," Sheriff Egbert said. "Mr. and Mrs. Savakis?" He stepped back as if giving them room to exit.

"I feel like we've been called in to the principal's office," she muttered under her breath as she and Ty fell into step.

"Like you ever were," Ty teased. Wren scrunched her mouth to stop from smiling. He wasn't wrong. The principal's office had been more her brother Aiden's territory. He never had done well with being told what to do.

"What's the plan?" she asked as they made their way slowly out to join the sheriff in the hall.

"Tell him the truth," Ty said. "Most of it, anyway. Follow my lead, yeah?"

Her hand tingled from where he'd grasped it. "I always do."

It felt oddly like a perp walk, Ty thought as he and Wren walked out of the hospital behind the sheriff. Strange, being on the other side of one.

"Sheriff!" Behind them a voice had called.

Ty glanced over his shoulder as the sheriff turned, and found a young man, barely out of his teens with shaggy blond hair and slightly panicked eyes. He wore a uniform of sorts, with an oversize dark puffy jacket with a security emblem on the left sleeve.

"Hang on a second." Sheriff Egbert motioned to the marked vehicle parked haphazardly across two spaces at the front entrance.

"Think he's going to run us out of town?" Wren said in her half-teasing tone.

"I bet he's trying to figure out where we fit in." Ty couldn't blame the man. Things had definitely gone a bit off the rails since Alice's accident. He dropped Wren's duffel onto the ground and leaned against the hood of the vehicle. "You get a good look at the guy's face?"

"Enough that I can play around with an ID program."

"On a scale of one to ten, how confident are you you'll find something if we can talk the sheriff into using his computer system?"

"About a three." She dug into her pocket, pulled out a wadded-up purple glove. "No scars, no distinguishing features that I could see. He blends. Dug these out of the pillar, though." Unwrapping the latex, she showed the bullet fragments to him. "Full metal jackets. Good ones," she added. "Military grade, if I had to guess."

And they would have to guess without a lab backing them up. "Military opens up a whole new can of worms."

"'Military grade' doesn't mean military." She chewed on the inside of her cheek, the way she always did when she was puzzling something out. "Private contractors can get a hold of stuff like this. Given that Treyhern's likely behind this, it would make sense he'd hire someone to take care of his witness problem. The hypo was empty, by the way. Probably planned to inject an air bubble into her IV line."

Ty's stomach clenched. "With her injuries, an embolism would be seen as natural causes."

"Risky, though, doing it with so many people around," Wren mused.

"Maybe they didn't have a choice." Disappointment crashed through him at her previous comment. "I thought you agreed with me about Treyhern being responsible."

"You say Alice wasn't involved in anything else that could be triggering this," she said. "I'm willing to trust you on that, but I'm keeping my options open. Going in blind isn't going to help us protect her. We need to be ready for anything."

Grudgingly, he had to admit she was right. Getting tunnel vision where a suspect was concerned was a surefire way to blow the case. And this was one case he couldn't afford to mess up.

"Sorry about that." Sheriff Egbert left the young man behind looking somewhat less…dejected. "Obie Farland. Been working security for the clinic for about three months. Feels responsible for what happened."

"He wasn't where he should have been," Ty observed. "Saw the 'away from the desk' note when we came in."

"Considering that up until now we thought Alice's accident was just that, Obie was exactly where he was supposed to be." The sheriff's eyes sharpened like a dagger's edge. "Doing his rounds through the clinic. He asked if it would be okay if he worked an extra shift." Sheriff Egbert glanced back at the clinic as he pulled open his car door. "He'll keep an eye on Alice's door specifically."

"Nice one, Ty," Wren muttered as she climbed into the back seat. "Shame the kid for doing his job."

Ty didn't respond. Guilt wasn't an easy emotion to deal with and he'd lived with his share of it. Funny, he'd have thought he'd gotten better at riding that particular wave by now.

"Gotta admit." Sheriff Egbert pulled out of the lot and turned left. "I've been sheriff of this town for going on seventeen years. Seen my share of fistfights and brawls, especially at The Icebreaker during hockey season—"

"Icebreaker?" Wren asked.

"Local bar. Pub," Ty corrected quickly at the glare he got in the rearview mirror.

"That back there isn't something I ever want repeated in my town," Sheriff Egbert told them. "Everyone should feel safe in a hospital."

"We aren't going to argue with you, Sheriff," Ty said.

"I'm a two-person operation here in Splendor. I don't have the staff to go running around looking for assault suspects with needles, or anything else, for that matter."

"But you were already looking for one, right, Sheriff?" Wren said. "The person who ran Alice down in their car?"

"Mrs. Savakis—"

"Wren is fine."

Ty bit the inside of his cheek. He'd been wondering how long it would take for her to get irritated by that.

"Wren." Sheriff Egbert glanced at her in the mirror now. "Yes, I've been doing my best, but something tells me I've been working under some misconceptions. Either of you want to tell me what Alice Hawkins got herself into?"

"She didn't *get* herself into anything." Ty's defense of the younger woman struck like second nature. It took precisely three minutes to drive from the hospital to the dedicated parking space in front of the blink-and-you'll-miss-it sheriff's office around the corner from the main drag of Splendor. This really was a blink-and-you-might-miss-it kind of town.

"I don't like the idea of leaving Alice alone at the hospital," Wren said as Sheriff Egbert parked. He flung open his door, then paused before climbing out.

"Neither do I, but I don't have any spare deputies." He slipped out, retrieved their bags from the back and waited for them to join him on the sidewalk. "Obie and his nighttime counterpart are going to alternate shifts. It's the best I can do." He hefted the duffel bag and pushed it into Ty's chest. It took all of Ty's effort not to *ugh* out loud. "Come on in." Sheriff Egbert pulled open the solitary glass door and waved them inside. "Let's chat."

To call the sheriff's office a hole-in-the-wall could be considered an exaggeration. The space couldn't have been more than twenty feet across, but it was considerably deeper than wide. Two desks sat across from one another, each topped with a computer and various trinkets and mementos. The wooden filing cabinet seemed both outdated yet completely in style with the rustic decor. As with most small-town station houses, this one boasted a pair of jail cells lining the back wall over which two narrow windows sat, the only real light other than the lamps currently glowing.

Cozy to the point of claustrophobic, but with enough personal touches that it worked.

"Have a seat." Sheriff Egbert pulled a couple of folding chairs out from between the filing cabinet and wall. Ty suspected Wren was surprised they hadn't been put in the cells.

"Let's start by reviewing the information you gave me a couple of days ago when we chatted, Mr. Savakis. If that's your real name."

"There's usually *FBI special agent* in front of it," Wren said.

"FBI." Whatever Sheriff Egbert had been expecting, it appeared it wasn't that. "Huh." He sat back, rested a thumping finger against his lips. "Well, that's something. And your relationship with Alice?"

"Professional," Ty replied. "Ten years ago Alice Hawkins was a witness in a murder case I worked. The suspect was a man named Ambrose Treyhern. Thanks to her, he's currently twenty-five to life in a maximum-security prison." He tried to get a bead on the sheriff's thoughts, but couldn't. "Treyhern was recently granted a new trial. My guess is he isn't thrilled with the prospect of her testifying again and he's hired someone to make sure she doesn't. I'm not here to cause problems, Sheriff. I'm here to find out who's trying to kill my witness."

Sheriff Egbert's eyes shifted between them. "Have to admit." He tapped a restless finger against the edge of his desk. "As disturbing as this is, it sits better with me than having to suspect someone in this town is responsible for the hit-and-run."

Ty kept his expression passive. He hadn't thought of that.

"I've spent the last week looking at people I've known for more than twenty years, wondering if they were guilty." Regret and a hint of anger tinged the sheriff's voice. "Would have been nice not to have to do that."

Ty winced. "In hindsight, I see where I should have handled things differently."

"Suppose you didn't know who you could trust, either." Sheriff Egbert's gaze flicked to Wren. "Except you."

"We've been partners for a long time," Wren said. "We have each other's back."

"Even when it means following him up here to the middle of nowhere?"

She shrugged and earned even more respect from Ty. "He needs me, I'm there."

"No questions asked?" the sheriff challenged.

"Oh, plenty to ask," she admitted with a wry smile. "But the answers wouldn't change anything."

She had no idea how much that sentiment meant to him. "I was on the phone with Alice when she was run down." Ty wanted the attention shifted back to him. Wren was going to have enough to deal with once their involvement in the case got out. And it would get out.

The more he could get the local authorities to focus on him, the clearer Wren would be. "She needed reassurances about testifying again." His head buzzed with the memory.

"Guess I have me an ear witness instead of an eye one, then," Sheriff Egbert said. "What did you hear?"

"Enough to believe this wasn't anything other than deliberate. No screeching brakes or tires." He refrained from sharing how the sound of Alice's scream and the heavy thud of her body hitting the ground haunted him.

The sheriff looked him straight in the eye. "As you know from our previous conversation, no skid marks at the scene, so I'd agree with your observation. The glass we found is one of the most common used for headlights, according to the crime lab in Anchorage, so no joy there. While it's not tourist season at the moment, we've had our share of visitors over the past few weeks. No one who's raised any alarm bells, other than you. But my deputy and I will ask around. Especially after what happened this morning at the clinic. Question."

"Okay," Wren said.

"That needle you found under Alice's bed." He shifted his attention back to Wren. "Your fancy FBI field office in Anchorage gonna be able to process that for you?"

"Ah." Wren glanced uneasily at Ty.

The office door opened, letting a cold blast of air in. Ty and Wren both turned in their chairs as a young woman shoved her hood off her dark head and stomped her boots. "All clear at Skyway, Sheriff. Kids are good. I went through the security camera recordings back to yesterday morning. Nothing strange that I noticed."

"Good to hear," Sheriff Egbert said. "Deputy Shelly

Adjuk, FBI special agents Ty Savakis and Wren..." He frowned, inclined his head. "It's not Savakis, is it?"

"It's McKenna, actually. Wren McKenna." She stood, held out her hand as Shelly approached. "Nice to meet you, Deputy Adjuk."

"Shelly, please. Wow. FBI, really?" Her eyes lit up with wonder and held more than a hint of excitement. "I would love to talk to you... Right. Sorry. Not now." She held up both hands and backed away. "I can bend your ear later."

"Fair warning." Sheriff Egbert eyed Wren. "She can do that better than anyone you've ever met. Now, about that needle." He reached for the phone. "I'm assuming you're planning on running that up to your FBI lab in Anchorage. Shall I let them know you're coming?"

Ty glanced at Wren, who shrugged. He may as well be sitting in church, given the amount of confessions he was making today. "Actually, we'd rather avoid any official interactions with the agency. My being here isn't exactly...sanctioned."

"Have you two gone rogue?" Shelly asked in a tone that sounded more enthusiastic than disapproving.

"Don't you have to file a report on Mrs. Tachino's prowler, Deputy?" Sheriff Egbert asked.

"Prowler, my left foot," Shelly muttered loud enough for them to hear. "A merry band of raccoons is more like it."

"Look, Sheriff." Ty sat up straighter and drew his legs under him. "I know my turning up is a bit of a complication—"

"*Our* turning up," Wren corrected.

"Right. We aren't here in any official capacity." He

stopped short of admitting that should his presence become known to his superior, those complications were going to increase. "Ten years ago I gave Alice my word she'd be safe. I'm not going to go away. Not until I know she is. That said, if our bosses find out we're here before we find the person or persons responsible for hurting Alice, chances are they'll get away with it." Considering Alice's condition, odds were pretty good they already had.

Sheriff Egbert met his gaze with chilling intensity. "My main concern is the safety of my town and the people who live here. I'm beginning to think Alice might be better off being transferred to a facility with more security. There's a hospital in Anchorage—"

"A bigger hospital could give them more cover," Wren said before Ty could. "I understand your concern, Sheriff, but you've taken new measures to keep her safe. People will be on the lookout for unfamiliar faces. I know it isn't your first choice, but these guys have worked themselves into a bit of a pinch point. Odds are better we'll find them here. We just need the leeway to look."

Wren's argument didn't require any backup from Ty. She'd hit it on the head.

"All right," Sheriff Egbert agreed but looked as if he wasn't entirely convinced. "Like I said, we're a two-person operation. It'd be pretty reckless of me not to accept help when it's being offered. Even unofficial federal help. I'd keep that information to yourself around here, though. Not everyone in Splendor has the best opinions when it comes to Feds. You fly low, I'll give you enough lead. But I'll snap it back the second I think you're overstepping with my people."

"Understood." Relieved, he looked to Wren for her reaction.

"What about a lab to process the needle?" she asked.

"I'll see what I can do with our contacts in Juneau," Sheriff Egbert said. "It'll take time."

Of course, time was the one thing Ty couldn't be certain they had a lot of.

"Appreciate your understanding, Sheriff." Ty stood, motioned to Wren's bags sitting by the front door. "I think it's past due we got out of your hair. We'll be in touch."

"Yes," Sheriff Egbert said as they headed out. "You will be."

Chapter 4

"Home sweet home." Ty unlocked the door to their fourth-floor apartment and pushed it open ahead of Wren. "For the next little while, anyway."

The walk from the sheriff's station to Skyway Tower had helped clear his head, but not completely. The closer they got to their temporary residence, the more anxious he became. The idea that his uncertainty had everything to do with Wren only added to the pressure building inside of him.

He hadn't quite been able to reconcile the odd anticipation he'd felt since Wren agreed to play house with him. They'd worked so closely together for the past seven years, it seemed strange to feel anxious or uncertain. They'd done this plenty of times before: gone undercover as a couple. But their obligation to the FBI had always been a kind of protective barrier between them. Here? On their own, without the agency backing them up, that barrier was nowhere to be seen or felt.

One more thing to throw him off his game. His pinballing emotions—anger, frustration, guilt—about Alice and Treyhern left him feeling as if his emotions were scattered all over the place and he lacked the energy to pull himself back together.

The hall of the fourth floor of Skyway Tower hadn't quite shaken that military housing feel. The reconfiguration and redesign had added more homey details, of course. The dark-colored patterned carpeting along the hallway. The soft beige walls. The wood color trim outlining the dozen or so apartment entrances. To Ty, it kind of felt like the building was trying a little too hard to be something it wasn't. But what it was, he reminded himself and as he'd just said to Wren, was home. For now.

A door behind them snapped open. Wren stepped back and the two of them looked to the elderly woman poking her gray-haired head out of an apartment a few doors down.

"Newcomers?" she called.

"Yes, ma'am." Ty rested a hand on Wren's shoulder. "Staying here a few weeks. We're friends of Alice Hawkins."

"Oh, Alice. Poor Alice." She emerged from the doorway, her bright pink tracksuit a startling blip of color. "Such a shame. How's she doing?"

"Last we heard, okay," Ty said and hoped that statement didn't come back to bite him. It was only a matter of time before word of what had happened at the hospital today got around town.

"Agatha!" Another voice echoed into the corridor. "I just got a double word and triple letter score. It's your... Oh. New people. Just moving in?"

Agatha rolled her eyes. "This is my twin sister, Florence. People just call us the Thistle sisters."

Ty's brows went up. He might have guessed sisters, but not twins. Agatha was short and squat where Florence was lean and towered over her sister by at least six inches. Where Agatha wore her gray hair neatly up and away from her face, Florence's dark frizzy curls framed her thin face.

"Welcome to Skyway." Florence waved and set the bangles on her wrist to jangling. "Do you like board games? We have a large collection if you're in need of any. Or join us for one! We promise not to win too quickly."

"Appreciate that, ma'am," Ty said with a chuckle. "We'll keep that in mind after we settle in."

"Come on by for tea anytime," Agatha called. "We love visitors. We've lived here going on fifteen years. Can never have too many visitors."

"Leave them be, Ag." Florence tugged on her sister's sleeve. "Can't you see they're wanting some alone time?" They were still bickering when the door closed.

"They're cute," Wren said. "And maybe a little lonely?"

"Probably why they're happy to see new people."

"Which apartment is Alice's?"

"Two doors down that way, left side." He pointed behind him. "Four G."

"Quiet floor. Soundproofing must be pretty good." She grinned. "Should work in our favor, yeah?"

Her statement sent a surprising array of rather erotic images shooting through his overstressed mind. Images starring him and Wren. Ty shook his head. Why on earth was he going down this road? They were adults. They knew how to keep their hands to themselves. Besides, they'd agreed a long time ago that their friendship and partnership were far more important than any physical attraction. Still. Ty's gaze dropped to her curves on display even beneath her puffy jacket. They'd probably been more intimate with one another than most lovers were.

Sleep, he told himself. He needed sleep. As much as he could get. That should reset the short circuit that had obviously taken place in his brain. And libido.

"Oh, this is cute."

Wren's surprise brought him fully into the apartment. Most of the space was painted a bright white—the walls, the massive floor-to-ceiling bookcase, the trim. No doubt that had been an effort to make the seven-hundred-square-foot space appear larger than it was.

He closed the door, bolted it out of habit. The splashes of color came courtesy of the furnishings and decor, which ranged from blankets and wall hangings of Indigenous patterns to the rustic bric-a-brac scattered about the living room.

"Shipping furniture out here costs a small fortune," Ty told her. "Doesn't make sense to take it with you when you leave, especially if you plan to come back. As you can see, reading's big in Splendor." The enormous multi-shelf bookcase was jam-packed with mostly genre fiction ranging from some of his favorite suspense titles to Wren's preferred epic fantasy novels. There was also a large selection of puzzles, which seemed a not-so-subtle warning of uneventful evenings. "Got plenty of movies to choose from." He indicated the selection of DVDs on a section of shelving. "The place isn't anything fancy, but it looked comfortable to me. We've got internet and cable, but again, they can be spotty."

"Being on the coast probably means a lot of outages," Wren said.

"Got your sofa—a sleeper, in case you were wondering."

"I wasn't." She wandered the room, no doubt making

a mental note of the television, comfy overstuffed chair and the narrow doorway leading into a well-organized and arranged kitchen. "It's small but I like that. We won't be falling over one another. Much." She flashed him a smile as she pulled off her knit cap, fluffed up her hair. The blond caught the sunlight streaming in through the window over the back of the sofa. Unzipping her jacket, she disappeared into the kitchen. "Kitchen's service-able. Better than yours, anyway," she called. "Fridge is bare, though."

So far he'd only eaten at a few of the restaurants in town or gotten takeout. "Didn't get around to shopping."

"Or you were waiting for me to get here because we both know you love my cooking."

He couldn't help but smile. "I'll plead the Fifth on that." He'd missed her these last few weeks. Being around Wren always centered him. Kept him on an even keel. She understood him, even tolerated him without adding drama. Not that she was responsible for his men-tal well-being. But her presence definitely helped. His vacation punishment hadn't put him in a good place. Hearing about Alice had only dropped him deeper into that spiral.

"Small-town grocery stores are a wealth of informa-tion," she said as she came back out. After removing her jacket and hanging it on one of the half-dozen hooks be-hind the door, she checked the half bath beside the afore-mentioned bookcase, then went into the bedroom. "If we hit that up later, we should get a feel for what people are thinking about what happened to Alice."

"Scared." He hadn't needed to visit any store to pick up on that. He followed her into the space where a king-size bed sat wedged between two anemic-looking night-stands. The apartment was a bit dated. No USB plugs or a lot of storage beyond the assembled MDF armoire that had been painted to match the blinding white of the walls, but the navy bedspread accented with bright red pillows added a kind of nautical feel. The character of the place seemed a bit disjointed, but they didn't need character. They just needed to be close to the Hawkins family. "They're scared. I got coffee this morning and the hit-and-run was definitely a big topic of conversation. Had a few odd looks shot my way, so the sheriff was right. They're more than aware when someone new is in town. I'd bet that's part of what's got them spooked. I dropped my name. Said I was a friend of Alice's. Just to see how they react to newcomers."

"Sheriff Egbert probably isn't the only person who's been wondering if one of their own was responsible," Wren mused. "If there's one thing a lot of British television has taught me, it's never commit a crime in a small town. The perpetrator won't ever get away with it, if only because everyone knows everyone's business. You know?" She poked her head into the second bathroom, this one with a full shower and claw-foot tub. He could attest to the water pressure being excellent. "It could be someone local. Small doesn't mean it doesn't have crime. And most everyone has a price."

"Presence of a sheriff proves that," Ty agreed.

"We should ask him about the troublemakers in town."

"Give it a day or two," Ty warned. "I think we've earned all the goodwill we're going to get for now."

"His deputy is interesting," Wren observed. "Young, though."

He'd thought the same thing. "Young enough to hurt our egos. Old enough to be competent. One thing." He crouched, pulled his folding pocketknife from his back pocket. The knife had been a gift from his first partner, the same partner who had helped him close the Treyhern case the first time.

"What are you doing?" Wren poked her head out of the bathroom as he slipped the blade in between two planks of the hardwood floor that he'd pried loose upon his first arriving.

"The really good thing about actual hardwood flooring." He pointed, then held out his hand. "Give me your badge and FBI ID."

"Oh, sure. Yeah." She handed him both. "You thinking we might get mugged on the streets and our secret identities will be revealed?"

"I'm not taking any chances with anything where Alice is concerned." He settled her items into the space under the floorboard, then pushed it back into place. He stood and stepped on it just to make sure it was solid.

Wren ducked back into the bathroom, leaving Ty unable to resist temptation.

He sat on the edge of the bed. Then, before he could talk himself out of it, he lay down. He didn't think he'd ever, in his entire life, found a pillow so perfectly soft.

"Now that we're in with the sheriff, that should make some things easier." Wren opened and closed cabinets in the bathroom. "If Sheriff Egbert's been suspicious, he's probably looked into a few people. Be interesting to know who."

"I got the feeling if he suspected anyone, he'd have let us know. Been here a long time." His eyes drooped.

"Yeah." Wren sighed. "He does seem to like his job. For the most part."

"He likes the town." He smothered a yawn. "He moved here with his wife and two kids. Kids have since moved back into the Lower 48. Wife runs the Books & Brews shop on the main street."

"Well, if we run out of things to read here, we know where to go." Wren popped back into the bedroom. "I'm gonna need something to occupy my brain with other than looking at your mug."

He managed a weak smile. Only when he felt the bed dip did his eyes spring back open. "Sorry." He pinched the bridge of his nose. "I'm about out of steam." It didn't escape his notice that it was only now that Wren was by his side that he felt comfortable enough to sleep.

"I can tell." She touched his leg and sent a wave of heat straight to his groin. He nearly groaned. He was more out of it than he'd realized. "I'm still a bit buzzed with adrenaline. Why don't I hit up the grocery, take a walk around town, get acclimated, and you can get some sleep."

"If you're sure." He rolled onto his side facing her, already feeling his body completely relax. "Second set of keys are on one of the bookcase shelves."

"Don't argue with me or anything," she teased. "I'll be back in a bit."

"Just need an hour or so."

"Uh-huh."

Her derisive snort was the last thing he heard before he dropped off to sleep.

at the end of the hall. The view put the ocean on full display. "It's a beautiful place."

"That'd be my opinion," Al agreed. "Maybe you two'll put this on your list of places to move to."

"Maybe." Ty must have dropped the hint around town that they were looking to move. "It's definitely shot up my list. As long as it's safe," she added, not wanting to get overly enthusiastic. "We have a lot of places in contention, though. A while back we spent a month in Sedona, Arizona. I absolutely loved it. Ty, not so much." While she always tried to stick as close to the truth as possible, lies were a necessary part of her job. Even when she was off book. "Now that Ty sold his company, we've got the means to consider almost anyplace in the world."

Al's bushy eyebrows arched and he shoved his hands into the pockets of his dark blue overalls. Koda let out a bit of a whine before sighing. "Glad to hear we've made the cut."

"Ty's a fan of unique communities." Wren did her best to stave off doubt. "I'm guessing you don't get many strangers around here."

"Get a few," Al confirmed. "You and Ty are the first new tenants since the holidays."

Interesting. "I don't suppose there's a thrift store in town, is there? I know we won't be here long, but I do love me a thrift store. They're such a representation of the area." They also tended to be a wealth of information. Thrift-store owners knew everyone and everything that happened. If they wanted to get the real pulse of Splendor, that was one place to start.

"Got a few stores, but sounds like you'll be wanting to visit Tundra Antiques and Treasures," Al said. "Callie

Haller owns the place." He winked. "She thinks putting *antiques* in the title makes it fancier than it is. Truth is the woman's a pack rat. Never throws much away, but she makes an effort at restoring things. Keeps the place pretty tidy. Might be a treasure or two lurking in there for you."

"Sounds like a fun place to explore." She touched his arm as she passed. "Appreciate the recommendation. Be seeing you around. Bye, Koda."

"You call me if you need anything!" Al called after her, his voice echoing down the corridor as she headed for the stairs.

The chill she got the second she entered the stairwell had her zipping up her jacket. Still, she memorized the number of steps, leaned over the railing to see if the stairs went the entirety of the building or cut off before the roof.

Emerging through the door that led to the lobby level, Wren found herself looking at a large open space filled with bright-colored walls and fun geometric carpeting, much like the lobby of a hotel near an amusement park where she'd once stayed. She hadn't paid too much attention when she'd entered the building; she'd been looking forward to unloading her bags and getting a look at where she'd be staying—and sleeping—the next few nights.

The entirety of the lobby level was dedicated to services and office space. The room for the complex's director near the front door had Wren turning back toward the elevator and walking down the east hall leading to the day care and school. She checked her watch. Just before lunchtime. She was hoping the chaos of mealtime might allow her a chance at observation.

She could hear the telltale sounds of singing and clapping. Structured activities, she assumed. That off-key enthusiastic caterwauling shot her straight back to kindergarten, when she'd been subjected to endless show-and-tells and story times. Sitting still had completely missed her DNA. Even now, she felt a bit jittery and jumpy.

Keeping her gaze steady, she scanned the upper corners of the walls, turned occasionally, getting a feel for what, if any, security measures were in place.

The wide hallways were accentuated by large windows. Nothing felt claustrophobic, despite the numerous amenities made available to residents. The beige walls gave way to colorful murals of children cartwheeling and tumbling their way around giant rainbows of bubbles that served as the entryway of the day care.

The second she approached the door, the back of her neck prickled. Leaning inside, she grabbed the door frame, then held up a hand in apology when the young Black woman sitting in the teeny tiny kid's chair shifted immediately to face her. There was an attempt at friendliness, but there was no mistaking the suspicion in her dark eyes.

"May I help you?" The way she stretched out her arm, as if providing protection for the handful of children in her charge, allayed some of Wren's concerns. She counted eight children in the circle, six boys and two girls of varying ages.

"I'm sorry. I'm new to the building," Wren said. "Just getting the lay of the land. Didn't mean to interrupt."

"It's story time!" a little girl of about five announced, her bright blond ponytail bouncing as she jumped to her feet. "We're listening to *Frog and Toad*. They're friends."

"I love *Frog and Toad*," Wren told them. "Again, I'm sorry to interrupt."

She backed away, and as she turned to leave the same way she'd come, she found herself facing a forty-something woman who definitely had the look of a school official.

"Hello." The woman's voice was a bit clipped. She hugged a stack of notebooks against her chest. Her fiery red hair was pulled away from her face, but springy gray curls erupted along her hairline. The color of her cardigan sweater reminded Wren of ripe blueberries.

"Hi." Wren did her best to appear contrite. "I'm not creeping around, I promise. I'm just new to the building. Wren Savakis." She held out her hand. Why did saying that name send chills up her spine? "My husband and I are friends of Alice Hawkins."

"Oh, you're Ty's wife." The woman visibly relaxed. "Nora Caldwell. I'm one of the teachers here at Skyway. I live in 2F."

"It's nice to meet you."

"Just a moment, please." She stepped around Wren and poked her head in the door. "It's okay, Gemma. She's a new tenant and a friend of Alice's. Oh!" She stepped back when a young girl with chestnut color hair worn long down her back stepped outside. "Esme, I don't think—"

Esme turned huge hazel eyes on Wren. "You know my mom?"

"I, ah…" Wren swallowed hard. She had no problem

lying to adults. Kids, on the other hand… "My husband does. His name's Ty."

"Is my mom okay?" Esme attempted to leave the classroom, but Nora blocked her with the gentlest of nudges.

"Last I heard." Wren approached, but kept a distance when she crouched down. "We thought we'd come out and see if you all needed some help while your mom recovers."

Tears exploded in the little girl's eyes. "She's hurt real bad."

"I know." The sadness on Esme's face made Wren's heart twist. "But you and your brothers, you're doing okay, yeah?"

"We're taking good care of them," Nora said as if defending herself.

"I'm sure you are," Wren assured her. Two little boys popped up behind Esme, one taller and slimmer than the other; the smaller one had bright blue eyes that sparked as if they'd been charged by the sun. "You must be River. And Bodhi." She looked to the older boy, who took his time following his brother's lead when it came to smiling. "I'm sure I'll see you all a little while later. After school."

"This is not school," Bodhi stated matter-of-factly.

"The rest of the students are on a field trip today." Nora bent down and set her notebooks on the ground, but Wren noticed the way the woman reached her arm out to keep a barrier between Wren and the children.

"We didn't get to go," Bodhi said with a scowl.

"Because Mom's sick and we need to stay together," Esme whispered loudly. "Dad said so. Go back and listen to the story. You, too, River."

"Okay!" River practically hopped his way back to the circle.

"You can go back, too, Esme," Nora said kindly but with a firmness that impressed Wren.

Esme didn't look convinced and met Wren's gaze with a steadfastness that felt a bit unnerving. There were questions in her eyes, questions Wren herself might have been asking in her place.

"I'll see you later," Wren assured the little girl. "When your dad's home. Okay?"

"Okay." Esme let Nora gently push her back inside and Nora closed the door behind her.

"Again, sorry." Wren didn't need to make enemies of the schoolteacher.

"It's all right." Nora picked up her notebooks and, not so subtly, steered Wren back down the hall. "Since you're aware of Alice's accident, I'm sure you can understand why we're being overly cautious." Her gaze fluttered up and to the right.

It was only then Wren caught sight of the camera in the corner of the wall overhead. It was pretty well hidden, thanks to the artwork, but it was definitely there, its little red light blinking away. "How are they doing? The kids?"

"As well as can be expected," Nora said. "I don't mean to be rude, but—"

"I took you a bit by surprise." Wren wasn't going to apologize again. That would be overkill. But it was clear there was more security in Skyway Tower than she'd expected. "I imagine things have been tense since Alice's accident."

"To say the least," Nora said in a way that led Wren to

believe she'd been holding that confession in for a while. Once they were in the main lobby area of the first floor, Nora appeared to relax. "It sounds so contrite, but things like this don't happen here. Let's start over." She took a deep breath, closed her eyes, and when she opened them, whatever hostility had been in her gaze was gone. "Welcome to Skyway."

"Thank you. I only wish it were under different circumstances."

"I'm sure Alice will appreciate seeing friends when she's able," Nora said. "Do you have children?"

"No." Why her face went suddenly hot she couldn't quite figure. "Not yet, anyway." At thirty-three she'd already started hearing that distinctive biological clock start ticking, but so far she'd been able to drown it out. "We're thinking about it now. Just need to figure out where we're going to settle down first." Yep, definitely no trouble lying to adults. "It's a unique situation you have here in Splendor. I like the idea of a self-contained community. School in the same building where you live. Is it open just to Skyway tenants or any of the kids in Splendor?"

"We're funded for up to fifty students."

"I was reading up on the town on my flight in." Talk about lies snowballing. "I think I saw where there are three teachers? You, Gemma and, um…" She pretended to have to think. "Celeste Wheeler."

"Four, actually." Nora straightened with pride. "We just got a new one a few weeks ago. Felix Oliver. He's an inventor by trade but teaches science on the side. You're very well-informed."

"I'm an attorney," Wren said. "Which means I'm a

details person. So Felix is new to Splendor, then?" At Nora's immediate frown, Wren hurried on. "It would be nice to talk to another newcomer. See what advice he might have for us as far as settling in."

"I can let him know to be on the lookout for you." Something in Nora's voice had Wren ready to move on.

"I'd appreciate that. Nice to meet you." She headed for the door.

"Hang on!" Nora hurried after her, then pointed to the basket on the table. "Gordy from the second floor leaves us a different kind of fresh-baked treat every day." She grabbed the handle of the basket and held it out for Wren. "Today is white chocolate macadamia nut cookies."

Wren's stomach still wasn't eager to be tested. "They look delicious." She took one and bit in. "Oh, my gosh." Unsettled stomach forgotten, she took another fast bite. "These are amazing!"

"Right?" Nora beamed and shook her head. "He hasn't struck out once. Do you bake?"

"Some," Wren admitted. "I'm a better cook than baker." Cooking was a lot of improvising. Baking, on the other hand, required precision and far more attention than she was willing to spend. Wren was more of a wing-it kind of person. In and out of the kitchen. "I'm just gonna take another…" She grabbed a second cookie and stashed it in her pocket. "For my husband. Maybe," she added with a sly grin. "If it makes it back. See you around, Nora."

"Yes," Nora said slowly. "See you."

Wren had no doubt the older woman could be a font of information, but she was also cautious and suspicious. That was going to take a little extra work to get around.

That said, the conversation had been productive. Wren now knew of a newcomer to Splendor that Ty didn't. She made a mental note to do a check on Felix Oliver.

Four teachers in one school of less than fifty students. An impressive student-to-instructor ratio.

The cold air blasted against her face when she stepped outside. Wincing, she drew up her hood, tightened the strings and turned herself into a half mummy. "How do people live like this?" She'd grown up in Boston. She knew cold. Or thought she did. Clearly she'd been wrong. Winter Alaska cold was like blades of ice stabbing into your bones.

A collection of park benches and picnic tables were arranged over a large area currently covered in snow. Wren could imagine families here in the warmer months, enjoying the sunshine. There was a fun direction sign at the end of the curving walkway, with giant arrows pointing toward various locations: downtown, marina, passenger air trams.

She shoved the last of her cookie into her mouth, considered having the second one, too, but told herself to wait instead. Tilting her head, she looked up into the sky. Sure enough, far off, there were thick wires stretching along one of the tallest mountains. Up, up, up… She gulped as a bright red cable car came into view and headed toward what she guessed was the top of the mountain hidden in the clouds.

"Gives you a view like no other."

Wren spun at the voice, feeling a bit panicked, which was not a good state for an FBI agent. It wasn't easy to sneak up on her. "Excuse me?" she asked the young man standing behind her. He looked like a walking rainbow, from his multicolored riot of curls that appeared to defy gravity to the colorful jacket covering paint-splattered jeans.

"The trams." He pointed back to where she'd been looking. "They offer a great view of Splendor any time of the day or night. And the surrounding mountains. On a clear day, at least."

"Where exactly do the trams take you? The closest glacier?"

He laughed, shifted his oversize bag higher up on his shoulder. "Vacation homes. For rich people. Very rich people."

Wren couldn't help but smile. "Why are you whispering?"

"No idea. I'm Doodle."

"Doodle," Wren repeated in disbelief. "Really?"

"Well, it's Leonardo, actually. Leonardo Doodle, but there's only one Leo." He winked. "If you get my drift."

"Ah, actor or artist?"

His grin widened. "What do you think?"

She shook her head. "I think I'm meeting some very interesting people in Splendor." Given her profession, that was saying something. "Hello, Doodle. I'm Wren."

"Ah, Ty's wife. The lawyer." Doodle nodded and sent his curls into overdrive. "Heard you were coming in. I'm so sorry about Alice." He inclined his head. "Are you close?"

"She and my husband have been friends for years." She could tell she was going to have this conversation a lot for the foreseeable future. Best to keep the details simple and easy to recall. "I'm doing a bit of exploring while my husband catches up on his sleep. Al told me about Callie's place?"

"Can't come to Splendor without visiting Callie's place." Doodle tilted his head. "Happy to show you the way. If you don't mind company."

"Not at all." She fell into step beside him, making mental note of every building they passed, every face she saw. She had a talent for recall, sight, sound, smells. It was one of her gifts, Ty had always teased. As far as she was concerned, it just made writing reports a lot easier. Which was probably why she typically got stuck writing them. As soon as she got back to the apartment, she'd put together a detailed sketch of the town. "So how long have you lived in Splendor, Doodle?"

"Going on five years. Came here with a bunch of friends during the summer after art school and never left." He swooped his arm out across the vista that included the marina, sea and the barest hint of his town. "No way I could walk away from this view."

"I have to admit, it's pretty glorious." There weren't many things, people or places that impressed her to the point of taking her breath away, but the beauty that was Alaska was another thing altogether. Biting cold aside, this state definitely put on a show of otherworldly proportions. "So you like it here, huh?"

"Best place on the planet." He hefted his bag. "Carry my easel and paints with me everywhere I go. Want to be able to capture that moment when it happens."

"So you're like a walking camera." They waited for a car to pass. She looked down the street, then in the other direction. "Don't see a lot of cars around."

"Entire town's barely two miles total," Doodle said.

"Only time we ever need a car is when we leave town. Most car owners supplement their income renting out their vehicles to tourists. But don't fall into that trap."

"What trap?"

"Most of them are complete junkers," Doodle said. "You need a car, talk to Sully at the Groovy Grub Grocery. He'll hook you up with someone legit. You can call for a cab to come in from the other side of the tunnel, but it'll cost ya."

Other than the plane she'd come in on or a water vessel, the tunnel was the only other way into Splendor. The traffic direction alternated every half hour, but it was only open from seven in the morning until ten in the evening.

Her mind did a quick calculation. According to what Ty had told her, Alice's hit-and-run had happened at nine o'clock at night, which, if the person who hit her had then tried to leave town, they'd only had a half hour to make it.

Or if the perpetrator had to wait, that still cut their escape time in half. She wondered if there were any security cameras at the tunnel entrance and exits.

Across the street and up a little bit she spotted a hanging sign over a door in the shape of a Victorian-style sofa. "I take it that's Tundra Antiques and Treasures?"

"You are correct," Doodle confirmed as they crossed over. "Be careful you don't get lost inside. Place is jam-packed with stuff."

"You're only making it more enticing." A screech of tires had Doodle jumping. His face lost a bit of color as he lifted a hand to his heart. "You okay?" She touched his arm, recognizing fear when she saw it.

"Yeah." He tried to shake himself out of it. "Sorry. Just jumpy. Alice's accident happened a few blocks that way. Still feels impossible. She's such a sweetheart. Why would anyone do that? Just hit her and drive away like that?"

"People do strange things when they're scared." Wren kept her voice sympathetic. "I don't think we've heard the actual details. Do you know what happened?"

"Only what other people have said. No one's come forward as a witness, apparently."

"Really?" Wren pushed the disbelief into her voice.

"Nine o'clock at night, town's pretty much shut down," Doodle told her. "Only reason Alice was out was because she was finishing inventory at the store."

"Right. That's... Wilderness something?"

"Wilderness Wonders Emporium." Doodle filled in some of the blanks. "Her own work's been really popular, so the owner offered her a management position. She and her husband. She'd sent Bradley home early to put the kids to bed. Then blam! She gets hit walking home. It's just creepy!"

"Definitely," Wren agreed. "And no one knows who did it?"

"Not that I've heard," Doodle said. "And I'd have heard. Course, there's the usual suspects."

"Splendor is big enough to have usual suspects?"

"Oh, sure." Doodle had stopped in front of Caribou Crafts, one of the many stores that featured locally made items. A beautifully woven blanket was displayed in the front window. "Davey Whittaker's usually top of the list. He drinks." Doodle dropped his voice. "I heard the sheriff didn't consider him for this, though. Even though no one's seen him since the accident."

"Really." That set off alarm bells for Wren for sure.

"Davey doesn't have a car, for good reason. He's always been harmless, near as I could tell. Like Alice. I hope she pulls through. I thought I'd stop by, take her some flowers." Doodle cringed. "Do you think that would be okay?"

Given Doodle had lived here awhile, she didn't think Alice's recently acquired personal security guards would take exception. "I think that would be lovely," Wren assured him. She hoped Alice would pull through, too. Not just for Alice herself, but for her family and, yes, Ty. Wren didn't want him spiraling further into a miasma of guilt. "I'm going to head this way." She pointed toward the thrift shop. "It was really great meeting you, Doodle. I'll have to check out your work sometime."

He brightened back up. "I have some pieces on display at the Northern Exposure Gallery. They're open from eleven to three most days."

"Thanks. I'll be sure to stop by."

She walked away, mind processing the information he'd inadvertently given her. If someone had waited for Alice to be off work, when it was typically a dead time of night, that meant they'd been in town long enough to know where she was employed. And to wait for the perfect moment to strike. Her gut told her it wasn't a local. Unless Splendor had its own hit man for hire. She and Ty needed to break down the time frame as far as when someone new in town would have arrived. People stood out here. Even people who lived here, like Leonardo Doodle, stood out. Made them hard to forget.

She pushed open the door to Tundra Antiques and Treasures, not surprised in the least when a bell tinkled overhead. The place had an immediate feel of the past, smelling a little musty, a little floral and more than a little promising. Wren offered a quick smile as she passed an older couple debating over a black iron bed frame.

The sheer amount of items should have made Wren feel claustrophobic, but instead she felt a bit enraptured. From old furniture to knickknacks, to cases filled with jewelry, knives, collectibles, and shelves filled with books. Exploring thrift shops in small towns always gave her a bit of a rush. She spotted a few old toys she'd had as a child, a sit-and-spin chair, a doll whose expression changed when you flipped her head around *Exorcist*-style.

Wren couldn't help but pick up a familiar fashion doll wearing a plaid dress. She lifted the doll's arm, a smile spreading across her face as the doll's chest expanded.

"Can't believe anyone would give that one up." The husky voice of an older woman had Wren glancing up. "Still have mine in a trunk in my attic."

"My brothers broke mine," Wren told her. "Then they stuffed her into GI Joe's helicopter and hung her from the ceiling."

"What are brothers for if not to torture us? Callie Haller."

"Ah, the owner I've heard about. Wren Savakis." Wren set the doll down and faced the woman with waist-length silver curls studded with baubles and beads. "Al suggested I stop by. My husband and I are staying in Skyway Tower for a bit."

"Heard you were on your way." Callie nodded knowingly. She looked out the window. "Seems like the storm coming in at your heels banked off. I'll thank you for that. Anything in particular you're looking for?"

"Do you have any embroidered dish towels? I collect them." It was one of her usual cover stories, but happened to be the truth. She appreciated the kind of needlework she had absolutely no talent for herself.

"Do I?" Callie waved her back, then shouted around Wren, "Vicki, you tell me when you and Theo are done arguing about that bed frame." Callie shook her head and sent her beads to rattling. "Don't know why they bother to argue over anything. Vicki always wins and Theo always grumbles."

"It's probably a tradition for them," Wren said. "My parents argue over who's going to cook the Thanksgiving turkey every year, even though we always know it'll be Mom." Mainly because every time her father forgot to remove the giblets bag.

"You're my kinda people, Wren." Callie steered her through the avalanche of items waiting to happen. "Tradition's why I opened this place. Things that mean something to someone can find their way into someone else's life. Now. Let's see what we've got for you."

Wren found herself surprised by the openness of the separate room. Whereas everything seemed a bit dark in the other area of the store, this space was bright and well lit by lamps with colorful glass shades.

"Anything in particular you like?" Callie asked.

"I know it when I see it," Wren said as she touched a beautiful appliqué quilt hanging on the wall. "You certainly have a lot to choose from."

"Twenty years I've been collecting. No place to keep

it all at home, so why not sell it. How about these?" She turned with a stack of yellow gingham towels with bright red milk jugs embroidered on them.

Wren wrinkled her nose. "Ah, anything a little less... frilly? I'm not a lace kinda person."

"Hmm." Callie's eyes narrowed. "Give me another second."

While Callie went on a search, Wren wandered the room, debating how best to approach the subject of Alice Hawkins. Callie Haller, much like Nora Caldwell, struck her as the kind of woman who would know everything that was going on in her town, but Wren had already asked Doodle some leading questions about the accident. She didn't want to raise suspicions by pumping everyone she met in Splendor for information.

Given the small-town effect, chances were everyone she met would be the kind of person who would know something. She needed to reevaluate her plan of action.

"Ah! I forgot about these. What do you think?" Callie popped back up with a stack of towels featuring embroidered cats and kittens. "Unless you're a dog person."

"I'm an all-animal person, actually." Wren took the towels and quickly went through them. "They're adorable." And they'd make great gifts for Christmas. "I'll take them all."

"Definitely my kinda people." Callie beamed and pointed at the other items. "You want to just look around some for a while? I'll keep these at the register, which is at the back of the store."

Chapter 5

By the time Wren left the thrift shop, she'd added a funny googly-eyed ceramic frog for Ty to expand his collection and a vintage camera her father would absolutely love.

Reusable tote bag looped over her arm, she headed for the grocery store next. According to Callie, the place was only a block down, but as Wren made her way back to the main road paralleling the marina, she began to wonder.

"Callie needs to redefine her definition of *block*." Arms burning, she was juggling the box into a less painful position when she finally spotted Groovy Grub Grocery. Given its name, Wren was surprised it wasn't painted in tie-dyed psychedelic swirls. The building was larger than she'd expected and boasted a long red awning noting that it was not only the grocery but also the postal annex, laundry and, oddly enough, offered homemade ice cream.

Sweet tooth activated by that cookie, she thought that might be easy enough on her still-queasy stomach. "Ice cream always smooths things out." She pulled open the door and stepped inside.

Immediately she could smell the sweet hint of Freon, no doubt used in the refrigerators lining the far wall.

She'd assumed the store would be limited in its offerings, much like the selection in the lobby grocery at Skyway Tower. But given the number of aisles in front of her, she realized she'd been completely wrong.

The walls were covered by a variety of colors, much like that tie-dyed effect the name alluded to. The style reminded her of the artwork outside the schoolrooms at the apartment complex. There were gaps on the shelves, as if they were awaiting new stock, but most items, like bottled juice and boxes of soda crackers, were plentiful.

The selection surprised her, but it was clear that shelf-stable foods were far more affordable than anything fresh. Or baby-related. Anchorage was only about sixty miles away. Given some of the prices she was seeing on things like diapers and laundry soap, she assumed most people would buy their staples elsewhere, probably when they had doctor appointments or other reasons to travel up north. Cookies, cereal and chips, on the other hand? She grabbed one of each and dropped them into the basket she carried.

"Smart woman," the silver-haired and fully bearded man behind the counter said as she passed by. The two other men standing on Wren's side stepped back to size her up. "Stocking up on carbs, I see."

"They're necessary to my survival." Nothing beat a chocolate sandwich cookie.

"You must be Wren Savakis." The man walked out from behind the counter and extended his hand.

"Must I?" she teased and accepted the greeting.

"Maisey Kirkpatrick described you pretty well."

Wren frowned. "Maisey…?"

"She's a nurse at the clinic. Word is you and your husband stopped someone from hurting Alice again."

"Oh. That was just…" She shot an uneasy glance to the other two men standing nearby. "I get these feelings about people, you know. That guy just didn't look right. Ty's always telling me I need to think more before I act."

"Well, glad you didn't think too much," the counterman said. "Poor woman's been through enough. Can't figure why anyone would try to hurt her while she's in the hospital."

"Maybe someone was worried about her being able to identify them," one of the other men muttered and earned a glare of warning from the shop owner.

"Before I go talking your ear off, I should introduce myself. I'm Sullivan Harper. Sully. I own this place."

"He's also the mayor," the second man said. "Funny enough, he tends to forget that part."

Ah, the mayor. Excellent. "Nice to meet you, Sully." She glanced at the other two guys.

Sully continued, "Met your husband a few days back. Plus, we heard the plane come in this morning. Welcome. Sorry your visit started off with a bit of a bang."

"I guess that is what one might call an entrance." Wren feigned embarrassment. "It's a lovely town you have here, Mr. Mayor."

"Sully," he said, his bright blue eyes teasing a warning.

"Right. Sure. Sully."

"This here is Cal Anderson and Nelson Finn. They work the *Fintastic Voyage*."

"My dad was a Jules Verne fan," the larger, rounder

of the two men said with more humor than his bearded face belied. "I'm fourth-generation fisherman."

"Hard life." Wren knew the reality TV shows she watched on the subject sometimes didn't come close to the actual "reality" of the profession. But she didn't think the depiction of long hours and rough seas were fictional. "A worthy tradition." She was seeing a recurring theme playing out in Splendor after only a few hours. "What's your main catch?"

"Halibut mostly," Nelson chimed in. The dark blue knit cap he wore was pulled down low to the point of almost covering his eyes. "But we get some salmon and rockfish in there, too."

"We keep the local restaurants in good supply," Cal said. "Sell the rest here or in Anchorage."

"Never lacking for fresh fish around these parts," Sully confirmed.

"Good to know. What did you bring in today?" Always happy to make inroads, she made the decision about what to cook tonight. "Thought I might fix dinner for me and Ty." She flashed a flirty smile. "Haven't seen him in a while. I'd like to catch up tonight."

"Catch up." Nelson snort-laughed. "Funny."

Wren genuinely beamed. She liked these guys.

"Well, now, you just come back with me and we'll see what we've got for you." Sully touched her shoulder and turned her toward the back of the store. He led her through a bit of a maze of items, including an entire wall filled with boxes containing harsh-weather boots and rain gear. There really wasn't anything she could think that was lacking in the store. "Now, personally, I think halibut is the way to go."

She tried not to balk at the list of prices tacked to the wall. For what a half pound of halibut would cost her, she and Ty could probably eat out for a few meals. Still, you couldn't get much more fresh than the catch currently sitting in a metal tray on a thick bed of ice. "Sounds good to me."

"I'll wrap it up for you, then. Got some fresh produce just down there. You're beating the crowd today. In another couple of hours, all this here will be gone."

She made quick work of choosing her veggies, then browsed the rather meager wine selection, settling on a chardonnay that would be good for drinking and cooking. She carried her basket to the counter, barely resisting the temptation of a fresh-baked pear pie sitting on the side rack next to the fruit. Tomorrow, she told herself. Tomorrow she'd come back for pie.

She eyed the small ice-cream counter on her way up to the register and debated her choices.

"Heard you and Ty are friends of Alice's," Sully said as he rang her up.

"My husband is, yes." She could feel Cal's and Nelson's eyes on her. "As soon as he heard about the accident, he headed up this way."

"Sounds like a good friend," Nelson observed. "He's a tech guy, yeah?"

"He was."

"And you're a lawyer." There was clear disdain in Cal's voice.

"White-collar," she said. "I specialize in insider trading and fraud. Big fish, so to speak," she added with a grin. "Those loopholes the rich try to jump through? I like closing them."

"You don't say?" Nelson's voice rose as if impressed.

"I'm a fan of the little guy," Wren said.

"Everyone's littler than us." Nelson chuckled.

Given both men were well over six foot and carried a good amount of weight, she got the joke.

"Okay, then." Sully rattled off the heart-stopping total. "Anything else you need?"

"I would love to try that maple bacon bourbon ice cream. On a cone."

"I'll get that for you," Cal told her. "As a welcome-to-Splendor treat."

"Well, thank you, Cal." She beamed up at him. "That's really nice of you." She'd bet beneath that beard she'd just made him blush. "It's just all so shocking, what happened to Alice," Wren mused as Sully bagged up her items, then headed off to scoop her ice cream. "I heard there weren't any witnesses to her being run down. No one knows who did it?"

"Nope." Nelson shook his head. "Not a clue."

Cal snorted as if he didn't agree. At Wren's frown, he shrugged. "Some of us have our suspicions."

"Now, Cal," Sully chided in a warning tone. "Don't go spreading rumors that have no foundation."

"Ain't no rumor if it's true."

"If what's true?" Wren asked innocently.

"My money's on Davey Whittaker."

The town troublemaker, Wren recalled from her conversation with Doodle. "I heard he was cleared," she said and earned raised eyebrows in response. "He doesn't have a car, does he?"

"He doesn't," Cal said in a leading way. "But his aunt Bea does, and it hasn't been parked in her driveway for going on almost a week now." He glanced at his friends. "Same time Davey's been missing."

"He's not missing," Nelson argued. "You know Davey. He disappears all the time. He'll turn up."

"Or maybe he already did this morning, so now he's beat it out of town for good," Cal countered.

"You're imagining things." Sully handed over the cone with two scoops. "Extra scoop on the house. Welcome to Splendor, Wren."

"Thanks." One mouthful of the creamy concoction and she nearly swooned. The salty bacon against the sweet maple flavor, then the smoky notes of bourbon. Pure heaven. "This is delicious. Do you make it?"

"My wife does," Sully said proudly. "She switches up the flavors every couple of weeks. Got her an industrial ice-cream maker for Christmas a few years back. Thing cost me a fortune, but it's paid off in spades. She loves creating new flavors."

"I'll definitely be back to try the rest of the menu." She shifted her attention back to Cal. "What does this Davey Whittaker look like?"

Nelson frowned. "Scrawny, scraggly blond hair. Always reminded me of a scarecrow."

Sully nodded. "Apt description."

"The guy I saw at the hospital definitely wasn't Davey, then." Nor was the guy driving the white SUV. "Why would you think he was responsible?"

"Who knows why that boy does anything he does? Been a mess most of his life," Cal said.

"He's twenty-six years old," Nelson chimed in. "Hardly a boy anymore."

"He had a hard upbringing," Sully said in Davey's defense. "His father was a big drinker, and Davey followed in his footsteps real early on. Does seem strange, Davey disappearing around the same time as the accident."

Not an accident, Wren thought. *Attempted murder.*

"Which is why it's the only thing that makes sense to me," Cal insisted.

"Davey's been picked on his entire life," Nelson said to Cal. "Never had anyone believe in him or even try to help him. Maybe give him a break until we actually know what happened. And like Wren here said, wasn't him who came after Alice at the hospital."

"I'll give him a break when he shows his face back in Splendor," Cal grumbled.

"Well, I hope he turns up," Wren said even as her mind raced. "And I hope whoever did hurt Alice is caught. I'm gonna get all this back to the apartment and see if my husband's awake. Nice meeting you all. And thanks for the ice cream, Cal." She hefted the two bags in her free hand and headed out.

A hand touched Ty's shoulder.

Still asleep, he reached up, locked his hand around the wrist and pulled forward. Hard. He'd barely blinked his eyes open as he followed through, shoved himself back and dragged Wren forward. She tumbled over him and sprawled on her back on the bed.

She glared up at him with that narrow-eyed gaze that had intimidated many a suspect. "Hey!" She twisted her hand, but he tightened his grip. "Ty, what the heck?"

"Sorry." The shock and embarrassment almost overtook him, until panic and desire struck and he gave in to what he'd been thinking about doing for...years.

He stared into her eyes, unblinking. Barely breathing. Waiting for something…understanding, maybe. Permission. Agreement. He leaned forward, ever so slowly, and watched as the color in her eyes darkened.

"Ty."

He kissed her, catching the last of his name with his lips. It was a mistake. He knew that from the instant his mouth touched hers. A mistake because he realized he'd only want more. He'd never look at her the same way again without knowing what it had been like to sink into her, to devour her in a way that set his entire body to singing.

He'd expected to be pushed away. He'd hoped to be. To be shouted down or looked at in disbelief or shock. If only to finally put an end to the desire he'd been feeling for what felt like his entire life.

But Wren McKenna had always been a woman who defied expectations. It was perhaps the most consistent thing about her. This was the one time he needed her to fall in line, follow the unwritten rule about partners becoming involved. And yet she didn't.

Instead her hands twisted free of his hold and slipped between them, grabbing hold of his shirt. She pulled him closer. And kissed him more deeply.

Reason grabbed hold as well and pulled him back to his senses. He broke the kiss, keeping his eyes closed. He couldn't bear to look into her eyes and see the regret he feared more than anything.

"Ty." His name was a whisper on her lips, a whisper that had him pushing through the doubt. "Ty, look at me."

He shook his head, squeezed his eyes tighter until

he saw stars. Stars that would explode and hopefully destroy the last few seconds from ever having existed.

"Ty."

"Sorry," he repeated, loosening his hold, but only then did he notice their legs were tangled together and he was looming over her, his chest pressing her into the soft mattress. "I'm...so sorry."

Her breathing was unsteady. Her breasts were pushing up against his chest in a way that had him, for a moment at least, debating about moving. Slowly, excruciatingly, he opened his eyes and looked down into her beautiful, confused, worry-filled face.

"I'm not." Her smile was sympathetic, teasing even.

He shook his head, refusing to believe. "That was—"

"A long time coming." She tightened her legs around his when he tried to shift away. "Did you get it out of your system?"

He let out a laugh that might have sounded like a sob, dropped his head forward to the point his forehead brushed against her chest.

"What is it?" She slid her hands up, clasped his face in her palms and forced him to look at her. "What's going on? Or maybe I should start by asking if you're awake now."

Oh, he was awake, all right. In this moment the yearslong effort of keeping his attraction to her under wraps threatened to break loose completely. He'd finally taken that taste he'd always been tempted to ask for and now...now he understood that kissing her had been a really, really bad idea.

Not because it hadn't been everything he'd ever wanted and dreamed about. But because he wouldn't ever be able to get enough. He freed his legs from hers and sat up. She followed him. Reached for him.

"Don't." His order was sharp, far sharper than he'd intended, but true to form, Wren ignored him and scooted closer. "Wren, please—don't."

"Don't what?" She took hold of his hand and squeezed his fingers. "Come on, Ty. We're each other's best friends. One kiss isn't going to change any of that. If you can't talk to me, you can't talk to anyone. It's been long enough. What's going on with you?" Her gentle tone crumbled his reluctance.

"I don't know." It was the biggest lie he'd ever told in his life. And he'd told it to the one person he'd never once lied to before. "Please, just forget this happened. That I—"

"I'm not going to forget kissing you, so let's get that straight off the bat." Her voice was so calm, so...accepting, he couldn't help but wonder why he'd stopped himself from initiating anything for the past seven years. "Something's wrong. It has been for a while. For weeks. And it's gotten worse since you called me." She paused, looked into his eyes in that way she had that made him admit hiding from her wasn't an option. "Is it Alice?" Doubt filled her gaze. "Was there something more to your relationship than you've said? Were you—"

"Involved?" He balked. "No, Wren. No, I'd never get involved with a witness in that way. Do you really think—"

"I don't know what to think because you won't talk to me. Not really." She sank back, her hair coming down from the knot she'd tied it in. The knot he'd wanted to untangle himself. She didn't let go of his hand. If anything, she only held on tighter. "Trust me, Ty. Everything

I'm coming up with is going to be worse than the truth, so please just tell me what's happening."

His throat tightened, as if trying to prevent the words from coming out. "Alex called me a few weeks ago. A month ago, in fact." He leaned against the makeshift headboard. Only then did he realize he was holding her hand as tightly as she held his.

"Did he?" He understood the suspicion in her voice. The barely restrained contempt. Before this call, he hadn't spoken to his brother in more than five years. "Why?"

He hadn't let himself think about the call. Not consciously, at least. But the conversation had been playing, over and over, in the back of his mind. When he slept. While he worked. "He told me it was time to come home." He pinched the bridge of his nose, willed the pain to stop him from talking. From thinking.

"Get it out, Ty. It's not doing you any good caught in here." She placed her fingers on his heart and the heat of her touch felt like a branding iron against his chest.

"It's my father. He's got liver cancer and the treatment isn't working." He heaved a sigh and opened his eyes, looked at her. "Alex said it won't be long."

"All right." She nodded as if processing the information he was still trying to. "What did Alex say when you told him you wouldn't be coming?"

Ty couldn't help it. He laughed. She knew him so well. Too well, perhaps. "What do you think he said?"

"I think your behavior these last few weeks suddenly makes an awful lot of sense." She moved closer, held on even tighter. "You don't owe your father anything, Ty. Absolutely nothing. You know that deep down. He was your childhood bully. An unloving, uncaring jerk who never should have had children. Although, to be fair..." She inclined her head in that particular way she had. "I'm glad he did, seeing as he had you. So I guess I owe him for that."

He loved her for the unwavering support. And humor. "I swore when I walked out of that house when I was eighteen I'd never go back." And he hadn't. Not for one second. Not even when his mother had died four years later. He'd gone to the funeral, but he'd been in and out within hours, long enough to say goodbye and lay flowers on her newly dug grave. "I left Alex with all of it. Everything. Why shouldn't I go back?"

"Stop right there. I mean it," she added firmly. "Alex was older than you and already out of the house when you got out, and more importantly, *he* left *you* there to take on everything yourself. Alex even chose to stay in the same town. He could have made a new life anywhere, just like you did, and he didn't. His situation is not on you. And your father's behavior, then or now, is not your responsibility."

"Isn't it?" It amazed him, how clearly she saw his family situation when she came from such an idyllic one. The McKennas were the kind of family others measured themselves by. The family was tight-knit, supportive, loving and, most importantly, welcoming to any and all hangers-on. Like him. Before partnering with Wren, he couldn't imagine a family like theirs. In truth, being around them only shone a spotlight on how bad his upbringing had really been.

"Did your dad stop drinking when you left? Did he

even try to get help?" Wren asked him. "Or, I should ask, has he finally stopped drinking?"

"Not according to Alex, no." And that, more than anything, was always the bone of contention between him and his brother. Ty could never get beyond the idea that his father hadn't stopped, and Alex couldn't forgive Ty for not accepting their father as he was.

"Then your father didn't do the bare minimum. He hasn't earned your visiting him and you can't save him, Ty." There was no pity now, only determined support and understanding. "Just like you couldn't save your mother when she refused to leave him." Wren made certain he was looking at her. "You saved yourself. That's what matters."

How did she always see the better side of him?

"I've sent money, in the past," he admitted. "For his treatment. To make things easier for him." He winced. "It doesn't seem like enough."

"It's more than he deserves." She traced a finger over the scar on his neck. A scar he'd received at the hands of his father on his tenth birthday, when he'd accidentally knocked over his dad's celebratory beer. "Hopefully Alex will keep some of that money for himself, if there's any left."

"I told him he could. He told me I couldn't buy my way to forgiveness."

Wren swore so violently and vehemently she broke through the confused grief that had settled around Ty's heart. "You've got to be kidding me. What a jerk. He's a—"

"I don't blame him, Wren."

"Of course you don't. You never blame anyone else

when you can blame yourself. I want you to listen to me, Ty. And just to make sure you do." She slid over him, her knees resting on either side of his hips.

"I don't think you sitting on me is going to make my ears work better." He'd gone rock-hard. It would be impossible for her not to know it. To feel it. But when he looked into her eyes, all he saw was defiance and determination.

"You cannot save everyone. You couldn't save your father from his drinking. Or your mother from her devotion to him. You can't save Alex from not being strong enough to walk away or at the very least not to throw the blame on you. But you know what you can do?"

He was definitely thinking about all the things he could do at that moment.

"You can work this case and find out who tried to kill Alice. You can keep your word to her and protect her and her family. We can do this together. And we will do it. Because that's what we do." She leaned forward, pressed her lips against his. She didn't close her eyes but bored hard into his. "All this guilt you're feeling about your father, I understand why it's there, and while it's easy for me to say, you need to set it aside. When we're done here, we can talk about what you want to do. If you want to go back, fine. Just be warned that if you do, I'm darn sure going with you and I've got more than a few harsh words for your brother. But for now, we work, yeah?"

His hands began to move. They'd lifted to rest on her hips, his fingers kneading into her in a way that had her gaze sharpening. And darkening.

"Don't start something you aren't willing to finish," she warned him. "Because you kissing me after all this time feels like a bit of a starting flag. You've got my engine revving. You want to see how many laps we can go?"

More so than anything else on the planet. But talking had helped reason and logic take over once more. "I'm not sure I'm in an emotionally stable place to be able to answer."

"Okay, then I'll ask later. After we eat." She kissed him again, quickly this time, and climbed off him. "Dinner's ready. That's what I came in to tell you, by the way. It's time to eat. So get yourself together and join me in the kitchen. I've got information from town that you're going to want to hear."

The bands of pressure around Wren's chest didn't ease until she was on the other side of the bedroom door. She stepped to the side, hand pressed against her chest, back resting against the bookcase as she willed her pulse to stop jumping like a salmon headed upstream.

The anger toward his selfish brother almost overtook the still-tingling sensations of Ty's kiss.

Her face warmed, but she didn't try to stop it or cover it. Or halt the smile that curved her lips. After all these years, all this time, he'd kissed her.

She supposed she owed his brother for twisting Ty up into so many knots her partner finally gave in to what Wren had only hoped he'd felt for her. He was, plain and simple, other than her father and brothers, the best man she'd ever known.

One look at Ty Savakis and most women would assume he had the kissing thing down. He had those classic Greek looks with the dark hair and bright blue eyes. He was...the epitome of romantic heroes come to life, right down to the invisible sword and shield he carried, white horse included. It was a secret she'd kept for going on seven years. Through her disaster of a marriage. Through his marriage. Until, it appeared, today.

And all bets may very well be off.

But her imagination about his kissing abilities hadn't come close to reality. That moment, those kisses—they'd been seared into her mind forever. Whatever happened now, at least, she'd have that. And maybe, for as long as they were in Splendor, Alaska, they could both get their fill and work out whatever attraction they shared.

Yes. That was how they should handle it. Like an off-the-books fling, no commitment. No strings. They could just go back to how they were before they'd come to Alaska. Easy peasy.

Right?

She blew out a breath, set her hair to ruffling on her forehead. She could hear him moving around in the bedroom, enough that she quickly went into the kitchen to finish the meal she'd come up with.

Her hands shook as she clicked on the gas burner, set the pan containing the seared halibut with a tomato-and-caper sauce to cooking. She tried shifting her focus away from what had happened in the bedroom to the notes she'd been scribbling in the book on the cluttered kitchen island.

"I see you haven't become any tidier when it comes to cooking." The humor was back in his tone when he joined her. The Ty she was used to. The Ty she...

She barely cast an over-the-shoulder glance at the mess that had overtaken the rest of the kitchen. "*Tidy* is barely part of my vocabulary." Personally, at least.

Professionally, she considered herself a real organizer with pinpoint efficiency. Her personal routine was an entirely different story. As far as she was concerned, if the kitchen wasn't a disaster, she hadn't made enough of an effort. "Notes are over there." She gestured toward the spiral notebook on the island. The cover had spatters of tomato and oil, which Ty wiped off with a dish towel.

"You had a busy afternoon," he said as he read through her copious thoughts and observations. "Even met the kids. What did you think?"

She set the water for the couscous to boiling on the back burner, dropped a lid on the pan. "That they're too young to get what's going on. Two of them, for sure. Esme struck me as a small adult."

"Birth order theory in play." Ty didn't pull his eyes from the page. "Visiting hours at the hospital end at six." He checked his watch. "Bet Bradley will be home soon after."

"I suggest we give him tonight, try to catch up with him again tomorrow." She hesitated. "We do need to know what, if anything, Alice told him about her past."

"I'm betting not much since he seems to be in the dark and he believes the story about my friendship with Alice."

Ty wasn't wrong. Bradley didn't strike her as the kind of man who could keep up any kind of pretense for long. He wasn't, she suspected, a very good liar.

"If we need an in, I can cook them dinner tomorrow." She rose up on tiptoe, checked to see where he was on her notes. "Two more pages and you'll get to something more interesting." She waited, stirring and adjusting the temperature and testing the sauce.

"Last I heard, four other tenants are alternating making them meals." He shook his head. "People go out of their way to cook when it comes to illness or death."

"It's a coping mechanism," she reminded him. One she recognized in herself. "And it's the way a lot of people show they care." She heard him flip the page, then again. "Get there yet?"

"About this Davey Whittaker guy? Yeah."

"It wasn't Davey at the hospital. Forget the fact his physical description doesn't match, but from what Nelson and Cal said, the man can barely stand up, he drinks so much. However, that…" She looked at Ty, waited for him to catch her train of thought.

"Makes him a good scapegoat, doesn't it?"

Satisfied he was back on track, she nodded. "Exactly what I was thinking. We've got the white SUV without plates, a missing local with a well-known drinking problem and…" She snapped her fingers. "I almost forgot." She hurried to where she'd hung her jacket up by the front door and pulled out the hypodermic needle. "We still have this. You didn't mention it before, but did you bring your fingerprint case?"

"No," he replied when she set the glove-covered needle on the countertop. "It wasn't in my go bag."

"I left mine back in Boston." Not that dusting for prints would do much good without a database to run them through. "Okay, so we table this for now. Tomorrow, we find ourselves a car—"

"I've got one," Ty said, cutting her off. "Rental. Grabbed it in Anchorage when I got back from meeting you in Seattle. It's parked in the underground lot."

"Oh." She blinked, impressed. "Great. Okay. I think

we should start with the tunnel. The one leading into Splendor."

"Why?"

"Because after doing some research, it might be a good place to disappear."

"Into Alaska, you mean."

"Eventually." She tasted another spoonful of sauce, nodded, shrugged, added more pepper. "There are emergency exit doors, the tunnel's so long. Even a comms room and more. In case the train breaks down or there's weather that makes it dangerous to leave the tunnel."

Ty raised his head. She could see the wheels turning.

"Couldn't hurt to check. Maybe talk to Davey's aunt Bea about her car that's gone missing?" The water boiled and she added the couscous, moved the pan off the stove. "I bookmarked the website about the tunnel construction. If you want to skim through it."

"I'm getting the gist of it from your notes." Notes he was still reading, so she started cleaning up. By the time he stood up straight and closed her notebook, the center island was gleaming once more, the black marble countertop displaying its thin gold lines and flecks.

"Sounds like you made more friends in a few hours than I've made in a few days."

She smiled. "I'm more sparkly."

"That you are." More often than not, their job was made easier by certain people's underestimating his very blonde, very pretty partner. "Trying to kill Alice a second time blew any chance these guys had of blaming Davey for the hit-and-run."

Wren nodded. "I figured the same thing. Throws her accident—" she used air quotes for emphasis "—completely into question and puts the entire town on edge, not to mention high alert. That's pretty desperate, if you ask me. Unless Alice has someone else from her past coming after her, which you believe is unlikely, it has to be Treyhern. He's the only one with a motive to make mistakes like this."

The fact she saw relief in his eyes at her statement made her wish she'd come around to his thinking sooner. "There is another option we haven't considered. It's not one I'm leaning toward, but it's one we should talk about."

"That Davey might have been hired to run Alice down?"

She nodded. "We'd need to know more about him to eliminate that idea. Addicts are unpredictable."

"Then we'll start with his aunt Bea," Ty said. "Sooner we can get a handle on Davey Whittaker, the sooner we can move on to more viable answers. That leaves me with one last question."

"What's that?" She put a dash of seasoning into the couscous, as well as some grated peel from a lemon that cost her more than her monthly streaming service charge. She fixed each of them a plate as he set the notebook aside.

The timer dinged and she turned to pull the homemade biscuits out of the oven.

"I'm seriously not going to starve with you around," he murmured when he tucked a golden-topped biscuit on the edge of his plate. "For tonight. You should take the bed. I'll do the sofa."

She wasn't entirely sure how to follow that. Her heart pounded in excited anticipation while the back of her mind sent out warning bells. "I'm not selfish. I'm happy to share the bed."

"You sure about that?"

"Yes." Suddenly she wasn't so hungry for food anymore. "What about you?"

He ate more, and again she could practically hear the gears grinding in his head. "We need to be careful about what might happen."

"You mean besides avoiding back strain on the sleeper sofa?"

"I meant our friendship." He winced, shook his head. "The last thing I want to do is lose you, Wren. And I'm just afraid—"

"Don't be. Afraid." She reached out, covered his hand with hers. "I've already decided—if you're amenable, that is—that whatever happens, it will stay here in Splendor."

Doubt shot across his handsome features.

"You don't think we can do that?" she asked.

"I don't know. That's what scares me."

"Then we take it a day at a time." Or in their case, a night at a time. "And we agree. When we leave, it stays here. But Alice and her family come first," she reminded him. "Agreed?"

"Agreed." He shrugged almost nonchalantly. She waited for him to say more, but he lifted a forkful of couscous to his mouth. If he could shrug off their sharing the same bed, so could she. But his less-than-enthusiastic reaction to her suggestion that they take their friendship to another level definitely required a glass of that very expensive wine.

Chapter 6

Turned out Wren was right. Sharing a bed with her wasn't an issue.

Trying to fall asleep beside her, on the other hand?

Ty could literally feel the heat of her body radiating across the blankets they shared, and the last thing he needed was to feel…warmer. It was like an ongoing pulse, feeding the attraction both had admitted to but neither had yet to completely act on.

None of this was what he wanted circling in his head at two in the morning.

It probably hadn't helped sleeping the afternoon away, either. Now, instead of falling into the blissful unawareness he longed for, he lay there staring up at the ceiling, unblinking, swearing he could hear her heart beating. Silence, it turned out, was loud. His city self was so used to noise, but up here he had the sneaking suspicion he could hear a fly buzz half a mile away.

Wren sighed a little, shifting and snuggling down to the point she pressed her bare feet against his leg. Ty stiffened, as if preparing himself for a nuclear launch rather than Wren settling back into sleep. He took a deep breath, inhaled the intoxicating scent of jasmine drifting off her skin.

Yeah, this wasn't going to work.

He slid out of bed as carefully as he could, tugging on the jeans he'd left tossed over the back of the one chair in the bedroom. Barefoot, he walked to the window, pulled the heavy curtain back. He had to stop his gasp before it escaped as he blinked, disbelieving, into the night sky.

The interplay of ghostly green light cascading down from the stars took his breath away. He'd heard of the aurora borealis, of course. Even remembered studying it in school. But seeing it now made him realize how completely otherworldly the event was.

His arm dropped and he stood there, watching the show as if it were the season finale of a grand epic. Yet another wondrous bonus of life in the north.

Just the sight of the intermingling lights with stars gentled the edgy thoughts cutting through his mind. He'd been unable to push aside the idea of an angry accusation Alice would aim his way if…when, *when* she woke up.

This was also a reminder that Wren was correct; he couldn't control the universe no matter how hard he tried. It was ridiculous to blame himself for what had happened to Alice, especially given how many years it had been. But he should have at least reached out to her as soon as he'd heard Treyhern had been granted a new trial.

He grabbed a T-shirt and went into the living area, where the enormous plate-glass window provided a big-screen view of the show in the sky. It was like the universe was trying to remind him that in the grand scheme of things he was one very tiny part. Trying to put himself in the middle of it was only asking for trouble.

His internal clock was as messed up as his head.

Everything felt like it was in flux. It had been that way even before the news of Alice's accident. Some days he felt completely trapped by the life he'd carved out for himself, despite knowing he was doing the job he was meant to do. He'd had doubts about a lot in his life, but from the second he'd held his FBI special agent badge and ID in his hand, for the first time his world had felt… right.

That was why it made no sense to him that he was making decisions that put his career at risk. His volatile behavior on the job meant his fellow agents questioned whether he could be trusted or relied on. His boss queried every case he was given. Wren was the only person who hadn't faltered in her support. She was there for him. No matter what.

Where would he be without her?

He sat back to contemplate that question and the sky.

A little over an hour later, answers nowhere to be found, he poured his first cup of coffee. He sat at the kitchen island, went over Wren's immaculate notes again. He had to admit, while he'd skimmed them last night, he hadn't exactly retained much of the information. It had been difficult to keep up the pretense of focus when she'd been talking about them sleeping together.

He was a man, and most definitely not a saint.

"Morning." Wren's slogging into the kitchen had him glancing at the clock. Where had the time gone?

Her bare feet shuffled against the wood floor as if she didn't possess the energy to lift them. "Ah. My elixir. Thank you." She didn't even look at him as she headed for the coffee maker and, after rooting around in the cabinet containing various mugs and cups and glasses, chose the absolute biggest tankard possible.

Coffee, two spoonfuls of sugar and a healthy splash of cream—three big glugs later and he watched her eyes visibly clear.

"Better?" He could think of fewer things more entertaining than watching Wren McKenna wake up.

"You know it." She looked outside, frowned into the darkness. "What time is it?" She glanced at her watch.

"Seven. Late sunrise," he reminded her and watched her eyes roll. "Takes some getting used to."

"Ya think?" She rolled her shoulders, bringing attention to the fitted tank top she used as a sleep shirt. "How long have you been up?" She eyed him with envy.

"Few hours." Long enough to shower, dress and map out a plan of action for the day. "We have to wait until after sunrise at least to visit Aunt Bea."

"It's your show. I'm just along for the ride. You get anything more out of my notes?"

"Davey Whittaker's still gnawing at me."

"Why?" She leaned her hip against the counter, held her mug of coffee as if it were indeed the elixir of life.

"I don't know." Because the few details he knew about the young man reminded him of himself? Of the path he could have easily found himself on. "It would make things easier if he was responsible for the hit-and-run." But he wasn't. Yesterday's events at the hospital had all but cleared him.

"You can't will someone into being a suspect."

"I know." Ty smothered a laugh and covered his eyes with his hand for a moment. He was so tired of complicated. A nice, tidy solution would be such a relief. But given Wren's doubtful expression when he looked back at her, it told him she was remembering what they'd both been taught early on at the Academy. Tidy solutions only happened in Hollywood scripts.

Real life was full of a lot more twists and turns than could be solved in an hour of television.

"What?" he asked at her pensive expression.

"I'm considering what the odds are that you have a copy of the Treyhern file."

"You mean because, legally, I should only be able to access that on my dedicated work laptop that is currently on my desk back in Boston?"

"Yes," she replied slowly. "That's what I mean."

He got up, returned to the bedroom to dig the jump drive out of the protective case he kept in his go bag. He sauntered to the kitchen and dropped it into her open palm. "This is my shocked face," she muttered and retrieved her laptop from where she'd left it in the kitchen last night. "I'll dig into this when we get back."

He could have suggested she email a copy of it to her phone, but that would be crossing too many lines for both of them. "I need you to help me stop spinning, Wren."

"About what? What are you thinking specifically?"

"Honestly?" He shook his head. "I don't know. That's why I wanted you here. I figured you could see what it was."

"Awww." That teasing lilt emerged in her voice. "You think I'm smarter than you."

"I don't think it. I know it." This was probably the one thing he was confident about. "Can you be ready to go in an hour?"

"Please," she scoffed. "I'll be ready in fifteen. Breakfast of champions is in the cabinet there." She pointed to the one near the stove. "Pour me a bowl, will you?"

"Wheaties?" he guessed, walking around the island to do as instructed.

"Be serious." She rolled her eyes and topped off her coffee. "Froot Loops."

"Only in Alaska," Wren said as she and Ty sat in the rented SUV watching a family of moose make their way slowly across the two-lane road headed out of Splendor. She cast a side-eyed look at him, impressed by the patience he showed when he put the car into Park and sat back to wait. "The pilot who flew me in says he's been bringing you up to Alaska pretty regularly."

"Yeah. Been doing that for a while now. It's a kind of reset for me."

"Always knew you disappeared somewhere. Never thought it was in Alaska." Wren returned her attention to the animals, who seemed more than happy to take their time. "Any reason you never mentioned it?"

"Not that I can think of." He reached down for his insulated tumbler mug and took a long drink. "The first time was a total fluke. Friend of mine invited me along for a spur-of-the-moment fishing trip. He didn't realize how much we'd be roughing it. Unplugging nearly drove him bonkers, but not me. I never expected to come back. Then I did." He shrugged. "I didn't keep it a secret on purpose. Just kind of worked out that way. You know, something that was just mine."

"Sure." Growing up in a house with three siblings, she could understand the need for solitary activity.

"You're welcome to come with me next time," he offered, still keeping his gaze firmly on the animals. "Honestly, I wouldn't have thought it was your kind of thing."

"No idea if it is or not," she told him. "But you're right. My family's never been exactly outdoorsy." Family vacations growing up had been limited to destinations within easy driving distance from Boston in case either of her law enforcement parents needed to get back for an emergency. The farthest she could ever remember getting was the Jersey Shore the summer she turned fifteen. "Not a fan of the cold, though."

The last moose finally cleared the road and stepped into the thick brush. "I don't come up during this time of year," Ty said. "Fishing's best in summer, especially for salmon. Hiking trails are pretty awesome. Still a few places you can access the glaciers."

"Listen to you, going all wilderness-camper dude on me." Next thing she knew, he'd be planning survival weekends for them.

He tossed her a grin, shifted the car back into Drive and headed off again.

"What?" she asked.

"Nothing, really." He hit the gas. "Just nice to know that even after all these years I can surprise you."

Oh, he was full of surprises, all right. But now wasn't the time to think about that kiss. Or how she hadn't wanted it to stop. Or how before she'd fallen asleep last night, she'd almost rolled over and...

Nope. Not now. Now was not the time. Officially or not, they were working. Finding the person or persons responsible for what had happened to Alice was the important thing. Everything else...could wait.

At least the sun had finally peeked over the horizon, and boy, was it spectacular. The color playing out around them almost stole her breath away. There really was something ethereal about this place, despite it wreaking havoc with her internal sensors. She couldn't quite shake that barely-there fog in her mind. Chances were she'd finally get used to the daylight and it would be time to head home. To the real world.

The real world...

"What if she's not up?" Wren asked as Ty pulled the SUV to the side of the road. Beatrice Mulvaney's home stood in the distance, in a bit of a clearing of a thick forested area. The weathered structure, from this far away, called to mind old fairy tales where magic and mystery awaited. "She might not be an early bird."

"Someone's awake." Ty gestured to the lights in the front window and the slow moving shadow on the other side of the curtain. He killed the engine and the sudden silence was deafening. The chill set in instantly and the windows fogged over.

"We sticking to our cover story? We're just nosy people looking into what happened to your friend Alice?"

"Seems to be working so far. No need to change it. If the sheriff's right, I don't want our employment status standing between us and who ran Alice down."

"Doesn't look like we'll have any neighbors to quiz about Davey." One couldn't exactly call the area a neighborhood. Wren was a city girl; she was used to homes being so close you could hear the neighbors' toilets flush. Here on the outskirts of Splendor, the closest house they'd passed on their drive had been a few miles back.

"People definitely get their privacy out here."

Ty sounded as uneasy as she felt. The drive through

town and to its surrounding area had provided a different view of Splendor. It was cute where they'd been, but the farther they drove, the more wild things seemed to get. Overgrown areas of shrubbery and fauna. The wildlife. She'd had her share of braking for squirrels or the occasional risk-taking feline in Boston. Up here you needed to keep your attention on the road for any number of creatures. Case in point, the aforementioned moose family.

"Would have been nice to get more information about her before we dropped by," Ty said.

"Google searches don't exactly get updated as fast as we'd like." It didn't help they were both on "vacation" and any logging in to their FBI accounts would alert someone to the fact they weren't exactly relaxing and doing nothing. "We could probably get some assistance from Shelly."

"The deputy?"

"Uh-huh." Wren nodded. "Something tells me she'd be more than happy to help." They just needed to be careful what they asked of her. They didn't want to burn bridges or get the young deputy into trouble. "I could give Aiden a call," she offered. "See if he can bring anything up on the aunt." But seeing as they were already parked outside the woman's house...

"Nah. We'll do things the McKenna way and wing it." There was the sense of humor she needed to hear.

"In that case, follow my lead." She pulled her 9 mm out from her waistband and left it under the seat. "I don't anticipate we'll be needing any weapons in there."

Ty nodded, but didn't repeat her action. "One of us should be carrying just in case."

"Paranoid," she muttered.

"Practical." He shoved open the door. "No one knows where Davey Whittaker is, remember? He could be holed up in her basement."

The chill shot through her the second she got out of the car. Her booted feet crunched in the icy gravel-strewn dirt. Her breath came out in huge white puffs, disappearing into the air around her as she fell into step beside Ty. "I bet people lose weight just stepping outside their homes." She hugged her arms around her torso, feeling the bite of cold seeping through the material. "We stay here for very long, I'm gonna need a heavy-duty parka." She'd seen one at Groovy Grub Grocery that would probably do the trick.

The sound of their walking reminded her of a path of dropped snow cones. *Snow cones.* She shivered and huddled deeper into her coat. She didn't think she'd ever eat another one for the rest of her life. Not without getting frosty flashbacks.

Whatever yard existed in front of Beatrice Mulvaney's house had been thoroughly blanketed by winter. The only pop of color against all the white was the Wedgwood blue of the house itself that was accented with a silvery-gray trim.

The gentle hum of the generator along the side of the house cut through the ear-pinching silence. Wren hopped up the trio of stairs onto the front porch and quickly knocked on the door with her gloved hands.

"Who are you?" The wavering voice came a few moments later. Definitely elderly. Definitely female.

"Ms. Mulvaney?" Wren spoke up and hoped that a female voice in response might be helpful in this situation. "My name is Wren Savakis. My husband and I are staying in town for a while. We're friends of Alice Hawkins."

"Alice?" The white lace curtain pulled back a smidge and a solitary brown eye peered out. "You know Alice?"

"Yes, ma'am," Wren said and swore her breath attempted to freeze into ice midair. "We were curious and hoped you could maybe answer some of our questions, if you don't mind?"

"Questions about what?" She popped open the door a crack, glared out, suspicion evident on her face. "And this early?"

"We're still on Lower 48 time," Wren said. "Please, ma'am. We'd like to speak with your nephew as well. Davey? He might have information—"

The door snapped open. The old woman stood just inside, wearing sturdy fur-lined boots along with a flowered housedress and at least two sweaters. Her short gray hair was neat and laid flat around her face.

"Davey's a good boy," she stated. "Troubled is all. He didn't have nothing to do with what happened to Alice."

"Yes, ma'am," Wren agreed. "You're absolutely right about that. Do you mind if we come in? It's awful cold out here."

"Sunbelters." Beatrice shook her head and waved them inside. "Y'all freeze if it dips below fifty. Come on. Come on." Wren stepped in far enough for Ty to move in behind her. It was only after Beatrice closed the curtained door that they saw the shotgun leaning next to it. "Can't be too careful," she said, as if reading her mind. "Never know what kind of whackadoodle might come knocking on my door at…" She glanced up at an old weathered cuckoo clock ticktocking its way through the morning. "Not even eight a.m."

She stepped in front of Wren, made her way down the wood-planked hall.

"Come on in. Might as well take the chill off ya and you can tell me what you're really doing here."

Wren cast a look at Ty, who merely shrugged. "Winging it."

She rolled her eyes and followed Beatrice into the kitchen. As weathered as the house was on the outside, the decor inside was surprisingly up-to-date and cheery. Bright yellow walls, beautifully stained cabinetry, and countertops that looked as if they'd been carved out of the finest of quarries. "I ain't seen my nephew for going on six days." Beatrice reached into a cabinet for a pair of worn mugs. "And like I said, he didn't hurt Alice."

"Are you sure about that?" Ty's voice was gentle but firm.

"As sure as you're standing in my home about to drink my coffee," Beatrice countered. "Sheriff Egbert already came out here twice last week looking for the boy. I'll tell you what I told him. Davey couldn't hurt a fly."

"With all due respect, ma'am—"

"That kind of respect ain't nothing but sass," Beatrice told Ty as she motioned for them both to sit at the kitchen table. "Davey had an awful time growing up at the hands of my reprobate brother-in-law. If my nephew were gonna hurt someone, it'd have happened long before now. And it certainly wouldn't have been Alice Hawkins he'd have taken his troubles out on."

"It's awful coincidental he disappeared at the same time Alice was hurt," Wren suggested.

"Coincidences ain't evidence." She straightened with pride. "I worked as a paralegal more than twenty years. Retired a while ago, of course, but I know what I know. And what I know is you aren't friends of Alice's." She shot them a dark look before turning back to the coffeepot. "Real friends would be at the hospital with her or looking after her young'uns, giving that husband of hers a break."

Wren arched a brow. The old woman had a point. "We're trying to find out what happened to her."

"Well, you're wastin' your time here." She set two mugs of coffee on the table. "Ask what you want to ask, drink up, then be on your way. *Paw and Order* starts soon and I don't like to miss Judge Payne's rulings."

"Paw and..." Ty turned somewhat confused eyes on Wren.

"Semi-reality TV show," Wren muttered under her breath. "Ma'am, we really would like to speak to your nephew. When was the last time you saw him, exactly?"

"Already said, didn't I?" She yanked the head off a cartoon-sheep cookie jar and pulled out a handful of what looked like chocolate-covered nuts. "He borrowed my car about a week ago. Haven't heard or seen him since. Ain't the first time he's disappeared for days on end," she lamented. "Won't be the last. Guess his timing coulda been better. Whole town's probably thinking he ran that girl down, then beat it out of Splendor to avoid getting caught."

"It sounds plausible."

"Course it does." Beatrice sat across from them, a shadow of concern flashing across her face. "That boy hasn't had anything but bad luck since he came out of the womb. My sister, she had a good heart, but a weak one. Didn't live much longer after Davey was born, and his father…" She broke off, her jaw tensing. "Too rotten for words."

Wren chanced a glance at Ty, who was looking anywhere but at her.

"One thing Davey's never been is a shirker. If he did wrong, he'd own up to it. Spent his fair share of time in lockup. Local, mind you. Nothing serious. Loitering, public drinking, the like. But he's harmless. The sooner people start listening to me on that front, the sooner they can get themselves looking for the person who did hurt that girl. Some people can't see nothing but the worst that people's done. Darn shame is what it is."

"Did you often loan Davey your car, Ms. Mulvaney?" Wren asked.

"Couple times a month, mainly to do grocery runs. Try to catch him early in the day about that. So he wasn't…preoccupied with other things." She frowned, her brow wrinkling. "You think maybe you can find him?"

"We're going to try," Ty said. "It would help if I could maybe look through his room? See if there are any clues as to where he might have gone? Does he have a computer?"

Beatrice looked Ty straight in the eye. "He's a good boy."

"Yes, ma'am." Ty nodded. "I'll be careful. And respectful. I promise."

She hesitated another moment. "All right, then. Down the hall, second door on the left."

"Thank you." He gave Wren a look that told her he'd

be quick. Then he left the kitchen and clomped down the hall.

"Handsome fella." Beatrice leaned over in her chair as if watching him walk. "Lucky girl."

"He's a good man," Wren felt obliged to share. Ty would understand, better than most, what Davey had been through. "We're really only looking to find out what happened to Alice."

"I don't know her well, but I've chatted with her a few times when I've gone into town. She even tried to give Davey a job at that store she works at a few months back. Stocking shelves mostly." Beatrice's eyes drooped with grief. "He's a good boy, Davey. Please. Find him. And if you can, prove he didn't do this terrible thing."

"We're going to do our best," Wren said as she sipped her bitter coffee.

"Mrs. Mulvaney?" Ty appeared at the kitchen door again, an old photograph in his hand. "I found this on Davey's dresser mirror." He approached Wren, handed her the picture. "Is this where he grew up?"

Wren looked at the faded image of a couple, the wife holding a baby. She was staring down at the infant with such affection, while the man towering behind her had a hand on her shoulder.

"It is," Mrs. Mulvaney said. "May I?" She held out her hand.

"Of course." Wren passed her the photo.

The tightness around the woman's face eased. "My late husband took this picture shortly after Davey was born. That's him, there." She touched a finger to the infant. "Back then we thought, or we hoped, Davey would help their marriage. Didn't really have a chance to, poor thing."

"Do you remember where this house is?"

Mrs. Mulvaney tsked and frowned at Ty. "Course I do. I'm not addled just yet. Place has been abandoned for years. It's Davey's, of course, but he never wanted it. Said it had too many bad memories. Ghosts, he called 'em. Never known him to go there."

"I'm thinking it might be worth a look," Ty said.

"Suit yourself." Mrs. Mulvaney shrugged. "It's down this road out here. Six, maybe seven, miles." She gestured back toward where they'd come in. "If you make a right at the twisted spruce grove, then keep going about two more miles, you'll run right into it."

"The twisted spruce grove," Ty mused with a look to Wren. "Guess that'll be our next stop."

Chapter 7

"I feel like I'm sitting on icicles." Wren squirmed uncomfortably in the SUV before reaching out to turn on her seat warmer. She checked her cell. They'd already lost the weak signal they'd had at Davey's aunt's place. "Is it me or are you purposely searching out potholes to drive over?"

He let out a sound that confirmed he'd heard her. She looked at him.

"You're awfully quiet. You find anything in Davey's room other than that photo?"

"The road not traveled." There was a bitterness in his tone and more than a little relief. "Other than a closet full of empty bottles, not much. Struck me as sad, really. Not a whole lot to represent almost thirty years of life."

"Depends on the years, I suppose." She appreciated the idea that Ty could see where his life could have gone if he hadn't made certain tough choices.

"Found a receipt for a winter season tunnel pass he purchased the day before Alice's hit-and-run."

"Can those be traced?" Instead of paying a toll each time a driver used the tunnel, people could buy a pass ahead of time to make travel quicker and easier. "Is there a way to find out if he's used the pass or not?"

"Not sure. Something to ask the sheriff once we get back to town."

The sun had finally risen enough to start the morning thaw. The trees they passed dripped sparkling drops of frozen water from their branches. The light streaming through the surrounding trees and mountains was the proof she needed that they were not on another planet, just in a unique part of the world.

"Have any idea what a twisted spruce grove looks like?" It felt as if they'd been driving forever, which reminded Wren about the locals' definitions when it came to directions.

"She said we'd know it when we see it."

"Is it me or are you having fun with this?"

"It's not fun, exactly," Ty said. "It's a change of pace, not handling one of our ordinary kind of cases. I mean, when was the last time you saw something like that?" He pointed to a bald eagle soaring overhead above the treetops. "We just don't see that in Boston. Or pretty much anywhere else."

"No, we do not." She leaned forward, looked out the windshield. Her experiences with forests were of the cement type; skyscrapers and buildings reaching up to the clouds in a claustrophobic cluster. "You think that's it?" She gestured to a twisted clump of trees on the right-hand side of the road accompanied by a snow-covered turnoff.

"Guess we'll find out." He slowed, made the turn and took the speed down considerably as they bounced their way along the snowy rutted gravel path. "Two miles, she said, right?"

"Yes, hopefully it's close to that." The farther they

went, the thicker the canopy of trees and overgrown brush. She held the photograph from Davey's dresser. The faded imagery was wreaking havoc on her heart. Baby Davey was far too young to know anything was amiss, but the vacant, somewhat worried expression on his mother's face shifted Wren's empathy into overdrive.

She never failed to notice those little fragments of people's lives that reminded her how lucky she'd been. The McKenna family was as close as you could get. There had never been a moment when she'd doubted she was loved, wanted or accepted. Despite the stresses that came with her mother's job as a police commissioner, time was always carved out to give each of the four kids the time they needed to grow into confident, stable individuals.

Davey Whittaker hadn't had that.

Neither had Ty. But Ty had something Davey didn't. He had her.

Eventually the break in the path came and the sky and road opened up. She was back to being focused on where they were headed. Fortunately for her backside, it wasn't a full two miles before they came across the house in the photograph, now dilapidated.

Ty parked and sat there a moment, then powered down his window. "You smell that?"

"Hard not to." The eye-burning stench of burnt rubber assaulted her senses.

She retrieved her weapon from under her seat as Ty hopped out of the car. The smell was stronger out here, so much so she used the cuff of her jacket to cover her mouth as she followed him. "Where is it coming from?"

They silently made their way through the snow, toward the two-story home. As they rounded the first corner, they both stopped and stared at the burned-out husk of an SUV, sagging crookedly near the edge of a small ravine. There was no smoke, but the leftover smell was unmistakable.

Ty coughed as he approached the front of the vehicle, swiped his own jacket sleeve across the ash-strewn plate. "It's Mrs. Mulvaney's car, all right. And burnt to a crisp." He grabbed a handful of snow to clean off his jacket. "No way of proving this was the car that hit Alice."

Wren heaved a sigh of frustration, wishing the grille and windshield were still intact. She stepped back to look up at the house. Part of the exterior wall was scorched nearly to the second floor. All the windows had been blown in, no doubt from when the car's fuel had ignited. "He must be inside." Her hand tightened around her weapon.

"Only one way to find out." Ty began to move back to the front door.

Windowpanes had been broken and covered with crooked plywood. Shingles hung off-kilter. Rain gutters had dislodged and looked like odd miniature water slides filled with icy moss and weeds.

"I have a question," Wren said.

"Only one? Because I'm closing in on about a dozen."

"Sheriff Egbert must have known about this place. So why didn't he come out to look for Davey?"

"A question we can ask him when next we talk to him. Come on." He waved her forward. "Let's check inside."

Wren followed, keeping a bit of a distance between them as they approached the porch. Ty knocked, then again more loudly. "Davey Whittaker? Your aunt sent us

to check on you." He pressed his hand flat on the door
and pushed it open.

The smell was worse in here, trapped, no doubt, by
the cold and frost. The house was as frozen on the inside
as it was outside. Wren tried to snuggle deeper into her
jacket as she took up the rear, weapon aimed and trained
and moving as they cleared the living room. The dining
room. The kitchen.

Old furniture sagged and collapsed all around them.
Broken china littered the floor. Papers fluttered in the
breeze, coasting through the entire structure.

"He's not here," Wren said quietly as Ty approached
the staircase. "Check upstairs if you want, but the place
would feel different if he were here."

"Still gonna look. You finish checking down here."

"Uh-huh." She kept her gun raised. Dishes sat piled
in the sink, covered in dust, cobwebs and mold. Cabinet
doors sat open displaying a smattering of plates, cups
and rat droppings.

She heard a rustling behind her, in one of the tall cup-
boards. She stepped back, giving the ajar door a wide
berth as she reached out and whipped it open.

A gray-and-black cat stood facing her, its mouth open
in a noisy hiss. The growling sound coming from the
back of its throat kept Wren at a distance. *Odd*, Wren
thought, as she stepped away, crouched and reached into
her jacket pocket for her cell phone. In her experience,
most animals would have scurried away upon being discovered. Unless…

She tapped on her flashlight app, aimed the phone
down and crouched lower. "Oh." She blinked at the sight

of three kittens pawing their way around an empty box lined with debris.

The mama cat hissed, this time with force.

"It's okay, Mama." Wren gentled her voice, emotion clogging her throat. "You're just protecting your babies. I get it." Wren met the cat's gaze, set her phone down and reached out her hand.

The cat's paw shot up, started to bat at her, but seemed to think better of it.

"That's right. I'm not gonna hurt you." She remained as still as she could, her legs aching as she remained crouched. "Come on. Give me a good sniff." The cat took a hesitant step forward and pressed her cold nose against the side of Wren's hand, then shoved her head under Wren's palm, clearly demanding a pet.

"Whatcha got there?"

Wren glanced over her shoulder to find Ty leaning against the door frame. The cat jumped, hissed and dived back into the cupboard. Wren stood and carefully closed the door. "New tenants. A mama and three babies." She'd spotted a vet clinic on their way out of town. "We can take them to the vet when we leave."

"Okay." Ty didn't sound entirely convinced that was a good idea. "You find anything else around here?"

"Not yet." She gestured toward the mudroom, where an ancient washing machine sat crookedly against the wall. Wren's boots stuck to the floor as she made her way over.

The back door stood wide open. But there wasn't a lot of snow on the floor. There was, however, a mishmash of footprints heading to the back door.

"See that?" She pointed at the floor as Ty joined her. "There's more than one set."

"Or he came and went multiple times," Ty reasoned. "But only that one set continues outside." He indicated the ghostly footprints on the back porch.

They skirted the prints, following them as far as they could. The only indication of anyone walking around here was straight ahead, into the line of trees in the distance. "Good place to try to hide, yeah?"

"Also a great place to freeze to death," Ty countered. "Temperature got down to below ten degrees last night. Hypothermia would set in within minutes, and that's an optimistic estimate."

"Always with the gray clouds," she muttered. "Let's go." She tried to keep her speed up, but soon the snow was calf deep. Her jeans were soaked. Her feet turned to ice blocks as they trudged on.

Her lungs burned. She could hear Ty huffing a bit by the time they reached the trees. "They need to add snow walking to the FBI training course." She stopped, leaned against a thick trunk for a moment, trying to get her bearings. "Snow isn't as thick under the trees." She pointed ahead of them. "See? I bet those are footprints. They pick up again." The indentations in the snow led them into darkness.

"Or we're on the trail of another family of moose."

"Moose or meese?" She inclined her head. "I never do get the plural of that correct."

"If this turns out to be a wild-goose chase…"

"No geese around here." Wren plowed ahead, convinced that there was something or hopefully someone at the other end of these prints. But Ty's estimation was right. It would be really difficult to survive out here for very long.

"Still believe someone was chasing him?" Ty called from behind her.

"I didn't say someone was chasing him," Wren countered.

"You were thinking it."

That much was true. "Here, look." She stopped, crouched and indicated a new scramble of footprints. "Whoever was behind him was stepping where he was. This one step here is a bit more uneven than that one."

"Or he started to run and they went wonky."

"Okay." She stood up, faced him. "Get going, then."

"What?" Ty blinked.

"Start running. Let's see how you do after having walked that whole bit back there." She shook her head. "And here you're supposed to be wilderness-camping dude."

"I come up here to fish and commune with nature, not take suspects on nature hikes."

Wren rolled her eyes. "You're the one who brought me up here. Let's try to run this to the end before we come to any conclusions."

"Fine. Just sayin'—"

"When we're done, we can get in the car and drive through the tunnel. See where that pass you found in Davey's room might get us." She took a step back, then another, ready to turn on her heel and walk away.

Her foot found only air. She spun as the snow beneath her foot collapsed.

She dropped straight down.

"Wren!" Ty's voice echoed from above.

She flailed, tried to grab out for something, anything to catch hold of. She tucked in just in time to avoid hitting feetfirst. The snow cushioned her landing, but it was still hard enough to drive the air from her lungs. She saw stars, felt that sickening feeling sliding through her stomach as she tried to keep her breakfast down.

"Wren!" Ty shouted again.

"I'm okay." Her voice came out a whisper, so she tried again. "I'm okay!" Her voice echoed as if she'd fallen into a hidden ravine. She pushed up on one hand that went elbow deep into snow. She focused on keeping her breathing even as she did a mental check—feet, legs, arms, shoulders. She ached, but nothing felt dislocated or broken.

She moved, shifting snow out of her way as she confirmed a lack of injuries.

"Hang on!" Ty yelled. "I'm going to see if I can get down to you. I think I see a way."

"Yeah, okay," she mumbled. "Be careful!" she yelled as an afterthought, knowing nothing she said would stop him from trying.

She shifted away from the rock face so she could look up into the line of trees overhead. She'd just stepped straight off the edge of a rock. She wasn't going to call it a cliff because that would just be mortifying. "Wait a minute." She stopped, looked up again. Looked back to where she'd landed. Then to where she stood.

She surveyed the edge of the rock face, how high up it went. She'd fallen a good fifteen, maybe twenty, feet and luckily hadn't hit anything on the way down. Definitely could have been worse landing-wise. She stepped backward a yard or so, only to have her foot collide with something solid yet soft.

The hairs on the back of her neck prickled as she crouched and brushed at the snow. When her frozen hands felt fabric, she jerked away, gasping.

Swallowing hard, she pushed the dread aside, resumed brushing. She kept at it until she'd completely uncovered the heavy knit sweater.

She recognized the brown-and-burgundy yarn as the same type and color that had been in Mrs. Mulvaney's knitting basket beside her chair in the kitchen.

"Ty?" she called as she touched the shoulder, gently rolled the body onto its back. Strands of wet, scraggly dark blond hair were frozen to the face and forehead.

She stared down at the lifeless eyes of Davey Whittaker.

"Yeah, almost there. I think." His voice sounded strained but seemed closer. "Give me a few—"

"Stop. Stop where you are." She would have blinked back tears if she hadn't thought they'd freeze on her face. "I need you to go back."

"Go back? I'm not leaving you—"

"You need to go back and call the sheriff. We need help." She rested her hand on Davey's chest. "I found Davey Whittaker." Something sticky coated her fingers.

"What? He's down there? Is he alive?"

"No. He's dead. But not from the elements." She lifted her hand, looked at the congealed blood coating her skin. "He's been shot."

Ty lost ten years of his life watching Wren drop out of sight and plummet through the snow. Ten years he suspected he would never get back. He held his hands up to the heat pouring from the SUV's vents and tried to replay how they could have avoided the events that might have nearly killed her.

After she'd managed the uneven and unofficial path he'd found running into the ravine, the trek back to the house had taken a lot out of her. Out of them both, really. Neither of them was in any shape to remain with the body. Not when there was a warmer alternative not too far away.

Ty forced himself to relax his jaw. He was giving himself a headache grinding his teeth and gnawing on something that couldn't be fixed. What had happened had happened. There were no do-overs. But the memory of seeing her disappear right in front of him fed the real fear he had of losing her. They'd had close calls before. More than their fair share. But this time...

This time he'd watched it play out in vicious, heart-wrenching slow motion.

He caught sight of snow pluming up as a vehicle approached and stopped behind him. Recognizing Sheriff Egbert's SUV, Ty flicked off the heat, shut down the engine and got out of the car. He looked beyond the SUV, half-surprised not to find any other cars following.

"You the only one coming?" Ty called as Sheriff Egbert and Shelly climbed out.

"Afraid so!" Sheriff Egbert tugged on a pair of gloves, tossed his hat into the car before he closed the door. "I've put in a request for a forensics team to come out when they can, but Juneau's been backlogged awhile. It'll be a few days at the very least. If it takes much longer, the request will go to Anchorage."

"Right." One of those quirks of a small town.

"Where's your partner?" Shelly asked.

"In the middle of a rescue operation." Ty hadn't even tried to talk Wren out of rescuing the cats. When it came to animals, there was no way to win. No sooner had he explained than Wren walked out the front door, a medium-sized cardboard box in her arms.

"Couldn't just leave them behind," Wren said as Ty opened the back of the SUV for her. "Mama's definitely not happy." She cringed at the howling coming from inside the box.

Shelly pried open the lid and peered inside. "Poor little things. You want to keep them?"

"No!" Ty said.

Wren chuckled. "I'd love to, but no. Thought I'd take them to the vet I saw in town."

"Doc Thompson, sure." Shelly nodded.

"Why don't you two head back?" Ty suggested. "I'll help the sheriff with Davey's body."

Wren nodded in agreement, mainly because they'd agreed to this course of action after calling the sheriff.

"Give me a call when you're on your way back," Wren said as she motioned for Shelly to jump into their SUV. "We can meet back up at the Salmon Run Café."

"Sounds good," Ty said.

"Okay with you, Sheriff?" Shelly asked.

"Keep your cell on you," Sheriff Egbert advised. "I'll run Davey to the clinic, get the paperwork started for the autopsy."

Ty climbed into the sheriff's SUV while the women drove off toward the main road. "Glad we're driving closer," he admitted as the sheriff slid in behind the wheel. "Wasn't looking forward to trekking through all that snow again."

"I'd think once a day for that is enough." The engine rumbled to life and they drove parallel to the tracks Ty and Wren had made both on their way in and out of the tree line.

"I've got a question to ask you," Ty said when the silence stretched thin. "You knew about Davey's upbringing. Where he grew up." He gestured back to the house. "Why didn't you check to see if he was hiding out here when he went missing?"

"Meant to." Sheriff Egbert winced into the bright sun streaming through the windshield. "I was headed up here a couple of days ago, then got called out for a domestic disturbance on the other side of town." He shook his head as if he could clear his conscience. "Went clean out of my head after that. To hear Bea tell it, Davey never wanted anything to do with this place even before his dad died a few years ago."

"Still." Ty wasn't buying it. "If Davey was a suspect in a hit-and-run, it would make sense for him to do something unpredictable. Having a whole house to hide in—"

"Hindsight's always clear. The place is uninhabitable. You saw that yourself. Given the temperature this time of year, it would have been suicide to come out this far without power or water."

"Guess maybe it was," Ty said, acknowledging the fact.

The sheriff swung the car around at the line of trees, backed up a bit before he killed the engine again. "Truth is." He heaved a sigh and Ty saw a flash of guilt he was all too familiar with. "I didn't chase Davey down because I assumed he was guilty. Figured he'd turn up in time. The boy always had a conscience and I assumed at some point it would win. I got enough to mind without worrying about a loose cannon whose only talent seemed to be getting into trouble. I know." He shook his head at Ty's assessing look. "Not very admirable. Or honorable."

"I didn't say that," Ty responded.

"You didn't have to. It's written all over your face." There wasn't just guilt shining in his eyes now, but sorrow. And regret. "I failed that kid. From the very first time I arrested him on a drunk and disorderly a dozen or so years ago. I should have done more to help." He opened his door. "I should have cared. Maybe then he wouldn't be dead."

These were not the words of a calculating individual, but of a man who would carry this loss for a good long time.

Recovery sled in hand, they hiked through the trees to where Wren had discovered Davey's body. The area had been more than a little compromised in Ty's rush to get down to her. When they reached the ledge, they both looked over.

"Wren fell straight down." Even now, the very idea made Ty's stomach hurt. "Hit a soft patch of snow when she landed. Davey's just there." He pointed to the barely-there splash of color a short distance away. "My guess, given the amount of frozen blood that's under his body, he was shot up here and then pushed over. It would take actual velocity to go out like that before landing. If he'd just fallen, Wren would have landed on top of him."

"You've seen more dead bodies than I have," Sheriff Egbert said. "I'll take your word on this."

"It would have been quick," Ty tried to reassure the older man. "I know that doesn't bring any comfort, but still, it'd have been quick." A shot straight to the heart like that? Couldn't have been anything but.

"You're right," the sheriff said as he started down the uneven path Ty had traversed earlier. "It doesn't bring me any comfort at all."

Wren was still trying to thaw out as she and Shelly stood beside the exam table at Thompson Veterinary Services back in Splendor. Personally she longed for a space heater to stick her hands and feet on, but that would have to wait. Right now there were more important things to address.

"Are they going to be okay?" Wren tried to keep the worry out of her voice. The three kittens—two gray-striped and one black—seemed to have no problem mewing their emotions. The wiggly little fur balls were gaining more energy by the second.

"I think they'll be fine." The forty-something woman with stark black hair and bright blue eyes nodded as she pulled out the third kitten and rubbed a gentle finger between its eyes. "They're a little malnourished, but not surprising, given their mama hasn't had much milk lately."

All three of their gazes shifted to the side table where the mother cat was eagerly gobbling up the bowl of food provided by Dr. Thompson's assistant.

"Once she's eaten some, her milk will come back in and she can feed them. In the meantime—" she smiled at Wren "—we'll give them some bottle formula and start bulking them up."

"Thank goodness." Wren breathed a sigh of relief. "What about finding them homes?"

"Shouldn't be a problem," Shelly said. "I can put the word out around town once they're cleared for adoption. It won't take long for them to be claimed."

Wren walked over to the other table, gently stroked her hand down the mama cat's sleek back. "Her, too?"

"She might be more difficult," Dr. Thompson admitted. "Older cats always are. People think they lose their cute factor. But we'll do our best. Don't worry. We're a no-kill town. If no one takes her, we'll keep her around the office as a bonus employee and comfort cat."

The mama cat lifted her head long enough to give Wren a quick lick on the side of her hand before she resumed eating. Wren took that as a thank-you.

"Can we get her spayed?" Wren asked. "If it's a matter of cost—"

"Way ahead of you," the doctor told her. "Thank you for bringing them in."

"Great. Okay, then." Wren sighed. "I guess we'll be going. I am in desperate need of some coffee." She looked to Shelly. "Why don't you join me?"

"Oh, sure." Shelly looked both pleased and surprised. "I've got time until Sheriff Egbert gets back into town."

"Back? Where did he go?" Dr. Thompson examined the ears of the black kitten.

"He took a drive out to the old Whittaker place," Shelly said without missing a beat.

"Looking for Davey, no doubt," Dr. Thompson said. "That reminds me—how is Alice doing this morning?"

"Last report was there's no change," Shelly said. "But the doctors believe that's positive news."

"Good to hear. I've signed up for the meal chain that's

got going for Bradley and the kids. Planning to make them my famous chicken enchiladas for tomorrow."

Wren's stomach rumbled in reaction.

"Thanks again, Doc," Shelly called over her shoulder.

"You bet."

"You handled that really well," Wren told Shelly once they were outside. It took her a second to get her bearings and adjust once more to the cold. "You didn't miss a beat answering her questions about the sheriff."

"I've learned to keep to the truth as much as possible. Makes it easier when the details really do come out." Shelly winced and tugged her gloves back on. "You really need to get yourself some gloves."

"I've been thinking that myself." Her fingers practically cracked when she tried to move them. "So, coffee?"

"Right. Salmon Run Café's this way."

For being such a small town, it always felt like a trek getting anywhere. *Probably the cold*, Wren told herself.

The instant they stepped inside the rustic-cabin-style eatery, Wren wanted to shout in relief. "Ah, nice and warm in here." The vet's office hadn't been cold, exactly, but here she could feel the heat blowing. She cupped her hands in front of her mouth and stomped her feet.

The interior reminded her of a classic-looking cabin with thick wood stained a rich, deep walnut color. Fishing was clearly the recurring theme, with numerous poles and tackle on display, along with photographs of people having caught some serious-looking salmon. A few pictures were in stark color, others in black-and-white, leading Wren to assume this particular eatery had been in business for a good long time.

"Hey, Aurora!" Shelly called to the woman behind the

ten-seat counter. "Gonna grab a table right over there, yeah?"

"Go ahead. Coffee?"

"Please," Wren laughed. "A tankard, if you have it."

The woman grinned. "Be right over."

It made sense the place only had a few customers, given she and Shelly had arrived right between break-fast and lunch. The pair of men sitting at the counter watched as Wren and Shelly claimed their table.

"Morning, Deputy." A young man with thick glasses smiled at Shelly from where he sat at a smaller table against the wall. He kept one hand on the laptop computer currently plugged into one of the outlets on the wall.

"Hey, Mason." Shelly's cheeks went slightly pink and she gave Mason a quick wave. "Uh, thanks for your help the other day with that computer glitch at the station."

"Not a problem." Mason's gaze shifted briefly to Wren, but it was clear he only had eyes for Shelly. "Happy to help."

"Mmm. I bet he was," Wren teased Shelly as they took a seat at a table for four by the window. "He's cute. What's the story?" She liked the young deputy. So far, she'd appeared unflappable and easily dealt with what-ever was thrown at her. In that way, she reminded Wren of her sister, Regan. There wasn't anything she couldn't handle.

Shelly rolled her eyes, but the pink in her cheeks only intensified. "Mason and I went to school together. We're just…friends."

"Uh-huh." Wren knew how that went. "He calls you *Deputy*. That's kinda hot."

"It's kinda not." But Shelly laughed. Sitting across from Wren, she shrugged out of her coat. "Since we've got the time, can I ask you some questions about the FBI?"

"As long as you keep your voice down," Wren warned as their coffee arrived. "Thank you so much." She had her hands wrapped around the steaming mug in record time. One sip and she nearly went to heaven. "Now, that's perfect. Hits the spot for sure, Aurora," she added, remembering the name that Shelly had mentioned.

"Good to hear. You're a new face. Pretty face," Aurora said, planting a hand on her hip and pinning sharp green eyes on Wren. She had a thick smattering of freckles across her nose and cheeks. There were a pair of turquoise glasses perched on the top of her head, either because she always needed them or because she'd forgotten they were there. "You must be Ty Savakis's wife."

"I must be." She was so grateful the mug was almost big enough to hide behind. "But call me Wren. Nice to meet you. I heard you fix a great salmon, bacon and tomato sandwich."

"You heard that, did you?" Aurora looked impressed and tapped her bright pink fingernails against the white apron tied around her waist.

"Gabriel Hawthorne mentioned it when he flew me in," Wren added. "He said I shouldn't miss it."

"Well, that Gabriel's a charmer." Aurora's face lit up. "I'll have to give him a free slice of pie the next time he drops in."

Wren's eyes went wide. "You have pie?"

"Oh, yeah." Shelly reached over and pulled the laminated card out from behind the napkin holder. "Made fresh every day." She leaned across the table. "You get a discount on the day's special if you order it with a meal."

"Yeah?" Wren's mood immediately brightened. "What's today's special?"

"Alaskan blueberry."

It was official, Wren thought. She was going to have to walk back to the Lower 48 after a few days in Splendor. "You'd better set aside two slices. My husband's on his way," she said.

"Sounds like a plan. Nice to meet you, Wren." Aurora moved off with an approving expression on her face.

"So, you have questions." Wren lowered her voice.

"Well, I have a lot of them. Not really sure where to start." Shelly scrubbed her palms against her thighs. "I've been thinking about applying to the FBI Academy."

"Oh?" Wren picked up her coffee. "Not enough excitement around here for you?"

"There has been since you and Ty got here. I mean, Special Agent Savakis."

"Make it Ty," Wren advised. "We aren't spreading the info about our actual jobs."

"Right. Sorry. Nervous, I guess." Shelly laughed and choked down a sip of her coffee. "Is it hard? Getting through the Academy?"

"It's not easy," Wren confirmed. "Getting in isn't a cakewalk, either."

"Oh, that I have covered, no problem. I've got my BA in sociology with a minor in accounting. Plus, I've been a deputy almost two years now, so, education, check, work experience, check-check."

Wren nodded. "You're more than halfway there." She looked to the door when it opened to let a trio of customers in. "They're going to ask when you apply, so I'll ask now. Why do you want to be an agent?"

Shelly's face fell a bit. "I'm… I don't know, really. It just feels interesting. You get to travel and do a lot of really important work. On all kinds of cases."

"You do important work here, Shelly." Local law enforcement, especially in a small town, was vital to the success or failure of a community. It was obvious Shelly and Sheriff Egbert were two of the good ones.

Shelly huffed. "But it's not…it's not anything special. FBI agents, they solve cases that really make a difference. Like you and Ty coming out here to help Alice."

"Yeah, well." Wren was nearly half-finished with her coffee and already longed for a refill. "You know by now we are here unofficially." And there would be a price to pay once she—once they—got back to Boston. But that was for another time. "I've seen you work, Shelly. You're good at your job. You're good with people. You understand them and they respect you. That's not easy to accomplish."

"I guess." She sagged and looked a bit deflated. "I just want something…more, something bigger to do with my life. I don't want to get stuck."

Wren nodded. "I can understand that. Look. When the time comes, and you make your decision, you give me a call. I'll write you a letter of recommendation."

"Really?" Shelly immediately brightened. "You'd do that?"

"I'd do that." Wren held out her hand for Shelly's phone and added her phone number into Shelly's contact list.

"That would be so amazing. And I hope you know,

if I can do anything to help you and Ty with this case, I'm more than willing."

As much as she appreciated the offer, Wren shook her head. "I wouldn't want to put you in a difficult position with your boss."

"I'd let you know if it was something I couldn't do," she insisted. "But I wanted you to know that you can rely on me." She broke off from saying more when the door opened again, and Ty and the sheriff walked in.

"Hey, honey." Wren rested her chin in her hand and beamed up at a rather sullen-looking Ty as the two men joined them. He looked a bit haggard, but just seeing his face seemed to erase the last of her sour mood. Maybe falling off the edge of a cliff—okay, she was calling it a cliff—had shifted some…priorities for her. "Hungry? They've got blueberry pie for dessert."

"Yeah?" He brightened. "I could handle pie."

"Deputy Adjuk." Sheriff Egbert looked to his second. "We've got places to be."

"Sure thing." Shelly jumped up and snatched her jacket off the back of the chair. "Where to, Sheriff?"

"Beatrice Mulvaney's place for the notification." The second he spoke, the quiet chatter in the diner went silent. "Might as well tell you all now." Sheriff Egbert stepped back, took off his hat. "Davey Whittaker's been found dead up at his family's old place."

"Oh." Aurora blinked quickly, touched her hand to her heart. "Oh, that's terrible. Was it…was it his drinking?"

"It was not," Sheriff Egbert said and triggered more than a few expressions of surprise. "I'm not in a position right now to say anything more, but we might as well get the word out. Mrs. Mulvaney's going to be needing our support and I'd consider it a personal favor if, when the time comes, you all pay your respects. I know Davey caused problems around here, but he had a rough life. He didn't deserve what's happened to him, so please. Just...keep that in mind moving forward."

"Sounds like he got what was coming to him," one of the men at the counter grumbled behind his coffee. "Good riddance."

Sheriff Egbert took a few steps toward the man.

Wren shivered against the chill she felt in the room.

"Davey Whittaker was a member of this town, Carl," Sheriff Egbert said coolly. "We don't have any proof yet that he was responsible for Alice's accident. You want to feel that way about him, you keep it to yourself. This isn't just a tragedy for his aunt. It's a tragedy for all of us. We've lost one of our own. That's all that matters." The man opened his mouth as if to speak again, but Sheriff Egbert held up his index finger. "For now, that's all that matters. Thank you, Ty. For the assist. Deputy?"

"Right. Thanks for the talk." Shelly tossed Wren a quick smile before she hurried after her boss, her braided black hair glistening against the overhead lamps.

The chatter started up again, no doubt this time focusing on a different topic. Ty took Shelly's empty seat, set her mug aside.

"Everything okay?" Wren reached across the table and grabbed hold of his hand. "Are *you* okay?"

"Shouldn't I be asking you that question?" He slipped his fingers through hers and held on tight. Tighter than normal. "You're the one who fell off a mountain."

"It was a cliff," she countered, feigning offense. "A small one, but I won't have you take that away from me." The air suddenly seemed charged between them. Something she couldn't bring herself to ignore any longer. Being with him here, in the middle of a snowy nowhere, with the way he'd kissed her yesterday…it felt like uncharted territory. "Seriously, Ty. What's going on in your head?" It was a question she needed to not only ask more frequently, but she needed to start demanding an answer. If only to ease her own worry.

"Uh, I just helped pull a missing kid off the side of a mountain with a bullet hole the size of a crater in his chest. So, yeah, today's been a great day."

"I know." She hated how he took on the pain of other people, as if he'd had any control over what happened to Davey Whittaker. "I know it's going to be tough, but we've still got a case to work. We might even have to start over, now that our prime suspect's gone. Especially if he wasn't responsible for what happened to Alice."

"I guess." He sat back as Aurora approached with a fresh mug of coffee for him.

"And you're Ty Savakis." The corners of Aurora's eyes were smudged with mascara, no doubt after shedding some tears for Davey. "Welcome to Splendor."

"Thank you." He accepted his coffee with a smile. "Long morning. This'll hit the spot."

"Word is you helped Sheriff Egbert bring Davey back." She nodded approvingly. "Not everyone will say it, but he had a good heart. A bruised one, but a good one."

"I don't know if that makes me feel better about it or not," Wren mused.

"He tried," Aurora said. "He even went back to those

Friends of Bill meetings they have at the church twice a week."

Ty's hand tightened around Wren's. "When did he start that?"

"Oh, about a month ago or thereabouts," Aurora said. "I thought it finally took. Said he met someone there who offered him a job working home construction. Really thought he had his stuff together this time."

Ty gave Wren the look.

"Any idea who gave him the job?" Wren asked. When Aurora frowned, Wren rushed on. "It would be nice for his aunt to know that he was doing better."

"Poor Beatrice." Aurora shook her head. "He did joke once that the guy was from out of town. Said that was probably why he was willing to take a chance on Davey. Didn't know the history." She shrugged. "Anyway, you two ready to order?"

Wren ordered for the both of them. She knew that look on Ty's face. It was his putting-the-pieces-together look. "What?" she asked once Aurora left again.

"Seems odd, doesn't it? Davey's just getting his life together, hits an AA meeting, makes friends with someone who might not even be from around here, and he's dead shortly thereafter?"

"You always say there are no coincidences."

"I do say that, don't I?" He took a large gulp of coffee. "Let's stop at the church on the way back, see when their next meeting is."

Wren looked down to where their hands were still locked together. "You, ah, have any other plans for the evening?" She stroked her thumb across the back of his knuckles.

"Nothing official. You have something in mind?"

"Maybe." She shouldn't even be thinking about kissing Ty at the moment, not with the mystery of Davey Whittaker's death added to the mix. Still, that drop down the mountainside had flipped a switch for sure. "Don't worry. I'll keep you in the loop."

Chapter 8

"Church is just up this way." Ty zipped up his jacket the instant they were outside the café. Funny, he would have assumed that it would get warmer as the day progressed, but he could not shake the persistent chill.

"We can't infiltrate an AA meeting," Wren said as she fell into step beside him. "Some lines can't be crossed."

"They wouldn't tell us anything, anyway." This little town really was growing on him. The laid-back pace, the small specialized stores, the friendly way everyone smiled or said hello as they passed. "They take the *anonymous* part very seriously."

"You know that for sure?"

"One of my high school English teachers recommended Al-Anon meetings to me when I was fifteen."

"The meetings for family members of alcoholics?"

"When you turn up to class looking like I did, the good teachers take notice." He'd shoved those memories down so far he couldn't believe they had the oxygen to resurface.

"Did you go?"

"Until I graduated. Saved my life. Gave me a support system of people to call when things got really bad." He didn't realize how much the memories stung until Wren wrapped her arms around his and held him close. The instant balm against his heart nearly made him trip over his own feet. "Of course, a massive growth spurt helped a bit more. Along with the boxing lessons I started taking." His smile was quick and cool. "Phone numbers were great, but seeing the look on his face when he realized I'd learned how to defend myself?" Now, that had been priceless.

"I hate that you grew up that way."

He did, too. But he wouldn't be who he was without it, and, for the most part, he was pretty pleased with who he'd become.

They found the church at the end of the main road of Splendor, looking as if it had been cobbled together out of various buildings. The wide arched windows were painted a darker brown than the natural wood that constructed the building. A beautiful shiny white wooden cross sat perched on the angled eaves over the front door. A solitary stained glass window sat below the cross, depicting a colorful scene of Alaskan beauty—the mountains, the water and an eagle soaring into the heavens.

A woman was crouched in front of a line of flower beds, digging through the snow to tend to the barely-there buds attempting to burst through the hard soil. She glanced up as they approached, shielding her eyes against the sun.

"Good afternoon!" Her greeting was warm as she got to her feet and pulled off her gloves. "Given the looks of you, I'm guessing you're the Savakises." She held out her hand. "I'm Pastor Lorraine Cunningham. But, please, call me Lori."

"Nice to meet you, Lori. Does everyone know who we are?" Wren asked in what Ty recognized as her half-teasing voice.

"Perils of a small town, I'm afraid." Her brown hair was cut short and on an angle and her thin face carried the barest hint of a sun kiss. She was well clad for a winter's day with her double layers and thick tights and boots. "You look like you've found what you're looking for." She turned to gaze up at the cross. "What can I do for you?"

"We have some questions about Davey Whittaker."

Pastor Lori shook her head. "Davey. I just heard." She touched a finger to the cross at her throat, looked at Ty. "You helped the sheriff bring him back to town."

"I did, yes, ma'am."

"He's having a little trouble processing the whole thing," Wren lied. "We've heard so many conflicting stories about him, we thought maybe you might have some insights?"

"Of course. Certainly." She gathered up her gardening bucket and motioned for them to follow. "Come on in. I was just about to fix myself some tea."

"Are we going to get struck by lightning for lying to a pastor?" Ty muttered so only Wren could hear him.

"McKennas have earned a fair amount of goodwill." She glanced to the sky. "Plus, it's for a good reason. And it's not all a lie. You are struggling."

It disturbed him that she saw that. But then whatever was happening between them seemed to have cracked whatever walls remained. Or the filters that kept them from commenting or speaking their minds.

Pastor Lori led them through the small quaint church

that on the inside looked as if it had been outfitted by master carpenters. The dozen pews sat neatly arranged facing a modest but elegant dais. The door to the right led to the pastor's living quarters, a practical area neatly displayed with even more hand-carved pieces of furniture and accent pieces.

"My grandfather helped build this church," Pastor Lori said as she urged them to sit at her square kitchen table. "He was a carpenter with a love of architecture."

"It's a beautiful building," Wren said. "Was he also the pastor?"

"No." Pastor Lori set a kettle on the stove and switched on the burner. When she turned, the knowing smile on her face said it all. "My grandmother was." She retrieved a tin of cookies from on top of the refrigerator. "Please. Save me from myself. My assistant makes the best peanut butter cookies. I need them out of the house."

Lunch at the Salmon Run Café had been filling and delicious, especially the pie, but Ty could never resist a cookie. "Thank you." He nudged Wren, who quickly followed suit. "We heard mention that Davey had recently started in a recovery program here at the church."

"Yes." Pastor Lori sat on the edge of her chair.

"Do you know the last meeting he attended?" Wren asked.

"I do." Pastor Lori nodded. "It was the night of Alice's accident. We all thought he was doing really well." She shook her head. "It's not an easy demon to battle."

"No, it's not," Ty agreed before he thought better of it.

Pastor Lori's gray eyes softened. "I'm sorry you understand that."

Ty resisted the urge to squirm. He didn't like being

under the microscope. One of the appeals of joining the FBI was to be on the other side of it. He cleared his throat. "What time did the meeting let out?"

"About five. We had bingo that night and I'm a complete stereotype when it comes to bingo." She chuckled as the teakettle began to whistle. "I didn't hear about the accident until the next morning."

"Any idea why everyone assumes Davey was the one who hit Alice?"

Pastor Lori glanced away. "I don't suppose it hurts to say. He was seen at the Outlaw that night. It's just a few doors down from Wilderness Wonders."

"Where Alice works," Wren clarified. "We were under the impression Davey didn't drive much."

"Oh, he did when he was sober," Pastor Lori said. "That was usually how anyone knew he'd stopped drinking. And he always drove his aunt's car. Couldn't keep a job long enough to pay for one himself."

"But he did get a new job, though."

"Apparently." Pastor Lori rose to pour the hot water into three mugs. "Is lemon tea all right for you?"

"Sounds great," Ty said. "You were saying, about his job?"

"Now, that I don't have many details about. I heard rumblings that someone he met in the program offered him a job. But it wasn't anyone local." She set their mugs in front of them. "Even if I was in a position to share their identity with you, I'm not sure it would get you anywhere."

"Oh? Why's that?" Wren accepted the sugar bowl and spoon Pastor Lori scooted closer.

"Well, let's just say I tend to know when people aren't

telling me the truth. It's a…gift." She raised her eyes to the sky again. "Just like I'm pretty sure you aren't asking about Davey because of any spiritual crisis you're going through. Or am I wrong?"

Feeling a door open, Ty walked through. "We're trying to find out what happened to Alice. And now to Davey. That's all we want to do."

"I see." Pastor Lori sipped her tea. "Okay, as I said, I'm afraid I can't be of any help as to who Davey might have met at the meetings. We had two guests in the past two months. Don't recall seeing them in town very much, but they were definitely at the meetings. Two, no, three."

"And since Alice's accident?" Wren pressed.

"We had our meeting last night. Not a sign of them."

"Could you describe them, maybe?" Ty asked.

"I cannot." Her expression said she clearly believed in the *anonymous* part of the group's principles. "All I can say is they stood out."

"Male?" Ty tried again.

She inclined her head. "What I noticed was that they definitely didn't look as if they had any interest in being at the meetings," Pastor Lori went on. "We pride ourselves on being welcoming. I got the impression they were both just going through the motions. But I try not to judge. It's kind of in the job description."

Ty chuckled. "Appreciate you spending the time with us."

"I'll do anything to help find out what happened to Davey, and whoever hurt Alice. It's such a tragedy. She and Bradley haven't attended services, but I stopped in after breakfast this morning. From what I hear, the doctors seem to think she's improving."

"That's great news," Wren said.

"I wish there was more I could do. That we all could do for Alice and her family," Pastor Lori said. "If you can think of anything, please don't be shy. Just ask."

"Believe me, neither of us is shy," Wren said.

"So, what do you think?" Ty asked Wren a few minutes later as they walked back through town. "She gave a pretty good description of bachelor number two in the white SUV."

"Yes, she did. Want to test our luck and check out the Outlaw?"

They did, but to no avail. The two employees working the night of Alice's accident—the night Davey supposedly fell off the wagon—wouldn't be on shift until tomorrow. Pushing would only make Ty and Wren stand out more, so instead they headed over to Groovy Grub Grocery.

"Hey, Sully!" Wren called as soon as they walked in the door.

Ty always marveled at how easily she got along with people. One of those McKenna traits, he supposed. They all knew how to interact with others in any situation.

"Oh, hey there, Wren. See you brought your other half today." Sully gave her a wave before returning his attention to the short line of customers at the counter.

Ty wandered while Wren perused the gloves and jackets. Her cold hands could explain her new tendency toward holding his hand whenever she could. Sure, that was it. She was cold. And keeping up the pretense of their "relationship." Still…

He couldn't help but wonder what she'd been talking about at lunch when she asked about his plans for the evening. He knew what he wanted to think about it, but he wasn't going to jump on board that particular train just yet.

"Find something?" he asked when she tracked him down at the back of the store. The selection of hunting knives, especially the carved ones and the more practical military type, captured his attention.

"One pair for me and one for you." She held the gloves up as if for his inspection, along with a new fleece-lined jacket the color of ripe plums. "Couldn't find one that came with a plug-in heater, so this'll have to do."

He trailed behind her to the register, keeping an eye on the customers milling about in the aisles. He got his fair share of looks and smiles and nods of acknowledgment. He received another from Sully, the burly man standing behind the cash register.

"You done good by our Davey," Sully said with a solemn expression on his whisker-covered face. "Heard you gave the sheriff a hand out there."

"Just doing what I could," Ty said as the man rang Wren up for her items. "Wish it didn't have to be done."

"Agreed," Sully said.

"Hey, Sully, I'd like to get ice cream for Bradley's kids," Wren said. "Can you give me a couple of pints of their favorites?"

"Sure can. You want a cone? Got a new flavor today. Mint chocolate chip made with Irish liqueur."

"*Irish*, you say?" Ty teased as Wren groaned. "You might have just said the magic word."

"If you aren't busy tomorrow night, we're having a town potluck to raise money for Alice's medical bills."

"Oh." Wren blinked and then glanced at Ty. "What a great idea. We'll definitely plan on being there."

"Six o'clock, the town meeting hall. You won't have to go far," Sully added with a deep chuckle. "It's in the basement of your building. Just take the elevator all the way down."

"Sounds good," Ty said, thinking that would be a great chance to see if anyone else had run into the two guys Davey had made friends with at his AA meetings. "Thanks for the heads-up."

"I'll have to put my thinking cap on as far as what to bring," Wren said as Sully included three pints of ice cream to her order, then went back to get her cone.

They were stopped again on their way out, more than once, by people thanking Ty for his helping the sheriff with Davey.

"You can see it on their faces," he said once he and Wren were on their way back to Skyway Tower.

"You mean that they maybe feel like they should have paid more attention to Davey while he was still here?" Wren asked. "I noticed that. Even saw it on Pastor Lori's face when we were talking to her. And she did try to help."

A new sliver of anger burrowed beneath Ty's mood. "It ticks me off, thinking Davey might have finally been ready for a change and someone was waiting to pounce on him."

"Wouldn't be the first time we've seen it." She licked the ice cream in a way that had Ty seriously wishing they were already in their apartment. Her gaze went up and her face lost a bit of its color. "Ugh. I've got to stop doing that." She squeezed her eyes shut, shook her head as if trying to erase an image in her mind.

"What?" He looked to where she had. One of the passenger air trams was gliding up the mountainside in the distance. Far above the ground. "You know, at some point you're going to have to get over this height thing of yours."

"Uh-huh, well, I've made it this long," she muttered. "There are some challenges I'm willing to let pass me by. Seriously." She pointed at the cable cars suspended high in the sky, her eyes wide with disbelief. "Why?"

"To reach places you can't get to otherwise?"

"Ha ha."

"It's not that bad, Wren. I took the trip up my second day here. They're automated, accessible 24/7, just someone overseeing the system in case anything goes…" He broke off at her glare. "You sit in the right place, you only see sky. You can almost trick yourself into thinking you're still on the ground."

"Please."

Okay, maybe that was a stretch. "Don't make me issue a dare," he teased. "You know you can't resist that."

"There are few certainties in life, Ty Savakis," she said firmly as she drew her tongue around the top edge of the cone to stop the ice cream from dripping. Every cell in his body tightened to attention. "But I can one hundred percent guarantee I am never stepping foot in one of those…things. What?" She frowned at him, examined her cone, then looked back at him. "What's wrong?"

"Not a thing." For once, everything felt very, very right.

"Want some?" She held it out.

"Of the cone?" he asked. "No."

He couldn't help it. He bent his head and caught her lips with his, tasting the cold of the ice cream along with the tempting combination of flavors that included Irish liqueur, chocolate and Wren. Her mouth opened beneath his, her free hand snaking up to the collar of his jacket to grab hold. She ignited something inside him he'd never allowed himself to stoke before. A fire, a desire that he'd had to bank for going on seven years.

He heard the telltale sound of giggles and whispers moving past him and he lifted his head, looking into her eyes as if she were the only life preserver in an ocean of emotions. After all this time…this, whatever it was between them, might finally happen.

"Is it just me," she murmured and patted a not-so-calming hand against his chest, "or am I the only one who's grateful that potluck is *tomorrow* night?"

"Not just you. Wanna go back to the apartment and compare…notes?" he asked with a grin he had no doubt came across as sly.

"Sure." Her smile matched his and set off all kinds of fiery images in his brain. "If you're sure."

How could he be, given everything making love to her would risk? He should say no. He should be the rational one, the responsible one, and remind her about their professional partnership. Their jobs. The undeniable fact that their attention would be…divided. But he'd spent years longing to touch her in ways he never could. Would he honestly walk away from it now? For so long all he'd had in life was his job, and now, even for a little while, he could have her, too. It was a long-ing he had to fulfill.

He took the bag containing the ice cream and her old jacket, slipped his free hand into hers. "I'm sure."

There wasn't a power in the universe that could have made him remember that walk back to the tower, or if they took the stairs or elevator to the fourth floor. All he did know was that closing in on that apartment door and the ability to lock the rest of the world completely out—even for a little while—felt like the culmination of a life's goal.

"Keys, keys," Wren muttered as she dug into her pockets. "Where on earth did I put the stupid— Gah!" She ripped the bag out of his hand, yanked out her old jacket and fumbled to find the correct pocket. It did something to him, deep inside where he tucked it safely away, to know she was as anxious and maybe as ner-vous as he was.

"Want some help?"

"No, I don't want— Oh." She blinked up at the key he held in his hand. "Give me that." She snatched it from him, laughing, and unlocked the door. She spun around, grabbed him by the front of his jacket and dragged him inside. The door had barely closed behind them before she pressed him to the wall and kissed him.

There wasn't a part of himself he didn't want her to touch. Every cell in his being cried out for her. His hands moved as if he were possessed by a restless fever, skim-ming up and down her back, frustrated by the thick fab-ric of the coat that separated them.

She pressed his mouth open with hers, dived in, took control of the kiss and swirled her tongue around his in a way that reignited that dormant core inside him. Breathing ragged, they worked at each other's jackets, letting them drop where they were as they went to work on buttons and…

"Wait!" She planted a hand on his chest. He almost couldn't hear her—let alone think—with the blood pounding in his ears. It shouldn't be possible that kissing her, having her in his arms, felt even better than he'd imagined.

"What?" He banged the back of his head against the bookshelves, flexing his hands since he wanted nothing more than to grab hold of her again.

"Boots. Off." She trailed her hand down his chest, scraped her nails under to where he could feel her fingers all but scorching him through his shirt.

"No fair," he teased as she bent down to untie her boots. He squeezed his eyes shut for a moment, getting his bearings before moving far enough away so that he could do the same. "Didn't realize what a hindrance these might be when I got dressed this morning." He fumbled with the laces, finally unknotting them. He hopped around on one foot, then the other, making her giggle while she watched him.

"So gallant," she teased as one boot, then his other, got tossed away. Her socks came next. He followed suit, only to find himself frozen at the sight of her shimmying out of her jeans.

The way she slipped her hands under her waistband and moved her hips so she could slide her legs free made him rock-hard in an instant. She reached up, pulled the band from her hair, letting it cascade around her shoulders.

Wren stood before him now in nothing but panties

and a thigh-skimming yellow T-shirt that clearly showed the outline of her bra. "Thought I'd save something for you to do," she said, a teasing smile playing across her lips. "Your turn."

He grinned, unbuttoned his shirt, but left it on. "Returning the favor." He reached out, clasped her wrist in his hand and tugged her forward. "The rest is for you."

Ty bent his head, caught her mouth again in a kiss that emblazoned itself so intensely, he couldn't imagine thinking of anything else ever again. The way she moved against him, the way she kissed him back, meeting him stroke for stroke. Feeling her still-cold hands flat against his chest, sliding restlessly over his bare skin.

"We should have done this ages ago," she whispered against his mouth as she pushed him toward the bedroom. Wren shoved his shirt off his shoulders and tossed it aside. She couldn't seem to get enough of touching him, something he could appreciate as he drew the hem of her shirt up until he exposed the tight muscles of her stomach that clenched when he touched her.

She moaned, directing his mouth back to hers as she hooked a leg around his. "Fast," she ordered, her hands fisting in his hair, her teeth blazing a trail down the side of his neck. "I want this fast, Ty."

"I can manage that." Reason sliced through his foggy mind. "Wait. I forgot." Trying to slow his breathing, he pressed his forehead against hers and squeezed his eyes shut. "I can't believe I'm going to say this, but I forgot condoms."

"Clearly not prepared. Tsk-tsk." She kissed him deeply, then looked him in the eye before stepping back and out of his reach.

He watched, dazed, as she kind of twirled her way to the nightstand on her side of the bed, pulled open the drawer.

"You know me." She ripped open the box and pulled out a foil package. "Ever hopeful."

If he'd needed any more confirmation that his desire for her was shared, he finally had it. She walked back to him, hands gripping the edge of her T-shirt, which she then pulled over her head. The resulting image of her there, wearing cute white panties and a bra, nearly had him exploding. She wouldn't even have to touch him again. The very sight of her was enough to push him over the edge.

"I thought that was mine to do." His legs felt weak as he stepped up to her, bit back a groan as her hands got busy on the button and zipper of his jeans.

"Changed my mind." She reached into his pants, slipped her hand around him and set off every synapse in his brain. The feel of her firm touch had him sighing with pleasure. When his eyes finally focused, he looked down at her, only to find her watching him just as intently. "Amazing," she whispered and kissed his mouth, releasing him so she could maneuver him to the bed. With one gentle nudge, she had him flat on his back.

She made quick work of his jeans, throwing them to the floor before she slipped her fingers beneath the waistband of her panties and pushed them down her thighs.

He cursed, hands fisting in the bedspread. He wanted nothing more than to touch her, but that look in her eye, that determined, demanding, powerful gleam, was something he never wanted to be rid of. When she reached back to unclasp her bra, every part of him stiffened.

She drew the straps down her arms, excruciatingly slowly, in his opinion. He'd always been impressed with how she could control a room, an interview. A suspect.

Now she was controlling him. Simply by standing there.

Until she wasn't.

She pressed her knee to the edge of the mattress, between his legs, and leaned over him, her hair skimming parts of his body in ways he'd never allowed himself to think of. Wren dipped, pressed her lips against his throat, opened her mouth and licked the side of his neck before returning to his mouth. He heard the crinkling of the foil packet in her hand, saw the slow, seductive smile curve her lips before she kissed him.

"I thought you wanted this fast." He lifted his hands to her hips, kneaded her soft flesh and felt her breath hitch.

She brought the condom packet to her mouth, clasped it with her teeth and tore it open. "Thanks for the reminder." It was clear by the slow shimmy she did down his body that she had every intention of drawing out his torturous pleasure. She pushed one of his hands away, placed his fingers into the bedspread for him to grip and then shifted back enough to roll the condom onto him.

There was no one else capable of giving him the pleasure he felt in that moment. The touch of her fingers as she protected them both had him shifting on the bed to the point of being unable to control his movements.

When she was done and she rose over him once more, she reclaimed his hands, wove their fingers together.

"Watch me," she said in a tone that would forever be locked around his heart.

She took him then, only enough at first to set her throat to humming. She closed her eyes, arched her back and deepened the connection, clenching her fingers around his as she began to move her hips. Her knees pressed into his and tightened with every thrust he gave. He couldn't look away from her. Mesmerized, he flexed his fingers and raised their clasped hands.

The soft, wet heat of her felt like the fulfilled promise of his life, but it wasn't enough.

It wasn't nearly enough.

He released her hands, grabbed her hips and, in one pulse-pounding movement, shifted their positions so she was under him, surrounding him. Fulfilling him.

She gasped, eyes open and shining into his as he drove himself deeper into her. The sensation of her legs locking around his back, holding him in her, was the only encouragement he needed as the rush overcame him. He thrust with every bit of himself, enraptured by the expression of pleasure crossing her face as she writhed beneath him. There wasn't an ounce of her he couldn't feel. Her heartbeat. Her breathing. Her…

Too much, he told himself as he held back that last bit of hope. It was too much to go there, so he kept it to himself as he began to thrust faster.

"Come with me," he whispered and pressed his hot mouth against her neck as she rose to meet him. "We go together."

She groaned, smiled and turned her mouth to his. "Together," she murmured. "Always. Ah!" She crested first, that look of utter bliss on her beautiful face carrying him over the edge as they rode the wave as one.

As if it was always meant to be.

Chapter 9

"You're thinking so loud I can't sleep," Ty murmured against the top of Wren's head.

"Sorry." Instead of moving away, she snuggled closer, reveling in the sensation of being in his embrace. "Got a lot going on in my head, I guess."

"Yeah? Me, too." His hand stroked down her arm, sending now-familiar and all-too-welcome chills racing through her body. "Anything you want to talk about?"

She lifted her head, found him looking at her with obvious affection, and it unsettled her. As dangerous as their…liaison was, she couldn't help but feel as if a part of her, a part she never wanted to acknowledge, was finally set free. "Why do you think it took us this long?"

He sighed, shrugged, shook his head. "Well, if we're looking at the facts."

"Oh, yes, please, Special Agent Tyrone Savakis." She shifted over him, rested her chin on her hands as his own moved down to her hips and curve of her butt. The latter a part of her anatomy he seemed particularly fond of. "Let's look at the facts."

"To start with, when we first became partners, you'd just gotten married."

"Oh, right." She frowned. "Antony." She'd almost forgotten about him. "Boy, there was a mistake. Poor guy didn't know what he was getting into." And neither, if she were being honest with herself, had she. At the time she hadn't quite figured out who she was. The last thing she should have done was get married, but it seemed like the right thing to do and she couldn't think of a good reason to say no. She had to give her parents credit. They'd supported her and kept their opinions to themselves, even after her divorce. "Mom calls that my rebellion phase."

"Does she?"

"Um-hmm." She loved feeling his hands on her. They had an oddly intoxicating effect on her still-humming system. "Each of us McKennas had one, I just waited the longest. Aiden's was the most typical. He went through his at fourteen."

"Really?" Ty raised a brow. "Can't really imagine Aiden McKenna going through a rebellious stage."

"It had to do with the wrong group of friends, a trunk full of illegal fireworks, a patrol car and a very bad sense of timing."

Ty's laugh drew a smile out of her. She couldn't remember ever feeling quite so...content before.

"What did your parents do?" he asked.

She suspected he was thinking about what his father would have done to him had he been in the same circumstances, and the prospect of that stabbed at her full-to-overflowing heart. "Mom and Dad employed the tough love with him. He spent three days in juvenile detention. They are firm believers in one's actions and poor decisions having consequences."

"I can't wait to ask him for the details the next time I see him," Ty said. "What about Howell? When did his rebellion hit?"

"Second grade. No kidding," she added at Ty's doubtful expression. "He took exception to this kid named Reno, who liked to bite girls on the arm."

"Sounds like a budding serial killer," Ty commented.

"Mmm. No doubt. The story goes that's when Howell developed *the look*."

"The look?"

"Howell has this…ability to just stare. He doesn't blink. He doesn't move. He just looks at you in a very particular way that stops you doing whatever it was you were doing."

"So he stared at this kid?"

"For about two weeks. Followed him around at recess, before or after school. Anytime a teacher wasn't around. He would just be there. But he didn't touch him. Didn't talk to him. Just…watched."

Ty laughed, covered his eyes with his hand. "Oh, man."

"Needless to say, the biting disappeared while Reno was fending off Howell, which was Howell's goal. Reno's parents tried to call for a meeting with our parents to get Howell to leave him alone, but by Reno's own admission, Howell hadn't touched him. And, considering the school hadn't done anything to stop him biting other students…" She shrugged. "Didn't really go their way. I was only in first grade at the time, so I don't remember it happening. I just remember the day Howell politely explained to the principal what he'd not done and, more importantly, why he'd not done it. We all went out and had ice-cream sundaes for dinner."

"I love your family." Ty continued laughing. "How different my life would have been with parents like that. What happened to Reno?"

"The family moved away before the next school year. Aiden says Howell stood across the street from their house the day they moved and watched, but I think that's just him adding to the legend that is Howell McKenna." She had no qualms with the pride she felt when it came to every member of her family.

"You McKennas do have a unique sense of honor about you."

"We are the watchers and protectors," she said, as if by rote. "Mom and Dad always told us to keep an eye on the people who could be easily preyed upon. Sometimes just standing in someone's corner is enough to make a difference. For some, knowing they aren't alone is enough."

His hand sank into her hair. "Like you've always done with me."

She shrugged. "With you, it was more out of obligation." She wiggled a bit and set his eyes to darkening. "I'm kidding. You do okay on your own, Savakis. You don't need a guardian angel."

"Maybe not need." He leaned down, kissed her gently on the lips. "But I'll take the one I've got. I'm enjoying this trip down memory lane with your family. Tell me about Regan. What was her rebellion?"

"It wasn't so much a rebellion as a disturbing dedication to winning." Something Regan had not outgrown.

"Winning what?"

"Anything and everything. Races, board games, bets. Being right." Under *stubborn* in the dictionary, there was a picture of Regan McKenna.

"I do seem to recall a rather vicious game of Scrabble at Thanksgiving one year that…"

"Vicious?" Wren paused, then nodded. "Yep. She hates to lose. And she goes after those triple-word scores with purpose."

"Probably comes from being the baby of the family."

"Don't let the baby hear you call her that," Wren warned. "She's thirty-one and carries her own badge and gun."

"Yeah, but she's ATF, so she's not really—"

She kissed him quiet. "Seriously, Ty. I cannot protect you from her if she ever hears that come out of your mouth."

"Noted for future reference."

Wanting a distraction from talking about the future, she shifted to the past. "So is now a good time to ask you what happened with Felicia? You never did tell me."

"Didn't I?" The overly innocent tone told her he was well aware he hadn't spoken of the breakup with his ex-wife. "Long story short? Never should have married her. It wasn't fair." He smoothed his hand over her shoulder. "To either of us."

"Would now be a good time to admit I never liked her?" A little levity in this moment couldn't hurt.

"Would have been better if you'd told me that before we eloped to Vegas." His hand was back to doing those touchy-feely things that would result in their not talking for a good long while. "Biggest mistake I ever made, but at the time it was a solution to a problem I couldn't solve another way."

"What problem?" She never had understood the impulsive wedding, especially since he'd never seemed particularly happy about the event.

He looked at her, an expression on his face she'd never seen before. An expression that caused her toes to tingle even as an odd panic settled in her chest.

"What?" she asked.

"I married Felicia because the woman I was in love with wasn't available."

"Oh. Well, that's just…" She didn't get it at first, but the longer he looked at her, the harder his heart pounded against hers, the truth settled. "Me? The woman you were in love with was…me?" How she had air left to breathe, she couldn't fathom. This man, this glorious, amazing, frustrating man, loved her?

"Pretty much from the second we met." His smile was quick and somewhat bittersweet. "Postcoital confessions are the ones that can get you in the most trouble, so I'd be grateful if we could just let that go and pretend I didn't say it."

"Then you shouldn't have told me." She curled her legs under her, straddled his hips and drew the sheet up and around the back of her shoulder. Bending over, she brushed her lips against his, her hair dropping around them like a curtain of protection. "All this time? You kept this to yourself all these years?" Even now, he had courage she lacked. The feelings, the emotions, were there. But she couldn't, no matter how hard she tried, push the words free to tell him she felt the same.

His hands ran from her hips up her rib cage and back

down. "I think you might be the only one surprised." He cupped her face in his palm, gazed up at her with such affection, such...love, she lost her breath. "The question is, where do we go from here?"

"We agreed." She swallowed hard, tried to remember what they'd said. "This would stay here in Splendor."

"Yeah?" He gripped her hips, kneaded her flesh with his hands as desire built up inside her once more. "You really think that's going to work?"

"We have to try." Figuring out how they could make this work outside this place, back in the real world, where their partnership could be at risk, wasn't something she wanted to contemplate at the moment. She didn't want another partner. She liked working the way they did. But...

She leaned over, shook another condom package free from the box. "Right now, I have other things on my mind."

"I can see why you went after Treyhern as hard as you did."

Ty didn't take his eyes off the scrambled eggs he stirred in a pan on the stove—the quick food was the only dish he was capable of making to any degree of success.

It had taken them until almost midnight before they realized hunger was the only thing that was going to blast them out of the bedroom. His offer to cook came from a purely selfish place. If he was busy with this, he couldn't dive deeper into a conversation about them that she clearly wasn't ready to have.

"Considering all the crimes he was suspected of committing, it's almost a miracle he killed that dealer of his in front of a witness."

"He made a mistake." Ty grabbed two plates from where they'd been drying beside the sink. "He completely underestimated Alice's loyalty."

"Mmm." Wren continued to scroll through the extensive Treyhern file, from the case's inception all the way through to his appeal. "He neglected to realize even people who are down on their luck have lines they won't cross."

"Alice was stand-up from the start." He could still remember how impressed he was looking at a then-eighteen-year-old Alice sitting in an interview room at a neighborhood police station, explaining that Ambrose Treyhern hadn't only murdered the nightclub dealer right in front of her, but had offered her a hundred thousand dollars to keep her mouth shut. "Don't think I have that kind of fortitude now at thirty-three."

"There you go, underestimating yourself again." It wasn't chiding, exactly, but it came darn close. "But that does explain why you're so determined to help her even now."

He popped two pieces of bread into the toaster, retrieved the butter from the fridge. His bare feet slapped against the wood floor. He wondered, not for the first time, if she had any idea how beautiful she was. Not just on the outside. She had that classic blonde-bombshell beauty Hollywood had made a fortune off of. But inside there wasn't any maliciousness to her, no hard edges to scrape past. She was the epitome of goodwill and justice wrapped up in an all too sometimes overwhelmingly appealing package.

"If...when Alice recovers," he said as he retrieved flatware from the drawer, "I might have to take a harder run at her when it comes to witness protection."

Wren nodded. "Good that you're seeing that. Treyhern's got a powerhouse attorney on his side this time around. His first one was good, but this guy?" She tapped the screen. "This guy could very well get Treyhern out. Of course, if anything else ever happened to her, he'd be the first suspect."

Guilt pitched inside him. "That wouldn't stop him. People like Treyhern, they're steeped in the belief that the rules and laws are for other people, not them. He'd take her out, along with her family, and then worry about whatever possible consequences there are later. Maybe not even then."

"I really hate guys like that." She finally glanced up, gestured to the stove. "Turn the flame off."

"Oh. Right." He clicked it off, flinched as he stirred the now-slightly-overcooked eggs. "Sorry."

"They'll be edible, don't worry." The smell of burnt toast coasted through the air. "Those might not be."

He dived for the toaster, but tossed the scorched pieces of bread into the sink.

"Seriously, I'll have to give you some cooking lessons." She pulled the jump drive out of the laptop and tucked it into the front pocket of his shirt that she was wearing. "Otherwise at some point you're going to starve."

"Will not," he argued as he reset the toaster settings and tried again. "Not as long as I've got my cell phone."

"Doubt they've got FlashFeast up this way." She closed

her computer, rested her chin in her palm. "What about calling Howell and asking him to come up and talk to Alice? Once she's better." She narrowed her eyes just as he turned his back on her. "You've already considered that, haven't you?"

"It crossed my mind." He dished out the eggs, stood watch over the toaster. "I didn't push her toward WITSEC the first time because with every other aspect of her life she was happy. I didn't want her to lose what she'd worked so hard to attain. But now…"

"Now there's more than just Alice to think about."

"Let's keep Howell in our back pocket." He buttered the golden toast and slid her plate in front of her. "I'd like to give it a better shot. Besides, we've got time before—"

The screech of the building's fire alarm had both of them jumping. Wren's toast clattered onto her plate as Ty raced out of the kitchen. He yanked open the apartment door, stuck his head out.

Strobe lights flashed in the hall, the high-pitched alarm blaring.

"You think there's a real fire?" Wren appeared behind him, stuffing her legs into her jeans.

"I don't smell anything." Doors up and down the hall opened. Some, like Ty, simply looked out, while others, like the Thistle sisters, emerged in their robes and curlers with their purses looped over their arms. "This happen often?" Ty yelled.

"Not in a long while," Florence called back.

"Take the stairs. Head on down," Ty suggested, then popped back into the apartment to grab a shirt, his shoes and their guns. "Here." He handed hers off and they each hid their weapons underneath their clothes.

Voices were muted, the alarm blared on, slicing through Ty's head like a knife. The lights had started flashing in apartments now, no doubt the next level of warning.

"This could be a false alarm," Wren said as they left with their phones and keys. "A coincidence, but still—"

"Not taking a chance. Did you see Bradley and the kids?" He scanned the flood of residents heading toward the staircase at the other end of the hall.

"No." They looked at each other for a brief moment, then ran to the Hawkinses' apartment. Wren banged both fists on the door. "Bradley!"

When the door opened, Bradley stood there, a sobbing and crying three-year-old River in his arms, seven-year-old Esme clinging to him. His hair was mussed, his eyes wide in panic, and there was little to no color in his face. "I can't find Bodhi."

"I'll get him," Ty said. "Wren, take Esme. Go on down."

"Sure, yeah, okay, honey. Come on. You remember me?" Wren crouched and held out her arms to the nightgown-clad little girl. "We met at your classroom."

Esme nodded, her big eyes filling with tears. "You're a friend of Mom's."

"That's right. Come on." She scooped Esme into her arms and pulled Bradley out of the apartment. "Ty'll get Bodhi. Don't worry. You've got your slippers on, right, Esme?" She glanced down at Esme's feet. "Good girl. And you've got your stuffie."

"But—" Bradley looked beyond terrified, and honestly, Ty began to wonder how much more the husband and father could take. "Bodhi has sensory issues. The noise and the flashing lights, he'll be so scared. I checked under his bed, but he wasn't there." The panic only made Ty more calm.

"I'll find him, I promise," Ty said. "I don't make promises I can't keep."

"He really doesn't." Wren sniffed the air. "That's smoke. And not from your toast fail." She pointed to one of the air vents. Smoke spewed out in puffs. "Ty?"

"Right. Go." The hall was almost empty now. "I'll meet you downstairs."

In the far distance Ty could hear the faint sound of sirens. Either that or he was imagining it. He knew about the police situation, but didn't have a clue about the fire department. Or if Splendor even had one.

He raced into the apartment, barely passing a glance at the mess and chaos a family with three kids could create. When he stepped on a LEGO, he thanked himself for putting on his shoes. Backpacks and schoolbooks littered the area around the coffee table in the living room.

The internal emergency lights continued to flash like some weird disco hall gone rogue. Shouting for Bodhi wasn't going to do any good and could, in his experience with people on the spectrum, be even more frightening.

The three-bedroom apartment was a completely different configuration than his and Wren's. He found himself in Alice and Bradley's room first. He dropped to the floor, looked under the bed, checked the closet. Then went to the bedroom across the hall.

Esme's room. Had to be, with an oversize unicorn that matched the one she was currently carrying painted on the wall. Again, he checked under the bed, the closet. Only one more to go.

"Bodhi?" Ty called loud enough to be heard over the alarm. "My name's Ty. I'm a friend of your dad's. He's really worried about you!" He dropped down; nobody under the bed. He checked the closet, bent to dig through the piles of stuffed animals and clothes. Nothing.

Frustrated, he turned, winced at the still-screaming alarm. "Where would he be?" Ty scanned the room. The pair of bunk beds for the boys, two different desks. A beanbag chair in the corner beside a large toy box wedged under the...

Toy box.

Ty shot forward, pulled up the lid.

The five-year old had buried himself among the toys, curled up almost into a ball with his hands over his ears. He wore pajamas with tiny trains on them. "Bodhi." Ty sat back on his heels, letting out the breath he'd been holding. "Hey there, little man. Did you hear me calling you? My name's Ty."

Bodhi nodded, pointed to the ceiling.

"I know. It's super loud, isn't it? But that's to make sure everyone knows we have to..." He heard a door slam, loud voices. Angry voices.

Torn between desperation to get the boy out of the building, and his instincts screaming at him, he made a split-second decision. "Stay here." He closed the lid again and returned to the door.

There was movement in the living room. "I've got this one!" a deep voice bellowed. "You check the other one!"

Ty flattened himself against the wall and carefully, slowly, leaned over to get a look.

A man in black, masked and covered from head to toe, moved through the living room, a SIG Sauer in his hand with a silencer attached. It was clear from the way the man moved without disturbing anything he was looking for people, not objects.

Ty returned to Bodhi and opened the toy box again. "Hey, Bodhi. Let's say you and me play hide-and-seek. We'll team up, yeah?" He held out his arms, wanting nothing more than to pick Bodhi up, but he didn't want to give the child a reason to cry out. "We need to be really, really quiet, though. Otherwise we won't win."

At the idea of winning, Bodhi's eyes cleared a bit. He sat up and held out his arms.

"Good boy." Ty grabbed hold, and hearing footsteps outside of the bedroom, he quickly ducked into the closet, kicking his way through the clutter, and pulled the louvered doors closed.

"It's loud," Bodhi cried in his ear. "I don't like noise."

"I know." He rubbed the boy's back. He could feel the child's heart pounding against his chest. "Just be really quiet for me for a little while, okay?" Ty tried to shrink back, but he was too tall for the closet and knocked his head on the top shelf. "Just hold on to me, okay? As tight as you can."

Bodhi's arms squeezed his neck with far more strength than Ty expected.

The lights still flashed. Ty could see just enough through the slats in the door. His mind raced. Reaching for his gun meant losing his firm grip on Bodhi, and right now, he had the feeling he was the only thing keeping the boy quiet.

Still…

Wincing, he readjusted his hold on Bodhi, shifting him over to one hip to hold him with one arm. "Shhhh," he whispered not only to Bodhi but to himself. He reached back, under the hem of his shirt, pulled his gun free and, releasing the safety, held it down at his side.

The man in black arrived, swept the room like a professional. Ty watched, memorizing every step the man made. The dim glow from the bedside lamp caught him in just the right light.

A shock of bright blond hair stuck out of the edge of the mask just above the man's eyes.

Ty's grip on the gun tightened. His head pounded against the continuing screeching of the alarm. The lights made it seem as if the man were moving in slow motion.

"I want Mama," Bodhi cried and began to sob.

"Shhhh."

The alarm cut off.

The lights stopped strobing.

Bodhi gasped. Ty shifted his feet, prepared to…

"We gotta go!" The second man slammed into the room, his gloved hand gripping the doorjamb. He was in all black as well, but there was nothing Ty could see to distinguish him. The other man, however… "Now. The police are here."

"They'll go after the smoke first and that's floors away," the first man said.

"Did you get it?"

Ty stiffened.

"Yeah. What about you? Anything in the other apartment?" He did a circle of the room, knocked a robot toy off a shelf.

"Laptop. Clothes. No IDs."

"What about the virus?"

"Installed. We'll be able to see everything they do on it when they turn it back on."

"Good. Okay." He moved to the window, looked out. Bodhi squirmed and began to make noises.

"Shhhh. Hide-and-seek, remember?" Ty whispered almost silently into the boy's ear. "We're going to win."

Bodhi turned his head and rested it on Ty's shoulder, heaved out a sigh.

"Let's go." The first man shoved the second one out of his way and they left. Ty waited until he heard the front door close before he breathed easy.

He reengaged the safety on his gun, shoved it back into his waistband and carefully set Bodhi on his feet. "You did really great, Bodhi. You were very brave."

"I don't like noise," Bodhi repeated with a bit more vehemence this time.

"Right there with you." Ty pushed open the doors, nudged Bodhi ahead of him.

His cell phone vibrated in his back pocket. He barely glanced at the screen when he answered. "Hey, Wren. I've got Bodhi. He's okay."

"Thank goodness. Bradley's been going nuts. Where are you?" Ty went to the window to look out. Dozens of people stood huddled around the entrance to the building. He saw the sheriff's SUV, along with a single fire engine. "Why didn't you—"

"Bodhi and I had visitors," Ty said. "Tell Sheriff Egbert and the firefighters to look for smoke bombs either on the first, lobby or basement level. That's what caused the smoke in the vents."

"How do you—"

"We're on our way down now." He hung up and found Bodhi picking up the toy the man had knocked over.

"Goes here." He put the robot back on the shelf, frowning and glaring up at Ty. "Did I win?"

"Absolutely." Ty touched a hand to the boy's head. "And you know what the prize is?"

"What?"

"Ice cream."

Chapter 10

River Hawkins turned a face-splitting grin up at his father and pulled the spoon out of his mouth. "Yum!"

Wren turned sympathetic eyes on Bradley as he reached out to touch his son's head. The expression on the man's drawn face could only be described as shock and dismay. "What do you say to Ms. Wren and Mr. Ty, River?"

"'Sank you!" He waved his spoon in the air before going in for another taste of the double chocolate chip that Sully had chosen for them.

"Come on, River." Carrying her own bowl of strawberry, Esme grabbed her little brother's hand and tugged him away from the table. "We'll go into the living room."

The little adult, Wren thought as the girl sent Wren a watery smile. Scared, but still determined to play protector for her brothers.

"Bodhi?" Esme called from the doorway.

"He's okay where he is." Ty smiled at Wren and set her heart to melting. The adoration Bodhi cast upon Ty was clearly reciprocated. She wondered if he had any idea what a good father he'd make. She coughed, almost choked and turned away before having to admit where her thoughts had taken her.

"Bodhi, why don't you go with Esme?" Bradley told his son. "I bet she can find an episode of *Proton Patrol* for you to watch."

"Okay." Bodhi slipped off Ty's knee, cradling his bowl against his chest. "Bye, Ty."

"Bye, Bodhi."

"Thank you again, for looking out for him," Bradley said to Ty once they were alone. "That's a level of terror I never want to feel again."

"I'm sorry you were put in this position."

"I can't believe I forgot to have them put on their coats." He rested his elbows on the table, lowered his head into his hands. "I just feel completely scattered and useless."

"You're far from useless." Wren touched his arm. "It's been a rough week for you. And them. But you're doing okay."

"I feel like I'm being held together by will alone." He sighed, and when he looked at Ty, there was an odd light in his eye. "You aren't a school friend of Alice's, are you? There's something else going on. That's why you're here, isn't it? That's why you're both here."

Ty glanced at Wren and she knew what he was thinking. That it wasn't his place to share Alice's story or past; that he didn't want to risk Alice losing the life she had because she'd lied to her husband about things she'd gone through. Things she'd done.

"We're here because Alice is in trouble and we want to help," Wren found herself answering. "I need you to believe that, Bradley. Alice loves you so much. We don't want you doubting that for even a moment."

"I don't doubt it." Bradley seemed confused she'd even say it. "I love my wife, and I know she dealt with a lot before we got serious. She told me most of it, about the trial, anyway. About testifying against her former boss because of the embezzlement. It was my idea to move. I wanted her to have a fresh start."

Any hope Wren had had that Bradley was up-to-date on Alice's past shriveled up and died. "She told you the case was about embezzling?"

"Yes. She worked in the office, knew about a second set of accounting books. She said..." Bradley's eyes went from bright to suspicious. "She said she turned the books over to the Feds and that..." He sat up straighter. "Oh, my God. You're Feds, aren't you? That's how you know Alice. But why...?" His frown returned. "But why are you here now?"

"Bradley, I need you to—"

"Wren." Ty's voice was sharp, sharper than she expected or appreciated. "Can I talk to you for a minute? Alone, please."

Bradley sighed, looked between the two of them. "I'll go check on the kids. Could you...please, could you just get your stories straight and be honest with me? Trust me." He got to his feet. "The truth cannot possibly be worse than what I'm coming up with in my head."

Wren sat stone-still in her chair, watching as Bradley left the kitchen.

"He deserves to know the truth, Ty," she rage-whispered. "He's been in the dark long enough!"

"It's not our place—"

"Those men created a fake fire to empty the building in the middle of the night, Ty."

"I am aware."

"Are you? Are you really?" Wren couldn't quite believe he was taking this tactic. "They evacuated hundreds of people in Alaska in winter so they could get into this apartment. So they could get into ours!"

"Again, I'm awa—"

"Stuff your awareness. That man needs to be able to protect his family, and he can't do that as long as he's in the dark."

Ty shook his head. "Alice would have told him if she'd wanted him to know."

Was he really this naive? This reckless? "Alice is currently in a medically-induced coma, maybe because she didn't tell her husband the truth. It's not just this family that's at risk now, Ty. It's the entire building. Maybe the entire town. They're using cars and smoke bombs as weapons against them. Protecting one person's past isn't worth risking everyone else's lives."

"That's not what I'm doing. I made her a promise."

It didn't escape her notice that Ty was staring down at the tabletop. He didn't look at her. Not once.

"You made a promise to keep her safe. Do you really think she wouldn't want you telling Bradley the truth if it meant putting their children at risk? You and I both know what would have happened if one of those men had found Bodhi in that toy chest."

"But they didn't find him. I did."

"Knowledge is power. Put that power in Bradley's hands, Ty. Alice can't speak for herself anymore. Maybe not ever again. He deserves to be able to decide for himself how he wants this to go."

"How I want what to go?" Bradley's voice was stronger now. He didn't appear as frail and dejected as he had just moments before. "It's funny how a few minutes with my kids clears my head."

"This is my fault," Ty said. "This entire thing—Alice's accident, the break-in tonight, the attack at the hospital. All of this happened because of me."

"Oh, for crying out loud." Wren stood up. "Martyrdom doesn't become you, Ty. This isn't your fault. It's not even Alice's fault. All of this is because the world is a messed-up place and bad things happen. You both got caught up in something that turned out not to be over. You made the choices you could make at the time. As great an agent as you are, time travel is not in your arsenal of weapons."

"You don't understand," Ty said. "I convinced her—"

"You gave her options," Wren corrected. "She chose the path to take. You said you'd back her up and you are. Now let's finish it once and for all. Tell him the truth!"

"I know she kept things from me," Bradley said. "I told her she didn't have to tell me anything she didn't want to. I love her. Nothing's going to change that. I promise. And like you," he told Ty, "I don't make promises I don't intend to keep." He shifted his attention to Wren. "You tell me, then."

Wren purposely didn't look at Ty. "It wasn't an embezzlement case Alice testified in. It was a murder case."

"Wren—"

She reached out, rested her hand on Ty's shoulder and squeezed. "She witnessed her boss, a man named Am-

brose Treyhern, kill a man who worked for him. Instead
of running or hiding, she gave a statement and testified
against him. He was convicted and sentenced to life in
prison. Only now—"

"Only now Treyhern's been granted a new trial," Ty
finished. "And he doesn't plan on letting Alice testify
again."

"Murder?" Bradley wandered back to his chair, sat
across from Ty, blinking quickly as if trying to process
what he'd heard. "All this time she said that trial was
no big deal."

"You didn't see anything in the papers about it?"
Wren asked.

"I was barely twenty. I was working full-time and
going to college," Bradley said. "I was lucky to see Alice."
He shook his head. "I don't think we've even spoken about
her testifying for years. Until you mentioned it, it never
crossed my... When did word of the new trial come out?"

"About three—"

"Three weeks ago." He dropped his head back. "I
knew something was wrong. Something was just off
with how she was. She was jumpy, nervous. I assumed
she was stressed with work and the kids." He took a deep
breath, looked back at Ty. "She called you."

"The night of the accident, yes."

A light flickered to life in Bradley's eyes. "You were
who she was talking to. The sheriff, when he found her
phone... Okay." He nodded, as if putting the pieces together. "She called and you were here the next day."

"I was one of the agents in charge of the Treyhern
case," Ty admitted. "I convinced her to testify. I promised to keep her safe."

"After she refused to go into witness protection," Wren added.

Ty glared at her.

"That's a big piece of this, Ty. Stop acting as if it isn't," she ordered. "Chances are, if she'd gone into WITSEC, none of this would be happening."

"I'm not going to blame her for making that decision," Ty argued.

"Fine," she snapped. "Then stop blaming yourself."

"Stop, please." Bradley held up both hands. "You two bickering isn't helping the situation. She wouldn't have chosen witness protection because of me. We were… getting really close around then. I was head over heels in love already and she… I'm super close with my family. A family that accepted her immediately. My parents, grandparents, siblings. They love her. Adore her. Probably more than they've ever liked me. She'd never had that before."

"She wouldn't have wanted to be cut off from them," Wren concluded.

"She wouldn't have wanted *me* to be cut off," Bradley corrected. "But I would have gone anywhere she was. In whatever circumstances. I just wanted her." Tears filled his eyes. "I just want her back."

"She's hanging on," Wren reminded him. "You have to hold on to that."

"I don't know how much longer I can do it," Bradley admitted. "Wren's right, Ty. I've been married to Alice for ten years. I know better than anyone that when my wife has her mind set on something, there's nothing that's going to change it. Not me. Not even the FBI." He took a deep breath. "I need to know our options. Moving forward, I want everything on the table. What could, what might, what can happen."

Wren shifted in her seat. "Does that include information on witness protection? Ty—" she blew out a frustrated breath "—if there's a way to get Alice out from under testifying, we'll find it, but right now, we have to go with what we know."

Ty cursed, shoved to his feet and walked out of the kitchen. Wren's heart twisted. She didn't want this to turn into a bigger fight than it already was, but she was in a position to help Bradley in a way Ty couldn't.

Bradley nodded. "I'd like to know what would be involved if we joined the program, yes."

Despite Ty's displeasure with the idea, the fact Bradley was open to it brought her some relief. "My brother is a US marshal. He's worked in the witness protection program for years. I can give him a call, ask him to come up and speak to you personally. One-on-one. No strings attached."

"He'd do that?"

"He can't say no to his little sister." She glanced out the window. Last she'd heard, Howell was working a case out of Idaho. Since she was going the unofficial route, it would take him some time to get here. "If that's what you want."

"I want my family safe," Bradley said. "All of them. I would like to speak with him."

"Okay." She nodded and sighed in relief. "I'll make that happen. So that's step one done. Now. What else do you want to ask me?"

Ty stopped at the apartment only long enough to grab his jacket before he headed out. He needed some fresh air, even if it was blistery cold air and it was still pitch-black outside.

He needed to get his mind clear and his anger under control before he said—or did—something he was going to regret.

As much as he loved her, Wren McKenna was the equivalent of a human steamroller when it came to doing things her way. It was his own fault, he supposed, for asking for her help. He should have realized once the tides shifted in a certain direction she was going to slip in ahead of him and take charge.

He took the stairs. It had been a couple of hours since everyone had been let back into their apartments. Skyway Tower was still relatively quiet, although he could hear the telltale sounds of chanting coming from the apartment of Zoe Marbury, who had apparently cornered the market on yoga and meditation.

All Ty wanted right now was to walk things off and come to terms with the fact that Wren had hit multiple nails on the head with her accusations and observations. He did feel responsible for Alice's situation. He'd spent an inordinate number of sleepless nights worrying that his inability to convince her to go into witness protection would result in something happening to her. Something like what had happened to her.

He needed to take some comfort in Bradley's declaration, that Alice was her own person with her own mind and she'd made a clearheaded decision.

Upon exiting the building, he found the sheriff's SUV parked where it had been for the past few hours. He turned back to the door just as the sheriff emerged from one of the hallways. He nodded at Ty and came out to join him.

"Figured you'd be out prowling around," Sheriff Egbert said. "Been a bit of a rough night for you."

"I've had worse."

"Bet you have."

"Where's Shelly?"

"I sent her home to get some sleep. She looked ready to pitch over into the snow." Sheriff Egbert eyed him. "Come on. Looks like we could both use a walk." He nodded toward the marina. "You have a chance to watch the sunrise since you've been here?"

"Not intentionally."

"A visit to Splendor's not complete without seeing one. Where's your other half?" the sheriff asked as they fell into step.

"Talking with Bradley." Probably being the proxy for her US marshal brother when it came to signing the Hawkins family up for WITSEC. "What's going in your report about the fire alarm?"

The air was so cold it didn't move. Not a ruffle against his skin. Not even coming off the water in the distance. He was getting used to not feeling his face and had the odd notion that once he left he was going to miss this place.

"That's a good question. Near as Shelly and I can piece together, someone hacked into the building's Wi-Fi, rode it into the security system and deactivated it remotely. They got in, set the smoke bombs off in the basement at the air-filtration unit, then another on the first floor under the smoke detectors. The rest took care of itself. Fortunately, the system acted the way it was supposed to and everyone followed procedure. Scared the life out of some people, but it seems to have also brought everyone closer together."

"Those two guys in black came in looking for something."

"So you said." Sheriff Egbert gave a quick nod. "Haven't gotten reports of anyone else's apartments getting hit. Just Bradley's and yours."

Ty wasn't certain he'd have known they'd gone into his and Wren's apartment if he hadn't heard the discussion.

"Any idea what they took from the Hawkinses' place?" Sheriff Egbert asked.

"None." And that bothered him. Whatever it had been must have been small since Ty hadn't seen the man carrying anything. "Bradley couldn't figure what might be missing, but he was pretty shaken up."

"At least we know they didn't come in specifically for him or the kids."

"That would make even less sense than what did happen." It was what he couldn't wrap his mind around. "Alice is in a coma. She can't talk, let alone testify against anyone right now. If they were smart, they'd lie low and wait to see if she dies." To Ty's thinking, that was the best-case scenario for Treyhern and whomever he'd sent after Alice. "Why expose themselves again by taking such a big risk?"

"If they needed something that bad, maybe it wasn't that big a risk," Sheriff Egbert said. "Evacuate the building when they wouldn't be seen or recorded. They couldn't pull that off during the day. Too many people around.

Everyone focused on everyone else. And this way they get the bonus of checking your apartment out as well."

"Did anyone report seeing anyone hanging around the building in the last few days?"

"Shelly checked the security footage going back more than a week. And I asked Al about that," Sheriff Egbert said. "He doesn't recall seeing anyone, but then most of the time he's inside the building. Aside from what happened tonight, we've never had any security issues with Skyway Tower. I checked with a lot of people tonight. The only thing people mentioned that was odd was Alice's accident and you and Wren moving in. Now's gonna be a different story. Everyone's on high alert and jumpy, especially where unfamiliar faces are concerned."

"Unless those faces aren't so unfamiliar." Ty racked his brain. "It's hard to be invisible in a small town, but they have to be staying somewhere close." He turned, looking behind them as they walked. The clear night cast the entire town in a glow he'd never seen before. Overhead the ghostly remnants of the northern lights played against the dark backdrop. "Someone mentioned to Wren about the vacation homes up the mountain." He pointed in that direction. "Any way to get a list of property owners or renters?"

"Property owners of record, no problem," Sheriff Egbert confirmed. "Renters would take some work-arounds. People who stay up here like their privacy."

Which would make it a perfect hiding place for someone who worked for Ambrose Treyhern. "Is the tram the only way up?"

"There's a narrow road that goes up that way." He pointed toward where the edge of town lay. "Most people prefer the tram, as it is not a fun drive. This time of year, the snow closes the road more than it's open. The entire tram system was overhauled last year. It's almost completely automated now and the cable cars are top-of-the-line. Takes about fifteen minutes."

"How high does it go?"

"About eight thousand feet. There's a gift and coffee shop up at the station, along with a bar that stays open until midnight." Sheriff Egbert pointed to where one of the two trams was parked at the station in town. "Makes for a beautiful observation area, especially on a clear day."

"If you could get me that list of owners, I'd appreciate it." They were at a distinct disadvantage in terms of accessing information since someone had gotten their hands on his laptop.

"I'll get to working on it as soon as I get some sleep."

"Is there anyone around here with some serious computer skills?" Ty asked.

"Sure—Mason Green. Shelly can hook you up with him. He's kind of a one-man tech guru. Makes a solid living hooking up entertainment and computer systems for people. I'll have her give you a call once she's back in the office."

The walk had done its job and taken some of the edge off Ty's ragged thoughts. The sound of the gently lapping water offered a surprising sense of peace as they approached the shoreline.

"Every so often this is where I find myself in the early morning," Sheriff Egbert said as they stood on the other side of the marina fence. "With the town behind me, and all that in front, reminds us what we have here. How special it is." He gestured to the water shimmering beneath the slowly disappearing moon. "I can see everything that's coming at us. Like that bank of clouds out there." He pointed off beyond the horizon. "You see that?"

"Not really." Everything looked like one big, massive blur to him.

"Take my word for it. Storm's coming in. Probably hit late afternoon, early evening."

"Okay."

"You get a feel for a place after a while. That said, I don't think I could've anticipated the last few days even with a crystal ball. I've had more crazy hours since you and Wren got here than I've had since my time on the police force in Chicago. Part of me is tempted to ask when you're leaving."

"As soon as we know Alice is out of danger and there's no more threat to anyone here in Splendor." He already felt a pang of regret.

"I appreciate that. Have to admit, last few days has me thinking about retirement."

"That would be a real loss to Splendor," Ty said. "We'll be out of your hair soon enough. Things'll get back to being uneventful once we are gone." But they weren't out of the woods yet. "Has there been any word from the medical examiner on Davey?"

"Time of death's going to be hard to pinpoint. His body's still thawing out." He shook his head. "But it's not out of the realm of possibility he was killed sometime around Alice's accident. Seeing as he couldn't have shot himself in the chest, I'm leaning toward someone using him as a convenient scapegoat."

Ty agreed. "Troubled local with a history of offenses,

a drinking problem and access to an easily-disposed-of car."

"Made him a perfect target. By someone who snuck right by me. That's what's got me spinning."

"At least one of the men in Alice and Bradley's apartment was part of the duo Wren and I chased down at the hospital," Ty told him. "Maybe take some comfort in that all those loose threads seem to be connected to one big knot. Near as we can tell, there's only two of them." He could only hope it stayed that way.

Sheriff Egbert smirked, shoved his hands deeper into his pockets. "Don't anticipate finding much comfort in anything for a while. Davey's death is going to haunt me."

"Davey was his own man, Sheriff." Ty was all too familiar with ghosts, and now seeing the sheriff wrestle with his own showed Ty what Wren must see when she looked at him. "He made his own decisions."

"Hard to make the right ones without a solid support system behind you."

There was no talking the sheriff out of his feelings of guilt and regret. But they certainly shone a certain light on his own internal demons. The ones Wren seemed focused on helping him exorcise. "Tell you what, Sheriff. You stop blaming yourself for what happened to Davey and maybe I can let go of my own guilt where Alice is concerned." Maybe if they tag-teamed each other, they could both get somewhere new. "I should probably give you a heads-up. There's a good chance Wren's brother's going to be coming up here in the next few days. He's a US marshal."

"Another Fed." Sheriff Egbert sighed. "Sounds about right."

"It's not going to be long before the truth about Alice's situation comes out," Ty advised. "Or about how Wren and I are involved. If the two men responsible for the evacuation know who we are—"

"I'm guessing since they tagged your laptop, we can assume that's true."

"Chances are they've been here long enough to realize the chaos blowing our cover could cause. Like you said, a lot of people around here don't have any love for the FBI."

"The FBI, maybe," Sheriff Egbert said. "But you and Wren are a different story. You came up this way to help one of our own. Folks will see that. Eventually. You get whatever was eating at you put back away?"

"I'm almost there." Admitting Wren was right really was half the battle. Telling her she was would be the other half. "Just working through some issues with my partner."

Another smirk from the sheriff.

"What?"

He ducked his head, rocked back on his heels. "I ever tell you about my first partner back when I was working for the Chicago PD?"

"Ah, you didn't really mention your previous job, Sheriff." Ty had just assumed the older man didn't want to talk about it.

"The most stubborn person you've ever met. Never knew anyone who could argue with me better but never once did I not think they were watching my back. We worked together for four, maybe five, years before we finally got around to admitting the truth. We've been married more than twenty-five years now." He lifted his head into the fading moonlight. "Partnerships like ours, like yours and Wren's, they're something special. Just so you know, one thing doesn't have to end in order to start another. The work-around is worth it. You've got the friendship necessary to make a go of things, Ty. Don't let fear or worry about what could happen get in the way of what's possible."

"Yes, sir. That's right." Curled up in the corner of the sofa facing the front door of their apartment, Wren looked up as Ty returned. Most of the knots in her stomach eased at the sight of him. The anger was gone. Mostly. The irritation as well. She pressed a finger against her lips.

He pushed the door closed.

"I understand this case is personal to Agent Savakis." Supervisory Special Agent Jack Frisco's rough voice crackled over her cell. "But we don't need anyone involved in the original investigation sticking their nose into Treyhern's reopened case. We can't risk tainting it any further."

"Ty's involvement has never been called into question before."

"His involvement, no," Frisco agreed. "But you and I both know he's not at his best when his personal feelings enter the picture. Keep him away from this case, Agent McKenna. That's an order."

"Yes, sir." She hung up and tossed her phone onto the coffee table. "Our boss sends you his best."

"I'll bet he does." Ty shrugged out of his jacket and hung it up. "Thanks for not ratting me out."

She frowned. Did he think she'd actually do that?

"Did you walk off your mad?" She had no trouble comparing him to a child who had thrown a tantrum. She'd done the same herself at times and therefore knew it rarely produced the desired result.

"I walked off my mad." He collapsed onto the sofa beside her and immediately reached out to take hold of her hand. "You were right. I'm too close to this to evaluate certain aspects properly."

It took all her self-control not to bask in the happiness that hearing the words *you were right* gave her.

"Bradley only wants information, Ty." Maintaining her hold, she turned to face him. "He hasn't decided on WITSEC."

"Yeah, well." He dropped his head against the back of the sofa. "Howell will probably talk him into it in about ten seconds flat."

"His record is seventeen minutes."

"So you called him?" Ty asked.

"I left a voice message, followed up with a text." At his raised brows, she shrugged. "When he's working a difficult case, he turns everything to vibrate. He'll call me back when he can."

"Good." He nodded and managed to only wince a little.

Ty was the kind of man who was quick to react, but often countered a flash of temper with putting some distance between himself and the subject at hand. He also often returned having come around to her point of view. It went both ways, but as their stats currently stood, Ty was the one often taking the walk.

She tried to smile, touched her other hand to his face.

"You okay?" Feeling his skin beneath her fingers eased the last of her tension. For a moment, a long few moments, she'd worried they wouldn't find their way back to one another. At least not in the sense their reinvented relationship offered.

"Yeah." He squeezed her hand. "Just tired. We've gone through everything as far as Splendor's concerned. Sheriff's going to get us a list of owner names for the houses on the hill."

"The vacation homes. Huh." That was an interesting turn. "You think there's something there?"

"I think those two guys are hiding somewhere nearby, yet we can't find them. They aren't roaming around town, only showing up to make very specific strikes. They could be coming in and out of the tunnel—"

"Not with the current operating schedule," Wren confirmed without hesitation. "The tunnel was closed when they hit here. They had to go somewhere afterward and that fire alarm and evacuation pretty much woke up the whole town. They're here in Splendor. They have to be. They couldn't have done what they have without staying close by, and hitting the tower took planning. Up the mountain makes sense."

"We're going to need evidence before we go knocking on doors." He smothered a yawn. Outside, the safety buoys clanged in the harbor. "Sheriff Egbert didn't come out and say it, but he treads carefully with the people up there. Too many toes to step on."

"Mmm." Wren shifted and looked out the window. The morning was dawning bright, with only a thin layer of cloud cover overhead. In the distance she saw the teeny figures of early-morning fishermen heading out on their catch boats. She shivered in sympathy even as she gnawed on her lower lip. "What about a boat?"

"You want to buy a boat?" He tugged her down against him, curled his arm around her shoulders.

"As a place to hide." She lifted her head as his eyes drifted closed. It was another avenue to explore.

"I can't think anymore right now," he said on another yawn. "Give me a half hour, okay?"

"Okay." She started to scoot away but his arm tightened.

"Stay with me." He turned his face into her hair, took a deep breath. "I like holding you."

She smiled and rested her cheek against his shoulder. "I like you holding me."

"Half hour," he murmured again.

"Half hour." She closed her eyes and followed him into sleep.

Chapter 11

"Let me see if I understand." Mason Green sat behind Deputy Shelly Adjuk's desk at the sheriff's office and blinked disbelievingly. "You want me to see if I can isolate, examine and extract a virus on this laptop that was installed specifically to track what you do on this laptop?"

"That's pretty much it," Wren said. "Can you do that?"

"Well, yeah, sure." It didn't sound like bravado. Exactly. "It's just an odd request is all."

"If you're worried about being paid—" Shelly planted her hands on her hips and glared at him. It was, to Wren's mind at least, a blatant throwing down of the gauntlet.

"No, no, it's not that." Mason waved both hands in the air. "I love the idea of a challenge. I'm just—" He leaned forward a bit, lowered his voice. "Is this legal?"

"It's my laptop," Ty said. "It's perfectly legal. What was installed on it, however, is not."

Wren tried to mitigate Ty's obvious frustration. "It's a weird ask, we know. But we don't have the resources we're used to currently available to us, and Shelly here said you're the best computer guy in this part of Alaska."

"She did?" Mason brightened.

"I did?" Shelly balked.

"Yep." Wren nudged Shelly with her elbow. "Why else would we have asked you to come in?"

"Exactly," Shelly said in an attempt to salvage the meeting. "Best in this part of Alaska. For sure. No one better."

"Don't oversell it," Wren muttered under her breath.

"I appreciate that." He touched the laptop, then stopped. "What resources do you usually have at your disposal?"

"Federal ones," Ty said. "We're trying to keep this on the QT. Wren and I are with the FBI. We're here to find out what happened to Alice and keep her family safe. We need your help to do that." He indicated the laptop. "Can we count on you?"

"FBI? Wow, really? You know, rumor was you two were some kind of private investigators." Mason rested his elbow on the desk. "What with all the questions you've been asking around town and—"

"Mason, we're really short on time right now," Wren said, cutting him off. "I promise, once all this is over, we'll be happy to sit down and chat and answer any questions you might have."

"Right. Sure, yeah, okay." He blinked his doe-brown eyes and gave Shelly a very personal grin. "Can I take you out as payment?"

"I'm not currency," Shelly said in a way that earned her another nudge from Wren. "But okay, I guess. When all this is over, but only if you're helpful." By her tone, it was clear Shelly was not convinced.

"Epic." Mason linked his fingers and stretched them out to crack the joints.

"Apparently they'd be able to track when I turned the machine on," Ty said.

"That's pretty sophisticated programming." He pulled his oversize tech bag onto his lap and dug into it. "I'm going to set up a proxy computer, open it in safe mode and then open yours as a kind of... Never mind." He shook his head. "I recognize those blank looks. Give me a few minutes. Can you help me make some room, Shelly?"

Shelly heaved a sigh, shot Wren an I'm-going-to-get-you-for-this look before helping Mason set up. Wren pulled Ty aside.

"Your grumpy side is showing," she accused gently. "You need another walk?"

"No. I'm just frustrated." He scrubbed his hands down his face and through his hair. "Doesn't help that you let me sleep a lot longer than a half hour."

"Only because I fell asleep myself." She had to admit, the fact they hadn't woken up until almost noon did feel like a hitch in their day. "You're worried about Bradley and the kids, aren't you?"

"I shouldn't be, I know," he admitted. "But Bradley wasn't happy when I told him to stay in the apartment."

"His home was invaded," Wren said. "Obviously, he'd want to get out. But you did a great job convincing him the tower was the best and safest place for him and the kids." But she didn't seem to be getting through. "You had the right idea asking Pastor Lori to check in on them. Hopefully she'll be able to help with Bradley's state of mind and she said she'll stay as long as she feels she's not in the way."

"Right. Yeah, you're right." Maybe their boss was right. Maybe Ty shouldn't be involved with this case.

The front door opened and the sheriff walked halfway in. The stony expression on his face had Wren doing a double take. "What's wrong?"

"Someone called me about an abandoned burned-out car out by the sawmill."

"What sawmill?" Wren asked.

"The one that was shut down before I was born," Shelly said. "Who called it in, Sheriff?"

"No clue. Came in as unknown. That's what had me stopping here." He looked at Ty. "You up for a ride-along, Agent Savakis?"

Shelly frowned. "But I—"

"I need you close to Mason while he works on that computer," Sheriff Egbert said, as if he'd rehearsed his response. "Man the phones. Storm's moving through the area soon, so send out our usual alert. The system may very well wreak havoc with cell service and you know how squirrelly some people get when their phones don't work. Ty?"

"Coming." He squeezed Wren's arm. "I'll be in touch. Hopefully."

"Be careful." Odd. Saying that to him now felt... different. As if she wasn't talking to her partner, but to the man she loved.

Her entire body froze at the thought. It felt right, somehow, to consider the idea. Loving Ty just made sense, and while it didn't freak her out on every level, there were enough questions and uncertainties to have her scrambling for a significant distraction.

"Guess I'll be staying here, then," Shelly grumbled.

"He's leaving the entire office and town in your hands," Wren said. "That's a pretty big statement of confidence. Hey…" She turned to the deputy. "I've been here a few days, never heard this sawmill mentioned."

Shelly shrugged. "Like I said, place has been abandoned for years. Only thing it gets used for really is a landing spot for teenagers and their parties. Keggers."

"So many keggers," Mason chimed in. "Just so you know, this computer thing is going to take a while."

"Why?" Wren asked.

"Because at first glance, what I'm seeing on the back end of this latest installation?" He tapped his finger against a line of code displayed on the second laptop screen. "That's military-grade spyware. Some of the best I've seen."

"Where have you seen it, exactly?" Wren peered closer and tried to make sense of the writing.

"Ah." Mason winced. "In my online training courses?" The high-pitched question gave away he was lying. "I have to be really careful getting into its guts to see where it's coming from."

"Then be careful," Wren said. "What else can I do?"

"Stop asking me questions," Mason said firmly, which had Shelly clearly impressed. "Just let me work."

Shelly waved her over toward the sheriff's desk. "Sheriff Egbert left this for you guys. It's a list of property owners Ty asked for." She handed Wren a stack of pages.

"Oh, right. For the vacation homes."

"I downloaded all the property information on record. That way if anyone noticed we were pulling anything, they couldn't tell which house we were focused on."

"Look at you, thinking like an agent," Wren murmured as she accepted the list. "Looks like there are—" she quickly flipped and counted "—eleven homes, valued anywhere from…" She let out a low whistle. "No wonder the sheriff doesn't want to go stepping on toes up there. Takes some serious funds to buy one of these. I can only imagine how much it cost to build them." When Shelly didn't respond, she looked to the deputy. "Something wrong?"

"Shelly's parents protested the sale of the land to build those homes," Mason called out. "Even got themselves arrested for trespassing about a half dozen times."

"Shouldn't you be working?" Shelly yelled back before she offered Wren a tight smile. "Those homes are a sore subject with native Alaskans. For a lot of reasons."

"Of course," Wren said. "Sorry to bring up a sore subject."

Shelly shrugged. "You asked me why I want to join the FBI? This is one of the reasons. To get away from things like those homes. They just sit up there, looking down on the rest of us like overlords. Makes it really hard to keep an objective attitude when it comes to offering them our services."

"I hear you. Just keep in mind…" Wren continued to scan the information. "You don't get to pick and choose who you protect and defend at the Bureau any more than you do here."

"Shelly, you're not thinking about leaving Splendor, are you?" Mason asked.

"Mason." Shelly's sigh said it all. "Nothing's written in stone, okay? I'm just exploring my options." The desk phones both rang. "Sheriff's office. Deputy Adjuk—"

She was cut off, listened, touched her hand to Wren's shoulder. "Okay. Thanks for letting me know. You're good staying with…Uh-huh. Great. Appreciate that. We'll get him back home as soon as we find him."

"Find who?" Wren asked with a ball of dread spinning in her stomach. "Who was that?"

"Pastor Lori." Shelly yanked her jacket off the hook over her desk, nearly smacked Mason in the head with the zipper. "She said Bradley went to Groovy Grub Grocery about two hours ago and hasn't come back yet. He isn't answering his cell."

"I'll come with." Wren grabbed her own coat and shrugged into it.

"Mason? You okay here on your own?" Shelly asked as she zipped up. "Can you answer the phone if it rings?"

"Like an assistant deputy or something?" His cheeky grin didn't come across as particularly reassuring.

"Or something. Please?" Shelly asked. "I really need to be able to trust you."

"You know you can." He seemed to get the message and turned serious. "Got your back, Shelly. Always. Go. Be safe."

Wren found herself grinning as she followed Shelly to the station's second SUV.

"What's the smile for?" Shelly demanded as she yanked open the driver's door.

"Nothing, really. That's just what Ty and I always say to each other."

Shelly rolled her eyes and climbed in.

"This is truly desolate." Ty leaned forward to look out the windshield as Sheriff Egbert took the winding road into the valley. It wasn't a part of Splendor that had been on Ty's radar before. Despite the snow frosting the area with its usual sparkle and ice, the jagged rocks and terrain on either side of the road felt far more eerie than beautiful.

"This land's first use was as a quarry going back about fifty years ago. After that, they turned it into a lumber mill, but transporting the trees got to be too expensive. Not to mention the drive down into this canyon's a pain. Mill shut down shortly before I got here," Sheriff Egbert told him. The strong winds had begun to howl and buffeted the vehicle, but so far the clouds had banked off and the snow had yet to fall. "My kids were teens at the time. You know the story. Tell a kid to stay away from a place, that's the only place they want to go."

"Looks like a definite temptation." The giant structure ahead was a reminder of just how horrible Davey Whittaker's old home had been. "An ideal location for parties."

"And ghost stories," Sheriff Egbert said. "'Bout five years ago a group of high school seniors from Anchorage got inspired by some TV show, thought it would be fun to make their own videos exploring the spot. Had themselves a pretty big following for a while. Until one of them took a wrong turn, stepped on a bad board and dropped about forty feet. Kid was in traction for three months. Broke both his legs."

"Kids will be kids." Ty was more than familiar with the level of foolishness of some teenagers.

"Don't I know it."

The sheriff eased up on the gas as they reached the base of the valley. The mill loomed large in front of them and blocked out anything behind it. "Place like this, you'd have to know it was here to ditch a vehicle."

"You'd have to know about this place to call it in." Sheriff Egbert slowed down even more. "Appreciate the backup. Call just got my nerves up, you know? No telling what might be waiting for us. Keep an eye out for the car, yeah?"

"Yeah. Those nerves of yours. They why you didn't want Shelly along?"

"Let's just say I'm glad I had someone else to choose from. There." He pointed off to the right as they slowly circled the four-story structure. "They weren't lying, whoever it was that called." He stopped the car a good ten feet away from their target vehicle. "Shelly's got potential but a lot of the job left to learn. Given what these guys did to Alice, tried to do to her in the hospital, I'd like my deputy kept as far away from them as possible."

Ty got out his sidearm while the sheriff checked his own pistol and chambered a bullet. "Does Shelly know you're expecting her to take over when you retire?"

"Not yet."

"Word of advice?" Ty grabbed the door handle. "She's looking beyond Splendor for her future. Asked Wren about applying to the FBI Academy. Says she wants to make more of a difference."

"Shouldn't surprise me, I suppose." There was no mistaking the disappointment on his face. "She'd make a good agent."

"She'd make a great agent," Ty agreed. "But that might not be where she belongs."

"That's up to Shelly to decide. I won't stand in her

way if that's what she really wants to do. What about you?"

"What about me?" Ty asked.

"You looking to make a change? If I can't pass this job on to Shelly, you'd be a good fit. I've been watching you. You don't seem particularly...settled with your life choices."

He didn't like the idea of someone reading him so easily. Especially someone he'd only just met. "I'm working through some things. There's an appeal to what you suggest...but..." He liked the town, the people he'd met. The laid-back life he'd found here. He couldn't imagine Wren here. Not permanently. She was made for the FBI. She was a stellar agent with a tremendous future. A future he wanted very much to be a part of. "I belong with Wren." As what, exactly, had yet to be decided. Partners? A couple? A family? He wanted it all, but he'd take what he could get. Life without her simply wasn't an option. No matter how picturesque and beautiful a place was.

"Spoken like a man in love." Sheriff Egbert left his keys in the ignition as he climbed out.

"Hopefully, maybe." Ty laughed as he opened the door. "I'm still working on it."

They walked side by side toward the burned-out vehicle. The acrid smell had dissipated but hadn't been left out here as long as the previous car they'd found at the Whittaker place. Thunder rolled around them as gray clouds overhead seemed to pick up speed.

"I didn't get a plate at the hospital." Ty circled around the car, looking for something, anything, that confirmed it was the one that had picked up the shooter from the hospital parking lot. "Suppose it could be it."

Sheriff Egbert remained where he was, weapon at his side. He shook his head, tipped his hat back. "I don't get it. Why out here? They could have taken it through the tunnel, ditched it on the other side."

"Yeah, but they'd have to come back, wouldn't they?" No, this fed into his and Wren's theory that the two responsible for trying to kill Alice were still here in Splendor. And apparently they were using every bit of local lore and information they could get their hands on. He completed his search and stopped a short distance from the sheriff. "My question is, who called you about it? And why? Do you get a lot of calls about abandoned vehicles?"

"I do not." Sheriff Egbert turned slightly. "As far as anyone knows, it's just a car."

A flash of red caught Ty's gaze. Small, almost imperceptible. Familiar.

It strobed once against the sheriff's chest.

"Down!" Ty yelled and dived for the older man. He tackled him around the waist as the sound of the shot echoed through the canyon. Sheriff Egbert grunted as Ty rolled, weapon raised. "You hit?"

"I am." Sheriff Egbert groaned and started to sit up.

Another shot went over their heads, plowed into the hull of the car. "Where?" Ty didn't dare take his eye off the horizon, trying to guesstimate where the shots were coming from.

"Shoulder. High. It's okay. I think."

"Can you move?"

"To save my life?" The sheriff laughed. "You bet."

Another shot. This one struck in front of Ty's knee that was planted on the snowy ground. One more shot, but this one sounded farther away. "I'll go for your car,"

Ty said. "You get behind what's left of that one, yeah? I'll come get you."

"Sounds good."

Ty could hear the pain in the man's voice, but he blocked it out. "Okay, in three, two…" He lifted his knee but stayed low. "One!"

He didn't allow himself the indulgence of checking to see if the sheriff had moved. He kept his eyes locked on the SUV, moving in various directions as he raced for the vehicle. More shots rang out, but they alternated, some at him, others at the sheriff. He lunged for cover just as a bullet ricocheted off the hood of the SUV. "Too close."

He yanked open the door, climbed in through the passenger side and shoved himself over into the driver's seat, trying to stay low even as a bullet cracked the windshield. Ty turned the key, barely had the car in Drive before he slammed his foot on the gas.

The car whipped forward. He swerved, trying to keep the truck moving unpredictably so the shooter couldn't get a good lock. The tires spun in the icy mud and sludge. When he screeched to a stop beside the sheriff, the car skidded a bit on its own, as if trying to find a place it wanted to stop.

Ty shuffled over to the passenger seat, then dropped to the ground. He knelt beside the sheriff, who had his right hand pressed against the wound low on his left shoulder. Ty swore. There was blood. A lot of blood. "You lied," Ty accused as he tucked himself behind the sheriff and dragged him toward the truck.

"I fibbed," Sheriff Egbert ground out. There was a weakness in his voice that didn't sound right.

He paid no heed to anything other than hefting the

sheriff into the truck via the open passenger-side door. The sheriff gasped and coughed, a wheezing sound emanating from his mouth.

The shot that exploded as soon as Ty jumped in from his side and slammed the door took out the front left tire. He swore again even as the SUV began to tilt slightly down.

"Tire's gone," he muttered as he threw the vehicle back into Drive.

"We'll never make it back into town on three wheels," Sheriff Egbert managed.

Ty glanced at him, looked in the rearview mirror as the telltale sign of someone with a gun stepped out from the cover of the mill. The sheriff's face was losing color. That all-too-familiar pallor of gray was taking over.

"You'll never make it," the sheriff said again.

Ty slammed his foot on the gas. "Watch me."

Chapter 12

"Bradley never made it here." Shelly walked out of Groovy Grub Grocery with more attitude than Wren had seen in her previously.

Wren, having checked with the stores on either side, hadn't gotten any sightings of Bradley Hawkins. "He left the tower what, more than two hours ago?" She planted her hands on her hips, turning back and forth as if she could spot him on the street. "That's not good."

"What'd they do? Just snatch him off the street?" Shelly accused. "That doesn't happen in—"

"Neither do hit-and-runs and vehicle burnouts." Wren grabbed her phone, hit Ty's number as the clouds rumbled by. The call went straight to voicemail. "Maybe the cell signal's down already."

Shelly's cell phone beeped.

"Or not," Wren murmured. The look on Shelly's face started an entirely new thread of panic. "What?"

"It's a text from my friend Nancy at the hospital. It's Alice."

Wren swallowed hard. "Is she—"

"She's awake."

Hope sprang anew. "Maybe that's where Bradley is."

They jumped into the car and raced to the hospital. Shelly screeched into the law enforcement–dedicated space minutes later. Running inside, they didn't stop until they got to Alice's room. Obie, the security guard, jumped up out of his seat, his young face alert and anxious.

"Everything okay?" he asked.

"Just here to see Alice." Shelly patted his arm as they stepped inside.

The doctor smiled at them from across Alice's bed. The badge on her white coat identified her as Dr. Maya Rodriguez. "Ah, here you go. Your first visitors. Deputy Adjuk. And friend."

"Alice, hey." Shelly seemed to struggle for control, but she maintained a calm voice as she moved into the room. Alice was still as pale as the bandages on her head, but those eyes of hers were struggling to stay open even as she managed a weak smile. "How are you feeling?"

Alice tried to wet her dry lips. "L-like I got run over by a truck." The monitors beeped irregularly, as if trying to catch up with her recovery.

"Unfortunately, you're close. It was an SUV." Shelly's attempt at humor fell flat. "Seriously, though, do you remember—"

"I'm sorry." Wren didn't want to interrupt but time was of the essence. "Alice, hi. I'm FBI special agent Wren McKenna. I'm Ty Savakis's partner."

"FBI?" Dr. Rodriguez went wide-eyed as she stared at Wren. Wren waved off her surprise.

"Ty?" Alice's voice crackled as she drew in a very ragged breath. "Is he here? Did he come? Funny, I thought

I heard him. Weird dreams." She began to hum a little. "Really weird dreams."

"He came as soon as he heard what happened," Wren assured her. "Ty'll be here soon. He'll be so happy to see you're awake."

Alice's smile dimmed and her eyes drooped. "Haven't seen him in an age. Is he still dreamy?" The arm unencumbered by IVs and tubes drifted into the air.

"As a matter of fact—" Wren grabbed her hand and held on "—he's even dreamier."

Alice laughed a little. "Awesome. Pretty man. Pretty, pretty man."

"Alice, have you seen Bradley?"

"Not yet. Said." She started to drift off. "Nurse said she'd call him. Need to see him. Need. To see. My…"

The monitors evened out again, the rhythmic beeping settling into place.

"She's just asleep again," Dr. Rodriguez said quickly. "You're really with the FBI?" she asked Wren.

"Yes. And I'm hoping you can tell us where Bradley might be?"

"I haven't seen him since last evening," Dr. Rodriguez said. "Check with the nurses. Maybe one of them—"

A gentle cough from the doorway had them all turning. "Excuse me. Hey, Shelly. You made good time." Wren recognized the young nurse from her previous visit to the hospital. She'd been the one flirting with Ty.

"Hi, Aiyana." Shelly's greeting sounded tense.

"This was just delivered for Alice." Aiyana held up a small cardboard box about the size of a paperback.

"Were you able to reach her husband?" Dr. Rodriguez asked.

"I'm afraid not. I left two voicemails, though."

"May I?" Shelly held her hand out for the box, cast an uneasy look at Wren.

"Go ahead," Wren said, urging her to open it. No postmark. Nothing to indicate it had been mailed. "Did you see who delivered it?" she asked Aiyana.

"No. It was left at the nurses' station while I was on break and everyone else was with patients."

Wren pulled Shelly off to the side while Dr. Rodriguez gave updated orders to Aiyana. Shelly pulled out a pocketknife, flicked it open and sliced the tape. Inside the box sat a framed photograph of Alice and her family. Bradley's face was marked with a red X.

Wren's stomach clenched. "That must have been what they went into the apartment for." She was careful when she lifted the frame up, mindful of leaving her own prints, and grasped the folded piece of paper beneath it. Every nightmare scenario that could play out in this situation came to mind. Wren tried to shake off the feeling. She needed to stay calm.

"What does it say?" Shelly asked when Wren finished reading.

"It says they have Bradley and that the only way to get him back is for Alice to refuse to testify in the retrial of Ambrose Treyhern. If she doesn't, they'll kill him and come back for the kids. One at a time." Wren gnashed her back teeth to the point of pain. She pulled her cell out, dialed Ty again.

"Yeah!"

"Ty?" She recognized that tone. "What's wrong? Where are you?"

"Heading to the hospital. I'll be there in maybe two,

three minutes." The sound of tires screeching came through the line.

"I'm here now. Are you hurt?" She stepped out of the room.

"No. Sheriff's been shot. Lower shoulder. He's losing a lot of blood. Why are you—"

"Alice is awake." She cupped the phone with her hand. "Dr. Rodriguez, is there an emergency entrance, room, trauma unit?"

"There's the ambulance bay at the back end of the hospital. Just to the left once you're in the lot. Why?"

"Ty, you hear that?"

"Yes. Be there soon."

"Sheriff Egbert's been shot," Wren told Dr. Rodriguez and the nurse. "It sounds bad. He's going to need blood. A lot of it. ETA maybe three minutes."

Dr. Rodriguez snapped into action, as did Aiyana. They raced out of the room, running down the hall past the outpatient clinic.

"The sheriff's been shot?" Shelly seemed stunned. "But...by who?"

"Not important right now." Wren pulled out the backup piece she'd borrowed from Aiden's stash of weapons. She cocked the hammer, handed the gun off to Obie. "You know how to use one of these?"

"Yes, ma'am," Obie said, straightening and standing taller.

"Good. You sit. In there." She pointed into Alice's room. "Doctors and nurses only. You don't recognize them, they don't get in, unless they give you the password."

"What password?"

"Winchesters."

"As in the gun? Or the TV show?"

Wren simply smiled. The family code word—based off their shared obsession over the latter—came in handy more often than not. "Anyone who uses that word you can trust them the same as you'd trust me or Shelly or the sheriff, yeah?"

He nodded.

"Alice. She's your priority, understand?"

"Yes."

Down the hall she saw Aiyana and Dr. Rodriguez running with a trauma stretcher between them. Two male orderlies raced after them. Wren followed with Shelly right on her heels.

The blast of cold air when they stepped through the automatic doors chilled her to the bone. She heard the SUV before she saw it, the grinding noise the same sound she had heard when she was speaking to Ty on the phone.

Sparks flew when the SUV barreled up to the hospital and Ty flew out. He raced around the front of the car and ripped the door open. Dr. Rodriguez shouted instructions to her people and within seconds they had Sheriff Egbert out of the car and on the gurney. As the medical team pushed him inside, Dr. Rodriguez flashed a hand-held light into the sheriff's eyes. "Olsen? It's Maya. Can you hear me?"

The sheriff's head flopped back and forth. "Going to take that as a yes. I want him checked and headed into surgery in ten minutes max. Go!" She blocked Wren, Shelly and Ty from coming any farther. "I've got him."

"But—" Shelly tried to dart around her, but Wren caught her arm.

"Let her do her job, Shelly." Wren nodded. "We're good."

The doctor vanished behind a pair of swinging doors.

Shelly shrugged out of her grasp. "I have to call his wife." Shelly's dull voice belied her shock. "I don't understand… How did this happen?" She swung on Ty. "What happened?" Anger filled her eyes.

"It was a setup. They lured him there," Ty said. "We didn't realize it until they took the first shot."

Wren touched his arm. "This isn't your fault."

Ty's glare was filled with disagreement, but he didn't respond.

"This isn't his fault," Wren repeated to Shelly, who looked unconvinced. "This happens, Shelly. It's part of the job."

"And I'm just supposed to get used to it? To be ready for it?" Shelly's voice went up an octave.

"Yes," Wren said firmly and released Ty's arm to grasp his hand. "It's part of the job."

"Well, this job sucks!" She spun on her heel, pulling out her cell phone as she stalked away.

"He knew," Ty whispered when they were alone. He stared unblinking at the double doors. "That's why he didn't want Shelly with him. He was afraid it was a setup."

"So did you." She'd seen it in his eyes before he'd walked out of the station. "You suspected that's what it was, so you went with him." Her heart stuttered. "It could have been you."

"It should have been me."

"No." She turned into him, rose up, wrapped her arms around his neck and drew him to her. "No, it shouldn't have been." Wren squeezed her eyes shut and held on when he tried to pull free. "Don't you dare let go of me. Don't you dare." She needed to feel him, every part of him she could, to remind herself he was still alive.

"Wren." Her name sounded like a prayer, a plea on his lips. Finally his hands moved around her, his arms tightened. And he held on.

"I love you." The admission nearly broke her in two. "Maybe it just happened or maybe I always have, but I love you, Ty. And I will not allow you to die on me before we get a chance at whatever this is going to be."

"Okay."

The simple response had her half laughing, half sobbing. She leaned back, looked into his eyes. Her feet were off the ground. He held her, supported her, comforted her all with a look.

"That's it?"

He kissed her. Like a man who had come too close to dying, he kissed both of them back to life. "That's it."

Shelly returned, her cell in her hand. "Mason called," she snapped. "He's got something."

"What about Sheriff Egbert's wife?" Ty asked.

"She's coming." Shelly visibly swallowed. "We should get back to the station."

Wren shook her head. "You should stay—"

"I'm done being left behind." Shelly cut her off with a furious look that had Wren shutting her mouth. "Let's go."

The short drive felt like they made it in light-speed mode. Wren and Ty didn't say another word, just glanced knowingly at one another as if to say, *Tread carefully with her.*

Shelly swore as she jerked the car to a stop. "Who the heck is this guy?" Yanking the keys out, she unlocked their doors. "I don't have time for this. No new people. Not today."

"Make time. He's here to help." Wren squeezed Ty's hand before she got out of the car and beelined for the man standing in front of the sheriff's station, some of her built-up tension melting away.

Howell McKenna had their father's height, their mother's fair Irish skin tone and the McKenna spark lighting his eyes. His passive expression didn't shift but his eyes did as Wren approached. Seeing him was like coming home. "Hey, Howell." She couldn't quite turn on her high-beam smile. "Thanks for coming."

"You called, I came. It's what we do." Howell pulled her into a quick hug.

"You got here fast." And she was so, so grateful.

"Called in a favor. Caught a military flight out of Boise. You doing okay?"

She nodded, her voice trapped somewhere between shock and dread. "Yep, doing okay." She thought she was handling the situation pretty well, but she absorbed the quick offer of comfort to reinforce her mental strength. A McKenna reboot she hadn't realized she needed. She stepped back as Shelly and Ty approached. "Shelly, this is my brother, US marshal Howell McKenna. I asked him to come up and talk with Bradley and Alice."

"Oh." Given the rapid rise of color in Shelly's face, she was rethinking her earlier comment. "Nice to meet you, Marshal McKenna." She held out her hand. "Deputy Shelly Adjuk."

"Deputy. And it's Howell, please."

"Howell." Ty reached out to her brother. "Good to see you again. Thanks for the assist."

"Ty." Howell offered a surprisingly easy smile. "Wren filled me in on the Treyhern case when she called. Want to bring me up-to-date?" He tucked his hands into the pockets of his too-thin jacket. "Preferably inside?"

"You'll get used to the cold," Wren assured him.

"Not entirely sure I want to." He held the door open for the rest of them before following. "Please tell me there's coffee."

"Pod machine's over there." Shelly pointed to the side table near the sheriff's desk.

Mason spun in his chair, his expression worried as he looked up at Shelly. "How's Sheriff Egbert?"

"Waiting to hear." Shelly's voice was uncharacteristically sharp. "Tell us what you found out."

Wren cleared her throat. "I should probably tell Howell—"

"I can play catch-up later." Her brother rested a gentle hand on her shoulder. "Go ahead," he urged Mason.

"Uh, sure." Mason frowned. "Who are you?"

"Reinforcements," Ty said simply and earned an appreciative smile from Wren.

"Okay. Well, buckle up." Mason turned back to his now three computer screens that were open and siphoning multiple lines of code. "I had to reach out to a hacker friend of mine. He's, ah, intermittently employed by some private companies."

"Everything's a free pass today, Mason," Ty assured him. "Speak freely. It'll save time."

"Right." Mason immediately brightened. "So it was this line here that stood out to me. I've seen it before. Hackers have their own way of identifying themselves in the code they write. They're like Easter eggs in an ego-boosting kind of way. According to my source, they were all written by a hacker named Inferno." He glanced up, clearly expecting a reaction.

"Never heard of him," Ty said.

"Me, either," Wren agreed.

"Make that three," Howell chimed in from where he waited for his coffee.

Mason frowned. "Okay, whatever. Three years ago, Inferno bragged about how he'd been contracted to work exclusively for a private security firm. TitanForge Technologies."

"Now, them I've heard of," Howell murmured as he moved in behind them. "They've got their hands in a bunch of pots. Global operation."

"How does this connect to the Treyhern case?" Ty asked.

"TitanForge is one of a number of subsidiary companies under the Titan Holdings name. They've got a law firm, health research-pharma company and a financial business. The financial firm is called Apex and—" He clicked on one of the screens. Images of a mini mansion popped up. "—they are the free-and-clear owners of this home up on the mountain." He grinned from ear to ear, spinning lazily in his chair again. "Am I good or what?"

"You're definitely something. Any chance you could access TitanForge Tech's current roster of employees?"

He glanced at Wren. "Wondering if our blond friend is listed."

"Be pretty stupid if—" Wren stopped, watched as a host of pictures exploded onto the smallest of the screens. "That's a lot of employees."

"Stop!" Ty stepped closer. "Go back. Slowly. Back. Back. And there." He stabbed a finger at the screen. "That's him. It's an old picture, but that hair." The shocking blond hair was slicked back and tamed but impossible to deny. "Barrett Lynch. Personal security specialist."

"That's your guy?" Howell asked.

"That's him, all right," Wren agreed, but didn't feel quite the joy Ty clearly did.

"What's wrong?" Ty asked her. "What's the face for?"

She shook her head. "Something's niggling at me. Titan. I've seen that somewhere." She pulled out the jump drive from her pocket. "Which laptop can I use, Mason?"

"Give it here." Mason cleared one screen and popped the drive in. The FBI's list of official files regarding the Treyhern case displayed. "What am I looking for?"

"Not sure." She scanned the file names. "I read through all of them the other night. Here." She pointed to the file titled Research and Associates. "Now scroll down...down." Her eyes moved back and forth, skimming as fast as she could. "There. Roy Calvin. He's a former associate of Treyhern's." She glanced at Ty. "You know him?"

"Not personally," Ty said. "He was a person of interest early on in the investigation. He and Treyhern grew up together. They remained friends for years. Gino cleared him."

"Gino?" Howell asked.

"Ty's first partner," Wren said. "Gino Bianchi."

"He was killed two years ago in an undercover sting gone wrong," Ty said.

"Good agent?" Howell asked in a way that had Wren wincing. She knew the subtext of that question. He wanted to know if Gino Bianchi was on the take.

"Taught me everything I know." Ty glanced at Wren. "Most of what I know."

Wren smirked. "I seem to recall skimming through a list of assets for Roy Calvin. Mason, is there a search feature—"

"On it." Mason clicked more keys. "This what you're looking for?"

"Oh, yeah." She moved in, leaned over Mason's shoulder and drew her finger down the lengthy list of assets. "He likes spending money. He likes his toys. And he likes to brag. At the time this report was created, he already had multiple properties all over the world. But…" She shot upright. "That boat. Yacht. Whatever you want to call it. The *Titanic Ego*. I've seen that boat." She spun around to Ty. "It's in the marina. Or at least it was the day I flew into Splendor."

"It's a place to start," Shelly said. "We should go."

"We need more evidence," Wren said. "We need proof of a current connection between Treyhern and Roy Calvin beyond the face of a security professional."

"I don't have—" Shelly snapped. "My boss is in the OR, I've got one murder, one attempted murder, an abduction and a town that's going to start panicking unless we get this under control. We should go to the boat. That may very well be where they're holding Bradley."

"Excuse me?" Howell's baritone pierced the room. "Holding Bradley? Explain."

"Sorry. Part of that catch-up." Wren cringed. "Bradley's gone missing sometime in the last few hours. Shortest version is Alice is awake, Bradley's missing. Their kids are safe in the tower with the entire building watching over them. And whoever took Bradley sent Alice a note telling her they'll kill Bradley unless she refuses to testify at Treyhern's new trial."

"When did that happen?" Ty demanded.

"You were busy trying to save the sheriff's life," Wren said. "Someone lured Sheriff Egbert into an ambush. He's alive." She nodded at Shelly. "Last we heard."

"Treyhern's reach has gotten longer," Ty said. "That's a lot for him to organize from behind bars."

"Impossible is more like it," Howell said. "I made some calls before my flight. With the exception of talking to his attorneys, Ambrose Treyhern has served almost every day of his term in solitary. Voluntarily, apparently. He does not play well with others. Especially in close quarters. He'd be closely monitored there. No cell phones. No outside communications. The only visitors he's had have been his lawyers."

"That must be how he's pulling strings." Wren noticed Shelly was getting antsy, pacing in frustration. "Ty, do you know what law firm is representing him?"

"Uh." He squeezed his eyes shut for a moment. "Brooks, Patel and Pendleton. They're based in New York, I think."

"They are." Mason clicked once on the second screen. "Brooks, Patel and Pendleton is the law firm owned by

Titan Holdings. And FYI, the Brooks part is actually Roy Calvin's daughter."

"There it is," Howell said with a nod to Shelly. "That's the connection you needed to lock in on." He turned back to Wren. "Where do you need me?"

On her six. Ty had been joking earlier, but Howell being here, backing them up, was tantamount to reinforcements having arrived. That said… "The hospital. We need someone watching Alice. Someone who can protect her if the need arises." She quickly explained Obie—the security guard's presence. "Someone who will know what to do."

Howell nodded. "Understood." He looked to Shelly. "I'll keep you apprised of your sheriff's condition."

"Thanks." She deflated a little. "I'd appreciate that. Can we go now, please?" She was already walking toward the door.

"She going to be okay?" Howell asked Wren as Ty followed Shelly out.

"Yes." Even though she had her doubts. "We'll make sure of it. If we get into a mess, you'll be my first call."

He squeezed her arm. "Stay safe, sis."

She flashed a quick smile. "You, too. Oh! The secret password is Winchesters."

Howell rolled his eyes. "Of course it is. Go. Do good work."

"I'm a McKenna," she said, heading out. "We always do."

Chapter 13

The wind whipped so hard that flags atop boat masts snapped soundly in the air. Shelly had gone to speak to the harbormaster, who also happened to be a distant relative, while Ty could see the *Titanic Ego* from where he and Wren were standing outside the marina. There were at least two dozen vessels tethered close to the yacht. Anyone on board those vessels could get caught in potential cross fire. It was important to know how many were occupied before they swooped down on the yacht. In the meantime, he and Wren waited across the street, not wanting to be seen until they made their actual approach to the *Ego*.

Anticipation and adrenaline built inside of Ty at an equal pace. He could almost hear the clang of Treyhern's cell door closing once and for all, but everything had to go perfectly in order to make that happen.

And perfectly hadn't exactly been in his repertoire as of late.

"Take it one step at a time," Wren said, as if, once again, she was able to read his mind. "Don't leap ahead, Ty. We get Bradley home. That's what we focus on right now."

Wren, always the voice of reason. "You give any thought to what comes after?" he asked.

"A long, hot shower." She shivered. "Feel like I haven't been warm since I got here."

"How about after that?" It was a distraction. One he needed before he worried himself through the cement under his feet. He'd obsessed over this case for so long; longer than he felt comfortable admitting. Treyhern had gnawed on him from the moment Ty arrested him ten years ago. That smug smirk on the man's face was haunting. It left him questioning himself in ways no agent ever should. Treyhern had known then this day was coming. Ty should have paid closer attention to his gut. "After we close the case against Treyhern."

"Well, I imagine we're going to be dealing with some disciplinary issues." She winced and turned into the wind. The clouds continued to move past at a clipped pace. Gray, full and threatening. Errant flakes of snow drifted down, a promise of what was to come. "Agent Frisco isn't going to approve of us being off book and ignoring orders. He might split us up."

"Did you mean what you said back at the hospital?"

"I don't say things I don't mean."

He could almost hear her heart pounding over the wind. "Wren—"

She faced him. "I'm not going anywhere, Ty. You're stuck with me. If you want a short, concise answer about our future at this moment, how about my place is bigger than yours and it's closer to work? I'm thinking you sublease your apartment for six months, or however long it takes us to accept that we're going to be in each other's lives until the end of days." She gave him a quick smile. "Does that answer your question?"

It was, he realized, the first time in his life he was looking forward to the future. "Given this some thought, have you?"

"A little." She put her back to him again. "One other thing you're going to need to accept. You're obligated to attend the same monthly McKenna dinners I am. We do this, you're one of us. No way out."

"Sounds like I'm joining the mafia."

"Hmm, in a way…" She trailed off as Shelly jogged over, gloved hands shoved deep in her jacket pockets. "What's the word?" she asked the deputy.

Shelly's breath came out in big puffs. "As far as Roscoe knows, all of the boats are currently vacant. Not many went out to fish this morning because of that." She pointed behind her to the storm approaching. "Doesn't mean someone isn't out there, but officially, they're all empty."

"Even the *Ego*?" Ty asked.

She shrugged. "Let's hope not."

"You need to make sure your mind's in the right place before we go in," Wren advised. "Bradley's our focus. We get him out and safely back to his family. Nothing else can factor into your thinking, Shelly. Not even revenge."

"I know."

"Do you?" Wren narrowed her eyes, waited for Shelly to meet her gaze. "We've got your back. Sheriff Egbert wouldn't want you doing anything to risk Bradley's safety. What you do is important, Shelly. Do it as well as you've done up until now and everything'll be fine. We've got you," she repeated.

A bit of the deputy's anger seemed to fade and Shelly nodded.

Understanding what Wren was trying to encourage, Ty said, "You know boats better than we do. How should we go about this?"

Shelly shifted to stare at the black-and-gold-painted yacht. "I'd send Wren to starboard and you and I take port. There's entryways on both sides of the main cabin."

"You know the layout of the ship?"

"Roscoe's nosy, especially when it comes to boats. He has a tendency to give himself tours when he knows no one is on board."

Ty nodded, impressed. She'd built up sources without even realizing it.

"We get Bradley home," Shelly repeated, as if she'd discovered a new mantra. "Our only goal."

"Our only goal, *for now*." Ty nodded in a way that told her they should get started.

They made their way to the marina entrance, stepped through the swinging gate and drew weapons as they neared the yacht. Their footfalls echoed dully against the wood planks, barely loud enough to be heard over the wind. The boat bobbed in the water, which swelled up and over the edges of the dock.

Shelly turned slightly, pointed to Wren, then to the right side of the yacht, where a short platform was attached. Ty fell in behind Shelly, mimicking her moves as they climbed the portside ladder. They landed quietly on the deck. Across the hull he could see glimpses of Wren's head bobbing as she crept along her side of the yacht. He focused on Shelly as they made their way, similar to Wren, toward the main cabin door.

He and Shelly stood on either side. Ty pointed down before pointing inside.

Shelly nodded, understanding he wanted her taking a crouched position once the door was open. He'd go high.

She reached out, slid the door open, and they ducked in. Ty took the lead now, moving his weapon from side to side as if clearing a room. The cabin space was larger than his entire apartment. The highly polished wood gleamed almost obnoxiously against the brass fixtures. Plush furniture and a well-stocked bar decorated the room. A ghastly garishly patterned carpet covered the floor.

Wren joined them, merging into their pattern easily. Ty held up a hand. They all froze.

He strained, listening. The roar of the wind was duller in here. But he could hear voices. Two, maybe three. He swallowed hard. Maybe more. Bracing himself, he walked forward, focused on keeping his balance as they reached the staircase that led down into the ship's belly.

Shelly tapped his shoulder, indicated she was going to go back out and around, then down. He took that to mean there was a separate entry into the keel of the boat. He glanced at Wren.

She nodded.

Shelly whipped around and went out the same way they had come in.

Ty placed a foot on the first step. He felt Wren at his back. Took another step. And another. The voices grew louder. He and Wren were headed in the right direction. Near as he could tell, however, he still couldn't see any faces.

He looked back at Wren, saw concern in her eyes

before she shrugged. They were in too far now. They couldn't stop. Below there were four closed doors, two on each side of the narrow passageway.

He pressed a hand against the first one on the right. It opened easily. Empty. He shook his head. Instinct told him the next door was going to be the one.

Wren tested the doors on the left. Both unlocked and empty.

The familiar tension built inside him. With it came the calm of having spent so long as an agent. He'd walked through the right doors and the wrong doors and come out alive in every instance. This wasn't going to be any different.

He felt Wren at his back once more. Even if he did have something far more important to worry about now, he took one more step and looked up.

Directly into a security camera aimed at his face.

He straightened, lowered his weapon and signaled to Wren. The door in front of them was ripped open and the blond-haired man they had been searching for emerged, pistol in hand. And aimed directly at Ty's head.

"Just returning the visit, Lynch." Ty raised his arms and let the gun spin out of his grip. The weapon dangled from his finger. "You have something that doesn't belong to you."

Lynch smirked, eyed Wren. "Put it down. Or he gets the first bullet."

Ty had dealt with men like this before. When he'd been up against seemingly impossible odds, Lynch would take them both out if it came down to his own survival. "Don't," he told Wren.

Her finger shifted from the side barrel of her gun to the trigger.

"You don't want to do that." Lynch stepped aside, away from the open door.

Inside the room, Bradley Hawkins sat tied to a chair. His face was battered and bruised. Blood trickled out of his nose and the corner of his mouth, but he was breathing. His swollen eyes widened with hope when he saw Ty and Wren.

"Not much space." Lynch gestured over his shoulder. "You miss me, you might hit your guy. And you don't want to do that, do you?"

"Alice got your message," Wren told him. "She's awake. She's agreed not to testify."

Lynch smirked. "You don't expect me to take your word for it, do you?"

Wren shrugged. "That's your choice. You said you'd let the husband go if she didn't testify." She cocked her pistol. "Let him go."

Lynch looked at her for a long moment, then at Ty. When his gaze flicked back to the stairs, an unfamiliar knot of fear tightened in Ty's stomach.

"Fine." Lynch lowered his weapon, did a little bow and motioned them into the room. "Go on and take him."

Wren's brow furrowed.

Ty's throat was dry. "Do as he says, Wren." He kept a solid gaze on Lynch's accomplice at the top of the stairs. He had one arm locked around Shelly's neck. The other held a gun to her temple.

Shelly's eyes were sparked with fear, but her jaw tensed as if anger was trying to take control.

"Guns down, please." Lynch motioned to the floor. "Now."

Ty bent and did as he was told. He nodded for Wren to do the same. Only then did she turn enough to finally see whom Ty had already spotted.

"Consider this a hostage exchange," Lynch said as Ty stepped into the room, holding out his hand for Wren to join him. "When you're ready to negotiate the deputy's release, you know where to find us."

Ty held on to Wren's shoulders, felt the tension in her body as she prepared to leap at Lynch. He squeezed his hands and she got the message to take a step back. Lynch pulled the door closed and locked them in, presumably to keep them from following.

Immediately Wren went to work on the door. The sound of Shelly's muffled cries echoed through the boat. Ty checked on Bradley, found the man's pulse to be strong and steady.

"Bradley?" Ty untied the ropes to free Alice's husband, then bent down to the point they were practically nose to nose. "You okay?"

"I think so." Bradley wheezed a bit. "Don't know why they did this. Never asked me anything." He spit a little blood.

Ty met Wren's raging gaze. "That's twice they've lured us. What's the endgame? What are they playing at?" She threw herself against the door and bounced off it. She swore and kicked the door. "What do they want?"

"Now? Me." It was the only thing that made sense. "They believe they've taken out the sheriff protecting Alice. So they're going after the agent in charge of the case. Alice doesn't testify, I don't testify, the charges go away. There's no reason Treyhern won't win his appeal."

"But leaving you locked up on a boat isn't really getting them what they want, is it?" Wren tended to get snippy when she was angry. And scared.

Ty looked around. There was a king-size bed, a pair of nightstands and a trio of portholes along the top of the wall.

"They left a way out." Ty yanked open drawers, cabinets, even rooted in the closet, searching for something, anything, he could use to... Diving equipment sat among the clutter. He sorted through the tanks and tubing, found what he was looking for. "Diving weights." He hefted them, scooted between Wren and Bradley and climbed onto the bed.

"What are you—"

The rest of Wren's question was lost against the banging of the weight against the porthole. He could feel time ticking away, feel Shelly's life possibly ticking away. Regardless of the noise, he had to try whatever he could to get them out of here. He hit the glass again and again. Finally he cracked it. The pane split like a spiderweb and so he hit it one more time and it shattered. Air whipped in. He dropped the weight, got off the bed and leaned against the wall to keep his balance as the boat swayed. "Out you go." Wren looked dubious when he shoved the discarded coat over the jagged window shards, bent over and cupped his hands. "I'll boost you."

She tucked her hair behind her ears. "If I get stuck, I'll never forgive you."

"You won't get stuck." He couldn't look at her when

he said it, though. "You should be able to drop down, then come around and open the door."

"Uh-huh." She shook her head, unzipped her jacket. "No way this is going to fit." Wearing only her jeans, T-shirt and a sweater, she planted her foot in his hands and he raised her up.

She cried out when she grabbed the frame of the window.

"What?"

"Glass shards. I'm fine. Brrrr." She shivered as she wiggled forward. "It's freaking freezing."

"Do you need me to push?" He had his hands out, ready at her butt.

"No, I don't need you to…" She grunted, shimmied some more. Let out a frustrated breath. "Okay, fine. Push."

He tried to be gentle, but that window wasn't forgiving.

"Harder!" she rage-whispered.

He did as she ordered, pushing hard enough that she dropped out of sight onto the deck. "Wren!" He climbed back up onto the bed and tried to see out the porthole, but his downward view was cut off. "Are you okay?"

No response. He shouted again but his voice disappeared into the wind.

The door busted open, slamming so hard against the wall that it bounced closed again. Wren shoved through. Her hair was disheveled, her palms bleeding, and, from her attitude, she seemed seriously ticked off.

"Next time, *you* get the porthole," she growled as she snatched up her jacket. She handed him back his gun and shoved her own into the back of her jeans. "Come on."

She grabbed one of Bradley's arms and tucked herself under it. Ty followed suit and they hauled Alice's husband out of the chair. They maneuvered down the hall, up the stairs and out. The boat rocked under their feet but slowly they made it onto the marina.

The storm was almost on them. Besides the howling wind, there was rain and sleet making the situation even more challenging. "Everyone's inside because of the storm!" Ty yelled. "We'll have to get him to the hospital ourselves."

He could see the conflict on her face. She agreed. But she was worried about Shelly. Wren paused and wiped the hair from in front of her face. "Wait. I see something! You got him?"

"Yeah." Ty accepted the full weight of Bradley Hawkins. She ran down the dock, heading toward a fishing boat pitching side to side. She waved her arms wildly and got the attention of two men. Ty focused on keeping his balance. "Hang in there, Bradley. We're going to get you help, okay? You'll be at the hospital in no time. The doctors will fix you right up."

"My kids?" Bradley whispered brokenly. "Are they—"

"They're fine," Ty assured him. The icy air had turned his fingers numb. "The whole tower is looking after them. And Alice is awake."

Bradley's head snapped up. "She's awake?"

"Woke up a little while ago. Wren talked to her. You should be able to see her once you're patched up." Wren raced toward them, two bulky men right behind her.

"Cal and Nelson are going to get Bradley to the hospital," she yelled.

"We've got him." The larger of the bearded men

took Bradley from Ty as if he were nothing more than a caught fish.

"We need to get your car," Wren yelled. "We have to get up that mountain and find out which house is Lynch's."

"Car won't do you any good!" the other man hollered. "They closed the road about an hour ago. Snowslide." The two men moved off with Bradley between them.

Ty could feel Wren's anxiety coming off her in waves. She looked to Ty, then over to the tram.

All he could do was shrug and nod. They had to get up that mountain—she'd said so herself.

"You have got to be kidding me." She stared at the dark sky.

"I'm not that funny," Ty said, attempting some humor. "I'm sorry. It's the only way we're going to get her back. We made a promise."

"I know." She shoved her hands into her wet hair and pushed it off her face. The fear was there, but so was the familiar determination of the woman he loved. "Come on. Let's go get our deputy."

Chapter 14

The race through Splendor to reach the tram left Wren's legs and lungs burning. Maybe it was the cold or perhaps the desperation she couldn't shake. Her mind spun around the possibility she'd never see Shelly again. But that was nothing compared to the fear that Ty was most probably Barrett Lynch's main target.

The killer had drawn out this entire thing like some sick game. Going after Alice had done its job. It had lured Ty here. They'd been kept here by the mystery of Davey Whittaker's involvement and the abduction of Bradley Hawkins. The only person left on their list had to be Ty.

The three flights of stairs up to the tram entrance was almost too much. The air had thinned with the incoming storm. She could feel her head spinning, as if she weren't getting enough oxygen. Beside her, Ty seemed to be doing just fine if not for the concern etched on his face.

"When this is over, I want a vacation." She heaved a breath, then another. "Tropical. Warm. Scorching. With nothing to do other than lie on the beach or by the pool."

"You got it."

They rounded the final platform. "Are you planning on being this agreeable for the extent of our new relationship?"

"I'm planning on taking things a minute at a time." His smile was quick and cursory. "I've had seven years to get used to you, Wren. I've been trained."

She laughed, then choked and coughed. She nearly tumbled on the last step, but he caught her and pushed her forward. The ticket booth was empty when they reached the main level of the tower. She slammed her hands on the glass.

"They must have shut it down because of the storm!" Ty said.

"Then how did Lynch— Wait!" She stopped, strained to hear. "What's that?" It sounded like whimpering. She darted around the corner of the ticket booth, saw the door and shoved it open.

Inside, a young woman sat curled up in the corner on the floor underneath the counter, arms tight around her knees as she rocked. Tears fell from her dark eyes to her brown cheeks. When she saw Wren she gasped, tried to push farther back into the corner.

"It's okay." Wren dropped down, held up both hands. "I'm with the FBI. My name is Wren McKenna. This is my partner, Ty."

Her eyes shifted with recognition.

"You've heard our names before, haven't you?"

"Y-yes." She swiped at her cheeks. "This morning. Mayor Sully was talking about you when I picked up my breakfast."

"What's your name?" Ty asked.

"Yara." She sniffled. "Yara Kato."

"Yara, two men scared you, didn't they?" Wren asked. "Two men with Deputy Adjuk."

Yara nodded. "I told them the tram was dangerous.

We always stop them during storms. I was supposed to be home, but I stayed here to study. It's quieter."

Wren could only imagine what noise there must be at her home. The wind was howling like a banshee and the entire tower felt like it was vibrating.

"They made me send the tram up." Tears pooled again. "I'm going to be in so much trouble. I'm not supposed to send them in the storm but they had a gun. They pointed it at me." The abject terror in Yara's eyes erased a good portion of Wren's fear.

"It's okay." Wren crept closer, touched the young woman's hands. "You did the right thing." She peeked up enough to see the second tram sitting in its bay. "Yara, I'm going to have to ask you to send us up in that one."

Yara shook her head. "It's too dangerous! The wind—"

"I know, you're afraid of getting in trouble."

"Not just that." Yara looked slightly offended. "I don't want you to die. Then no one will be able to save Shelly."

"Hey." Wren needed every ounce of reassurance she could find. "We aren't going to let anyone hurt Shelly. She's our friend. And we promised we'd have her back. But we can't go get her without your help. We'll be okay." Even as she said it, the fear tasted like a lie in her mouth. "The system's mostly automated, right?"

Yara nodded.

"Okay, then just tell me what buttons to push."

Yara's eyes cleared. "You're really going to go up there to get her?"

"We really are," Ty said.

Yara took a trembling breath and let Wren pull her to her feet. "It'll have to go slower than normal. Otherwise the tram—"

"Don't!" Wren ordered sharply. "Just do me a favor and don't tell me what could happen."

Yara nodded.

"Can you hand me your notebook and a pen?" She flexed her hands, praying she could make them work properly. When Yara gave them to her, Wren scribbled down Howell's number. "If anything goes wrong, I want you to make a call. This is my brother. He's here in Splendor. He's going to need to know."

"Okay."

Wren gave her a quick hug. "Thank you for your help. Open the doors for us, yeah? Then send us up."

"You sure about this?" Ty asked when the two of them were back outside.

"Absolutely not." Never in her life had her heart pounded this hard and fast. At this rate it was going to be able to live outside her chest. She didn't stop moving. She didn't dare to. Arms stiff at her sides, her hands clenched into fists so tight she couldn't even feel them, she approached the shiny red thirty-passenger cable car and stepped through the open door.

"Hold on to me," Ty said and reached for her as the door slid shut behind them. She grabbed hold, tried to remember to breathe. Her feet felt like they were stuck in cement, but she moved an inch, maybe two, to the side, grasped the metal pole with her free hand as the tram glided away from the tower.

As it picked up a bit of pace, the car lurched from one side to the other, buffeted by the strong wind. She let go of Ty and locked her other hand around the pole, hugging it as the tram made its way up, into the foggy storm.

"We're in this together." Ty stood next to her, his

arms around her as if wanting to remind her he was
there. As if she could forget. The rocking got worse. She
could hear the cables overhead straining and whining.
The padded plastic seats around the perimeter of the
car looked comfortable; she wished she had the courage to try to sit.

"I'm not going anywhere, Wren."

She laughed nervously. "Where would you go?" Her
voice sounded like a mouse's squeak. "This is pathetic.
I have no idea where it even comes from. But it's just—"
she struggled for breath "—paralyzing." The tram seemed
to be moving in slow motion. "It's never going to end."

"Nothing lasts forever. And look at the bright side."

She stared at him with narrow-eyed suspicion as fog
blanketed the tram.

"After this, I'm betting heights won't bother you so
much. Maybe you'll even be willing to go zip-lining with
me."

"Keep dreaming, Savakis." But the idea made her
smile. They rumbled past something. "What was that?"

"One of three towers," Ty said. "Perfectly normal."
He shifted his feet farther apart as the tram swayed more
violently. "That's one down and two to go."

"I'd say a prayer if only I could remember any of
them."

"I thought you all went to church every Sunday. Another McKenna family tradition."

"Did." She choked down the bile rising in her throat.
"Didn't really pay that much attention. Oh, hey, here's a
silver lining." She cleared her throat. "If we die, you're
off the hook with monthly McKenna dinners."

"Then I've got another reason to stay alive." He pressed

his mouth to hers. "I think I'm going to like being a Mc-
Kenna."

She sob-laughed and grabbed hold of him. "I really,
really hate this."

"I know. But in fact, it could be—"

"Do *not* say it," she ordered.

"Worse."

No sooner was the word out of his mouth than the
overhead mechanism let out a jaw-dropping screech. The
tram slammed to a stop. Wren and Ty were thrown to
the floor as the doors on either side slid open.

Wren screamed, flailing frantically for the metal pole
as she felt herself sliding toward the opening.

"Hang on!" Ty yelled and gripped the nearest post.
With his free hand, he grabbed a fistful of her jacket and
tried to tug her toward him.

The storm shot through the tram, filling the thinning
air with fog and rain and now snow.

"Ty!" She could feel herself slipping out of the jacket.
The weight of her body was pulling her free. The tram
shuddered and lurched. Her body twisted and suddenly
she could feel her feet, then her legs, dangling free of
the tram.

"No!" Ty yelled and groaned at the same time.

She dropped another inch. Wren screamed, fingers
flexing uselessly. There seemed no way to stop herself
from falling the thousands of feet to the ground.

Panic surged. The edge of the cable car pushed hard
into her stomach. Almost the whole bottom half of her
dangled out of the tram. She had one hand on the edge,
the other barely holding on to Ty's. She turned her head.

"Not. Going. To. Happen." Ty spit out each word as

if it were an oath. "Don't look down, Wren. Wren!" he yelled. But she was unable to resist temptation. "Wren, don't!"

It was an odd moment. Certainty descended. She felt the absolute acceptance that she was about to die. She didn't want to, of course. She'd miss her family and she knew they'd miss her. And Ty. Her breath froze in her throat and she felt the tears in her eyes turn to ice. What she could have had with Ty.

The thought reignited her spark to live.

"Wren!"

She looked up, saw Ty had shifted position. He now had his other hand free. A hand that reached out for her now.

"Grab hold!" he hollered. "I won't let you go. I promise. Trust me and grab hold."

He promised.

It took every ounce of strength she possessed to release her grip on the tram. But she did and shot her arm up to where he could latch on to her wrist. Holding both her hands now, he nodded when she met his eyes.

A fierce gust of wind hit the tram and she closed her eyes, surrendered and put her trust in Ty.

He tugged hard, quickly jerking her toward him as the tram rocked. She flew up and cried out as she landed, his hold gone. But in the next second he locked his arms around her and rolled her to safety at the back of the car.

She clung to him, insisting; she told herself that she'd never let him go, not in any sense of the word. Her breathing slowed, his, too, and she tried to remember how to think. Her brain was blank.

The overhead mechanism clanged before they started

moving once more. She laughed, long and loud, and felt the tears on her cheeks as she held on to the man who'd saved her life. Just as his hold on her tightened.

"Amazing," he whispered into her ear, his breath hot against her skin. "Thank you. Thank you for trusting me. I love you, Wren." He squeezed his arms so tight he stole what was left of her air. "I love you so much and I'm never letting you go."

"Okay." Her muffled response had them both laughing.

They remained where they were, huddled together as the tram made its way slowly to the highest deck. She didn't think she'd ever heard a more beautiful sound than that of the tram locking into place.

The rocking stopped. The doors slid closed before one side slid open again.

"The thing's possessed," Ty muttered. "Can you move?"

"Right now, I think I can fly." She shoved to her feet, held out her hand to help him up.

Every inch of her ached to the point she'd probably be unable to walk tomorrow. But right now? She checked to make sure her gun was still in place. "You good?" she asked Ty as he seemed to need a moment to get his legs under him.

"I will be." He bent over, planted his hands on his knees. "You ready to finish this?"

"More than and we'd best make it fast. Now even their machinery is trying to kill us."

"What do you mean?" Ty asked. He followed her out.

"That thing. The tram system?" She pointed back at the car of death. "It was built by TitanForge Technologies."

"They hacked into it," Ty said dazedly. "That's why it stopped."

"That's what I'm betting." And the very idea really, really ticked her off.

Apparently sixty-mile-an-hour winds and snow coming down was nothing when in the presence of Wren McKenna.

Ty trudged along beside her, keeping an eye out for the side road located about a hundred yards from the tram deck. The house owned by Apex shouldn't be much farther, but if they didn't get there fast, the windchill was going to take him and his partner out.

"There!" Wren shoved her hood back and pointed to the left.

They headed up a slight hill, found themselves in front of the house almost immediately.

They flanked the door and brought out their weapons. Ty continued to pray that his frozen hands would work. "We expect anything," he told her. "They're expecting us."

"Unless they think we fell out of the cable car." She grinned. "I'm really hoping we surprise them."

She was about to touch the handle when the door opened.

Ty went low this time. Wren went high. They left the door open as they moved through the marble foyer.

They made it as far as the main seating room before a slow clap of applause exploded through the house.

"Impressive." Lynch's voice rang against Ty's ears. "If I hadn't been hired to kill you, I'd recommend TitanForge hire you. Both of you."

"It's doubtful you're going to have a job for much longer," Wren said as the man stepped out of the shadows. The house was cold, unlit and monstrous. Ty bet the power had gone out at the beginning of the storm. "Where's the deputy?"

"She's resting. It's been a long day."

Ty's ears perked at the squeak behind him. He spun and fired.

Lynch's second flew back off his feet and landed dead on the floor.

Lynch rolled his eyes. "Told that moron to get better shoes." The shooting was evidently cause enough for Lynch to draw his own weapon and aim it at Wren. "Put your gun down, Savakis."

Tired of being a puppet, Ty ignored him and advanced. "No."

"Put it down or she's dead."

"You put your weapon down, Ty, and I'll shoot you myself," Wren warned.

"Feisty," Lynch said. "I like that."

Ty took another step forward. Then another. And saw a flash of doubt on Lynch's face. "There's nowhere to go. Storm's locked everything down. Once you leave the mountain, there's a US marshal waiting in Splendor to take you into custody."

Lynch's eyes narrowed. "I don't believe you."

"Howell McKenna," Wren said. "My brother. And trust me when I say you can't hole up in here waiting him out. He'll come get you. Especially if I don't turn up."

"Can he fly?" Lynch asked. "Because in about eight hours a helicopter is going to be arriving with my boss and I'll be out of here." He shifted his gun from Wren to Ty, then back to Wren. "Which one to shoot first?"

"How about you?"

Ty and Wren both jumped at the sound of the gunshot.

Lynch's face went completely white, shock barely having time to register in his dark eyes before he pitched forward and landed on the floor.

He didn't move.

Shelly, leaning heavily against the door frame, dropped her arm to the side and sagged forward. Ty dived for her, caught her before she collapsed. "Hey. Hey, Shelly. You okay?"

Wren was at his side immediately, helping to prop Shelly up, narrowing her gaze as she checked for any indication of injuries.

"Using your X-ray vision?" Shelly mumbled. "You two sure seem like superheroes to me."

Wren smiled.

Ty slipped the gun out of Shelly's hand, set it aside. "Where did they keep you?"

"Basement. Back there." She pointed behind her. "They drugged me. Offered me water and I fell for it. Ick." She lifted a hand to her bruised throat. "I made myself throw up. I hate throwing up."

"You are going to make a brilliant agent, Deputy Adjuk," Wren said.

"Hmm." Shelly grinned. "I'm tired."

"That's okay. You got the bad guy."

"I did, didn't I?" Shelly managed one more smile before she gave in.

Wren straightened and smiled. "I think we did it. I think we closed the case."

"Not quite yet," Ty said, as a new plan began to form. "But soon."

* * *

Three hours, almost to the minute, and Wren and Ty were settled on a sofa in the living room of the mini mansion owned by Apex. They'd moved Shelly into one of the bedrooms for her to sleep it off. She and Ty planned to get the deputy to the doctor as soon as they were back in Splendor. But, for now, they were enjoying the calm after the storm.

"No, we're fine, Howell. But we will eventually need a full team from Anchorage to help clean this matter up." Wren looked over at Ty before she snuggled closer. "Lynch and his buddy are dead. We're just waiting on one more to arrive. As soon as the tram's been cleared for operation, Ty, Shelly and I will be on our way down. Yes." She laughed. "Yes, I said *tram*. It's a long story. Talk soon, okay? Love you." She ended the call, rested her head on Ty's shoulder. "Sheriff Egbert's okay. He'll be away from the job for a while. Rehab's going to be tough, but he's out of the woods."

Ty heaved a sigh of relief. "Now, that's good news."

"Would you like more good news?" She was just getting started. "Apparently my brother took it upon himself to call our boss." She couldn't seem to stop smiling.

"Oh?"

"Mmm. He explained that it wasn't just a witness who was in danger of lethal retaliation, but one of Frisco's own agents, namely you. It turns out, thanks to all of us, that several cases across various agencies were closed. Justice has triumphed yet again, and due to my brother's extra-fast talking, you and I are not only *not* in trouble, but in line for a commendation." She actually giggled.

"I bet Frisco had a hard time saying no when he heard. He's not going to be able to fire you or suspend me. Yay!"

Ty didn't respond.

Concerned, she turned her head to look at him. "What?"

"I'm just… That he'd do that." He shrugged. "That's pretty awesome of him."

"It's what family does," she said. "Best get used to it because the word is out. Howell also called my mother, so you're officially on the dinner-invite list."

"No place else I'd rather be." He pressed a kiss to the top of her head. "I do have a favor to ask."

"Anything."

"You say that now," he teased. "You mentioned that if I decided to go see my father and brother, you'd come with me. Did you mean it?"

"I did." She didn't like the idea. She knew how much he'd been hurt by his family. She didn't want him stepping into the line of emotional fire again. "Do you want to go see them?"

"I think I have to. Not for them," he added quickly. "For me. I need to close that book before I can start writing another one."

"Then I will come with you. Can I bring my gun?"

"No." He laughed and they both looked up. There was the distinct sound of whapping helicopter blades. "You ready to do this?"

"More than." But neither of them moved. They simply sat there, on the sofa, staring at the front door.

The key in the lock had them shifting away from one another, both sitting forward as Roy Calvin entered the house. He wore a long beige wool coat, his hair slicked back, his cheeks red and ruddy. He carried a large metal suitcase in one hand that he set on the floor almost immediately.

"Barrett? Is it done?" He took off his jacket. "I've got your money."

"He won't be needing it." Ty's voice froze the owner of Titan Holdings just inside the living room. "Nice to finally meet you, Mr. Calvin." Ty gestured to one of the empty chairs. "Please. Take a seat."

Wren watched with a certain growing pleasure as Roy Calvin walked stiffly toward them. "I take it we don't need to introduce ourselves?"

Calvin remained silent.

"You're a smart guy, aren't you, Roy?" Ty said. "You've stopped talking because you don't want to further incriminate yourself. Good play. It won't help, of course." He set the cell phone they'd found on Barrett Lynch's body on the coffee table, beside the gun they suspected had been used to kill Davey Whittaker and the rifle used on the sheriff. "Funny thing about Barrett Lynch. He didn't trust anyone. Not even you. He recorded every conversation the two of you had over the past month and a half. He even called you when he made contact with Davey Whittaker. Said he'd found the perfect patsy for Alice's accident. She's fine, by the way, in case you were wondering."

Calvin's face went stone-cold still. "What do you want?"

"So many things," Ty said.

Wren's pride in his patience and composure soared. Her joy at seeing him be able to close this chapter of his life once and for all, immeasurable.

"But we're going to start with Titan Holdings writing a very generous check to Beatrice Mulvaney, for the death of her nephew."

"I won't—"

"And then you're going to resign from Titan. You'd have to do that anyway," Ty said before Calvin could interrupt. "Because the Justice Department has just opened an investigation into all aspects of your business practices. Trust me, you aren't going to want to deal with that. You'll have other things to worry about."

"What other things?" Calvin began to sweat. Tiny beads of perspiration dotted his upper lip and forehead.

"You're entering the witness protection program," Ty said. "You'll have to after you testify about your dealings with Ambrose Treyhern. You're going to admit that your law firm took on his case with the intent of eliminating the witnesses against him. I don't think new attorneys— his old ones are being notified of their possible disbarment in the near future—will be easy to find. You're both going to be held responsible for the actions taken against Alice Hawkins, her husband, Sheriff Egbert and Deputy Adjuk."

"I really like that last part." Shelly entered the room, slowly, as if every step she took hurt. Her face was bruised, her lip bloodied, but she stayed on her feet and stood behind Wren and Ty.

"You will testify against Treyhern," Ty said firmly. "You will tell the truth about everything, and you'll be the one who will lock him in his cell forever. It'll let Alice off the hook, so in a way, your plan worked. She won't be testifying. And she and her family will stay here in Splendor, safe. For the rest of their lives." Ty took a deep breath and glanced at her. "Is that everything?"

"For now," Wren said. "You can relax for a little while," she told Calvin as he sat awkwardly in his chair. "The Marshals will be waiting for us once the trams start working again." She stood. "Can I get you something to eat or drink?"

Calvin glared at her.

Wren grinned. "All right, then. Ty? Shelly?"

"I, ah, want to thank you both." Shelly hugged her arms around her torso. "For everything. For coming to get me."

"We promised," Ty said. "Simple as that."

"I, um…I don't think I'm going to be applying to the FBI."

Wren met her steely gaze. "Please don't tell us this incident scared you out of law enforcement. You're a natural at this, Shelly."

She nodded. "I know. That's why I'm going to stay here in Splendor. So I can take over when Sheriff Egbert retires. These guys showed me something that I forgot. This is my home. My people. My town. I'm sticking with it and will make sure every citizen is safe."

Wren's heart skipped a beat. "That sounds like a great plan."

"You'll come back, I hope? To visit?" the deputy asked Wren.

"Oh, we'll definitely be back," Ty said, and he got to his feet to stand beside Wren. "I've had some savings stashed away for a long time. And I think I'm finally ready to invest in a property. Say an apartment in Skyway Tower?" He turned expectant eyes on Wren. "Our home away from home?"

Wren pressed her lips together, hope soaring inside of her. "Do I still get a vacation in the tropics?"

"Absolutely."

"Sounds like the deal of a lifetime to me." She threw her arms around his neck and kissed him. "Partner."

* * * * *

HARLEQUIN
Reader Service

Enjoyed your book?

Try the perfect subscription for Romance readers and get more great books like this delivered right to your door.

See why over 10+ million readers have tried Harlequin Reader Service.

Start with a Free Welcome Collection with free books and a gift—valued over $20.

Choose any series in print or ebook.
See website for details and order today:

TryReaderService.com/subscriptions